AFTER YOU HAVE READ . . .
TRADE IT FOR CREDIT!
PAPERBACK EXTRA
1220 Vantage Drive
Little Rock, AR 72204

Double FANTASY

CHERYL HOLT

St. Martin's Paperbacks

DOUBLE FANTASY

Copyright © 2008 by Cheryl Holt.

Cover photo © Shirley Green

ISBN: 0-312-94256-7
EAN: 978-0-312-94256-4

Printed in the United States of America

St. Martin's Paperbacks edition / March 2008

St. Martin's Paperbacks are published by St. Martin's Press, 175 Fifth Avenue, New York, NY 10010.

10 9 8 7 6 5 4 3 2 1

Chapter
ONE

Anne Carstairs walked down the path that wound through the woods. Warm June sunlight drifted through the trees, dappling her shoulders in shades of green. The air was thick with the tantalizing odors of a verdant summer day.

Off in the distance, she could see Gladstone Manor. The mansion was nestled against the rolling hills and surrounded by acres of manicured gardens. Horses grazed in the pasture. It was a bucolic site, yet she scarcely noticed.

At any moment, Jamieson Merrick, the recently installed Earl of Gladstone, was due to arrive, accompanied by his twin brother, Jackson Merrick. There were two horses tethered in the drive out front, so apparently some of Jamieson's entourage had already appeared. Soon, his fancy coach-and-four would follow his outriders, and the Merrick family crest would be insultingly visible for all to witness.

As babies, the twins had been sent away from Gladstone, forced to make their way in a cruel world. They'd been called pirates, thieves, smugglers—and those were the polite descriptions. Gossip abounded that they'd committed hundreds of murders, that they would kill at the drop of a hat. Jamieson Merrick, especially, was reputed to be violent. He ate small children for his supper; he drank their blood for his wine.

He was coming to Gladstone, demanding justice, demanding recompense and admissions of guilt. What might such a brutal individual do to pursue his goal of vengeance?

Since he held her fate in the palm of his hand, she was terrified to know the answer. Such an angry, evil criminal might be capable of any perfidy.

She approached the stream and stepped out on the ancient rock bridge. It was slick with moss, and she tiptoed carefully, bound for the other side, when movement out on the ridge caught her eye.

She halted and stared.

A man was there, fists on hips, feet spread wide, and he was covetously taking in the view. He was smug, in his element, as if he was finally standing precisely where he was meant to be.

From his shabby condition, he had to be one of Jamieson Merrick's disreputable sailors, down from London to help him lawfully seize the estate from her cousin Percy.

Percy had been Earl of Gladstone for eighteen of his thirty years, having assumed the title at age twelve. But now, with the discovery of a tattered birth certificate and a stained, crumbling marriage license, Jamieson Merrick was earl and Percy Merrick was not.

Anne never ceased to be fascinated by how such a simple event could totally alter the lives of so many. Her future was winging toward her like a bad carriage accident, and now that she'd glimpsed the first member of Merrick's crew, she was more distraught than ever.

What would become of her?

When Percy had initially broached the problem regarding the earldom, the story had seemed too fantastic to be believed. Supposedly, Percy's father had impregnated and secretly married a housemaid who'd died birthing the twins. Afterward, he'd panicked and hid evidence of the union and his two lowborn sons. He'd subsequently wed the appropriate debutante, had sired Percy and *his* twin sister, Ophelia, and they'd all proceeded on with Percy as the heir, as if the siring of Jamieson and Jackson Merrick had never occurred.

But after three decades of silence, someone had come forward and told the truth, and the whole estate had been pitched into chaos.

Anne had embraced Percy's false hope that everything would be fine. She had dawdled and delayed, had made no contingency plans, but Jamieson Merrick had proved a wily adversary. He'd won every legal skirmish, and he was eager to claim what was his.

Anne and her only sibling, Sarah, were an unwanted pair of hangers-on, two dedicated spinsters with no skills and no money. They had nothing to recommend themselves to Jamieson Merrick—not even kinship. Yet Gladstone was their foundation, the only home they remembered. Where would they be when he was finished with them?

What if he tossed them out on the road? Anne couldn't envision herself trudging away, a satchel slung over her shoulder, like a common vagrant. The concept was too bizarre to imagine, and the man strutting before her was the complete embodiment of all that had gone wrong the past few months. She couldn't quit gaping.

He was tall, every inch of six feet, and he was whip-cord lean, his anatomy honed by arduous labor, with Merrick as his brutal taskmaster. His shoulders were broad, his waist narrow, his legs impossibly long. He looked strong and tough, ready to fight, ready to win.

His hair was black as a raven's, and it was untrimmed and messy, lengthy enough to be tied in a ponytail with a strip of leather. He was wearing what had to be a red soldier's coat, but most of the gold buttons were gone, the cuffs frayed, the hem torn, and she uncharitably wondered if he'd stolen it from the corpse of one of his victims.

His boots were scuffed, his trousers faded. He resembled an impoverished farmer who was down on his luck, yet he exuded a power and determination she couldn't deny.

As if he perceived her attention, he turned toward her, and she was disturbed to note that he was the most handsome man she'd ever seen. He had a perfect face, aristocratic nose and generous mouth, but his eyes! Oh, his eyes! They were a startling sapphire, as dark and mysterious as the waters of the Mediterranean were said to be.

He assessed her from the top of her head to the tips of her toes, his rude appraisal as thorough as if she'd been a slave or prized cow. He lingered on her lips, her breasts, her stomach, each torrid glance like a caress that had her squirming and wanting to cover herself even though she was fully clothed.

She was the dreaded *poor relative,* with no dowry or prospects, so she hadn't spent much time around men. As a consequence, she wasn't overly familiar with seduction, but still, she recognized lust when she saw it. He was a cad of the worst sort, one who might do any reprehensible thing to her. And he'd enjoy it, too!

He seemed to read her mind, seemed to realize the moment she'd decided she should be afraid of him, and he was humored by the notion. He smiled, a roguish, mesmerizing smile that promised all kinds of naughty behavior, and he started toward her, his fleet strides quickly crossing the grass to where she was perched on the bridge.

It was a strange impression, but she felt as if he was her fate, as if Destiny had pushed him into her path when she didn't want him there. He was Doom and Destruction, descending on her like a thundercloud she couldn't outrun.

With a squeal of alarm, she spun to hurry away, but the stones were very slippery. She wobbled, then plunged over the edge into the cold stream. The water wasn't that deep, nor was the current brisk, but the weight of her garments dragged her under before she could gain her balance.

She had a brief instant to consider the ludicrousness of her predicament—would she die in sight of the manor on her last day at Gladstone?—when he reached in and fetched her onto the bank as if he were a fisherman and she a trout.

"There now, I've got you," he murmured, his voice a rich baritone that tickled her innards.

He sat and pulled her onto his lap, their positions appallingly intimate. Her torso was stretched out with his, their chests and bellies melded, her hip wedged between his thighs. One of her breasts was pressed to him, and the placement had a riveting effect on her nipple. It hardened and ached, and she suffered from the most peculiar desire to rub against him like a lazy cat.

"I could have drowned," she said, amazed by the

petty disaster she'd averted, and she shivered, which earned her a tight hug.

"You're too pretty," he replied. "I wouldn't have let you."

She was stunned that he'd throw out the word *pretty*. In her entire life, she didn't think anyone had told her she was pretty before. With her auburn hair and green eyes, her petite frame and shorter height, she was too different from her statuesque, blond cousins, and his opinion was exciting to hear.

"And if I'd been an ugly old hag," she asked, "would you have allowed the stream to carry me away?"

"Maybe."

He grinned his devil's grin, and she was shocked at how her heart pounded. She wanted to fall into that grin, wanted to wallow in it forever, which was embarrassing and horrifying.

He was a wicked one, indeed, and she had to beware, lest she linger when she oughtn't. She shifted, desperate to regain her footing, but the attempt only brought them into closer contact.

"Help me up, you bounder," she scolded.

"In a minute, my little maid. I rather like having you just where you are."

"Well, I don't, and I'd appreciate it if you'd keep your hands to yourself."

His long, crafty fingers were stroking up and down her arms and back. She was chilled to the bone, and the stirring caresses warmed her, but she wouldn't surrender to how marvelous they felt. If it hadn't been so improper, she'd have lounged there all afternoon, letting him massage and fondle.

She put her palms on his chest and shoved him away, creating space, behaving herself.

"Help me up!"

"If you insist," he sighed.

As if she weighed no more than a feather, he lifted her, and he followed so that they were both standing. He peered off into the woods, and whatever he saw made him frown.

"Dammit," he muttered. "Get down."

"What?"

"Get down!"

He was dragging her to the grass, again, and she dug in her heels.

"I will not. I am—"

Like a madman, he tackled her. They landed with a painful thump, with her on the bottom and him on top, his body shielding hers.

A loud bang—that sounded like a gunshot—rang out and echoed off the hillsides. Birds squawked and flew away in a huff; then all was quiet.

Anne was bewildered, speechless and aggrieved, and struggling to figure out what had transpired.

He raised up slightly, shrewdly scanning the trees. Apparently, whoever had been there had fled. When he realized there was nothing to see, he relaxed onto her, but his large torso didn't seem heavy. He felt welcome and thrilling.

"Are you all right?" he asked.

"Yes, I'm fine."

"Good."

He shuddered with relief and rested his forehead against her own. It was a tender gesture of affection, and when he drew away again he assessed her oddly, as if he didn't know what to make of her.

He dipped down, and for a hesitant second, he brushed his lips to hers. He was very tentative, as if to pretend that the hasty advance had been an accident. Then he pulled away, acting nonchalant and blasé, so she tried to ignore the liberty he'd taken, but it was difficult to feign apathy.

It had to have been the quickest, most fleeting kiss in history, but it was her very first, and she reveled in it. For a man who was so rough-and-tumble, his mouth was incredibly soft, his breath sweet and intoxicating, and she knew she'd lie awake many nights in the future, pondering the bizarre encounter.

"Let's get you home." He rose and tugged her up.

"What . . . what happened?" she stammered. "What was that noise?"

"Someone shot at us."

"At *us*!"

"Yes."

At having him affirm the absurd event—in such a cool and calm manner, too!—she was incensed.

She'd been with him for all of about two minutes, and she'd nearly drowned, then been murdered by an unknown assailant. If she loitered in his company for a whole hour, how would she survive it?

"No one shot at me!" she declared. "I'm the most pleasant person in the world. If anyone was being shot at, it was you!"

"I'm sure you're correct."

She studied the forest, and it seemed much more dense and threatening than it had previously.

"Shouldn't you search for him or something?"

"There's no need. He's gone."

"How can you be so certain?"

"I have a devious mind, so I understand how devious people think. He fired; he missed; he ran."

"What if you're wrong?"

"I'm not."

He was so annoyingly positive, and she couldn't abide such arrogance. She almost hoped their attacker would strike again—merely to prove he was mistaken.

"Why would someone shoot at you?"

"Probably because they don't like me. Why would you suppose?"

"Aren't you the least bit concerned?"

"No. I'm too tough to kill."

"I'll just bet you are."

She was much smaller than he, so he towered over her, and with him being so close, it was easy to see what she hadn't noted prior. There were age lines around his eyes, brackets around his mouth, his skin tanned from outdoor living. He couldn't be more than thirty, but he looked much older. Obviously, he'd had a difficult life, his face providing evidence of years of toil and heartache.

The brief connection they'd shared had vanished, and she was scared of him again. He had a raw, desperate edge that was frightening in its intensity. She didn't care to tarry, didn't care to experience the anxious, disturbing feelings he ignited.

"I'd best be off," she told him.

"What's your name?"

She was about to blurt it out, then thought better of the idea. "It's none of your business."

"Tell me anyway."

"Miss Carstairs."

"Are you Anne or Sarah?"

She scowled, wondering why he'd been apprised of her and her sister.

Anne was twenty-five, and Sarah was twenty-six. After the back-to-back deaths of their parents, they'd been orphaned, tiny girls requiring shelter. Their aunt Edith, Percy's mother, had brought them to Gladstone. For over two decades, the Merricks had grumbled about Anne and Sarah being a burden but had fed and clothed them nonetheless.

Anne and Sarah lived dull, quiet lives filled with monotony and routine. There was no detail about their existence that was curious, that might pique a stranger's interest. Who had informed him about them? *Why* had he been informed?

"I'm guessing you're Anne," he ventured when she didn't reply.

She neither confirmed nor denied his deduction.

"Thank you for rescuing me from the water. Good-bye."

She was eager to be far away from him, and she was about to spin and go, when he asked, "Don't you want to know my name in return?"

Nothing would have pleased her more. "No."

He laughed, but his voice sounded rusty—as if it didn't occur often.

He shrugged out of his shabby coat and held it out to her.

"If you're going to the manor, you'll need this."

"No."

"Trust me. Put it on."

The last thing she'd ever do was prance into the house wrapped in a man's coat. She'd never be able to explain it, but he was staring at her so keenly, his hot gaze drifting to her bosom and remaining there.

She peeked down to see what had captured his attention, and she was shocked by the state of her wet garments. The moistened dress was stuck to her breasts and delineated them so clearly that she might have been wearing nothing, at all. The bodice hugged every curve and valley, especially the pointy tips of her nipples in the center.

"Aah!" she shrieked, and she clasped an arm across her chest. "Shut your eyes, you despicable scapegrace!"

"No. I'm enjoying the view too much."

He reached out, his finger on her chin, and she stood, frozen, as he traced it down to the neckline of her gown. For a mad instant, it seemed that he'd burrow under the fabric, that he would touch her, bare skin to bare skin.

Her cheeks flaming with embarrassment, she whipped away, and he draped the coat over her shoulder, waving it like a flag, urging her to take it. Without further argument, she grabbed it and stuffed her arms in the sleeves, and she was overwhelmed by how his scent clung to the material. It was such an alluring fragrance that she could hardly keep from rubbing her nose in the weave.

Disgusted with herself, she stomped off, but she could feel him watching her. Just as she arrived at a bend in the trail and would have disappeared from sight, he called, "Miss Carstairs?"

Don't turn around! Don't turn around! She whirled around.

"What?"

"I hope to see more of you again. Very soon!"

Even though she was a sheltered spinster, she recognized the salacious innuendo underlying the comment. Burning with mortification, she ran all the way home, more of his rusty laughter ringing in her ears.

Chapter
TWO

I s the family assembled in the parlor as I requested?"

"Yes, sir."

"Then announce me. And be quick about it."

At his being forced to tarry in the foyer like a supplicant, Jamie Merrick's infamous temper flared. He glared at the reluctant butler who hadn't moved a muscle.

"How . . . ah . . . how would you like to be named, sir?"

"Lord Gladstone. How would you suppose?"

The butler's eyes nearly bugged out of his head. He'd spent his whole life referring to Percy as Lord Gladstone, and Jamie's demanding the change had to sound as absurd as if Jamie had suggested he jump off a cliff.

"But he is . . . that is . . . I am—" the butler stammered.

"Is Percy here?" Jamie interrupted.

"Yes."

So . . . the sneaky weasel had mustered the courage to be present, which was a surprise. Percy was Jamie's half brother, but they were nothing alike. Percy was too much of a coward to stay and fight like a man. After the failed murder attempt out in the forest, Jamie would have predicted Percy's flight from the property.

Jamie had met Percy on several unpleasant occasions. Initially, Percy had been hostile and threatening, but as the legal tide had turned, he'd grown fawning and conciliatory. Jamie was aware that it was a ruse, that Percy had many schemes fomenting in hopes of reclaiming the estate, but Jamie wasn't concerned about any of them.

Percy wasn't smart enough or driven enough to do what was necessary, so he'd never effect any real damage.

Still, Jamie had instructed Percy to vacate the premises before Jamie's arrival. The transition would be difficult, and having Percy around and underfoot would only make matters worse.

But then, Percy probably had nowhere to go. Jamie had offered him a cash settlement and a London house, which Percy had proudly and stupidly refused. He'd been incredibly ungracious about it, too, so Jamie wouldn't offer again. From this point on, Jamie had no intention of being courteous or sympathetic. He'd waited three decades for this moment, and he would revel in his triumph.

He stepped to the butler so that they were toe-to-toe, and he towered over the smaller man.

"I'll announce myself," Jamie seethed, "and save you the trouble. As opposed to you, I know my true title. But when I next ask you, you'd best proceed immediately, or you won't work here anymore. Am I making myself clear?"

The butler gulped. "Yes, Mr. Merrick."

Jamie raised a brow.

"I mean *Lord* Gladstone."

Jamie flashed a cold, lethal grin. "That wasn't so hard now, was it?"

"No, no, it wasn't."

"You're excused."

The butler raced away, and Jamie glanced over his shoulder at his twin brother, Jack.

"Worthless bastard," Jack muttered.

"He's harmless."

"You should have skewered him with your dagger as an example to the others."

Jamie chuckled. Typically, Jack was the pragmatic, rational sibling, while Jamie was the wild, impulsive one. If Jack would voice such a remark, he was more unnerved by events than he let on.

Jamie and Jack were close as any two brothers could ever be. Jack could read Jamie's mind, could finish his sentences. Jack was the only person in the world who understood what Jamie had been through. Jack was the only person in the world Jamie cared about or trusted.

"Are you ready?" Jamie inquired.

"Of course."

"Watch my back."

"Don't I always?"

Jamie's wry expression reminded them both that Jack had been nowhere in sight when Percy had risked an assassination, but Jamie wouldn't judge Jack too harshly. Neither of them had anticipated the attack, and in a way, Jamie was glad Percy had acted.

Jamie had been preoccupied with Anne Carstairs, so he hadn't been paying attention. With Percy's desperation so blatantly exhibited, Jamie would be more cautious.

"Let's get this over with," Jamie said.

He marched down the hall, Jack directly behind him, and they entered the parlor. The Merricks weren't expecting him to appear without a grand pronouncement, so he was able to scrutinize them without their noticing.

They were attired as the rich, lazy nobles he detested. The four women had on fancy gowns and ribbons, while Percy wore a fussy, expensive outfit that had likely taken his tailor a month to sew. In contrast, Jamie was in frayed woolen trousers, dust-covered boots, and a shirt that he'd pilfered from a dead sailor.

He didn't even have a coat—Miss Carstairs had robbed him of it—so he didn't have the advantage of pretending he'd been taught how to dress. He'd have to meet them in his shirtsleeves, and if they didn't like it, they could all go hang.

On the sofa off to the right, Anne Carstairs was whispering with her sister. Anne had had no clue as to his actual identity, and he was eager to see the look on her face when she heard who he was.

With her hair tidied, and her garments clean and dry, she was even prettier than she'd seemed out in the forest, and he frowned with dismay. He'd enjoyed their encounter much more than he should have, and the realization had him so vexed that he noted he was distractedly massaging his wrist, which was always a sign of extreme distress.

It was an old habit, picked up after he'd almost had his hand chopped off when he'd been caught stealing some bread for Jack when Jack had been ill and starving. Jamie had been very young, just seven or eight, and already a dangerous, cynical criminal, but the near loss of his appendage had been a frightening affair, the terror of which had never totally faded. All these years later, he still occasionally had nightmares that the blade was about to slice down.

He couldn't comprehend why the incident had remained so vivid in his memories. The episode was nothing out of the ordinary. His childhood had been one long trial of misery and woe, a violent and tragic saga of betrayal and duplicity. As a result, he never attached himself to others, never bonded or befriended. His father's cruel decision to forsake him and Jack had seen to that.

Although Jamie's mother had married the despicable swine, Jamie had been treated as a shameful, dirty secret, had been discarded like a pile of rubbish.

He often wondered if his father knew—when he'd cast them out—the sort of existence he'd sentenced his sons to endure. Had he plotted for them to die as a consequence of the indescribable torture and strife they'd suffered? Or had it all gone horribly wrong? Maybe he'd meant for them to be raised by some kindly widow down the road, but without his being aware, they'd been kidnapped, instead.

On considering the notion, Jamie scoffed. He'd discovered the hard way that children were expendable, so most likely, his monstrous father had intentionally delivered them to what he'd prayed would be their abrupt demise.

During Jamie's slavery and servitude on the High Seas, he'd seen and done things that would have killed the average person a thousand times over. He'd survived the ordeal, but not without a steep cost.

He was a callous man, a brutal man, who'd learned early on that it was pointless to trust or hope, and he didn't like it that Anne Carstairs had rattled him so easily.

She'd been humorous and sweet, bumbling and in need of male protection, which had stirred his masculine instincts in a disturbing manner. He hadn't planned to like anything about her, had wanted their introduction to be cool and formal, but circumstances had determined that they'd commence on a different footing.

Time would tell how the alteration would affect their relationship, but he was certain it would be to his benefit. He always got his way. He always came out on top.

"I am Jamieson Merrick, Earl of Gladstone," he said, causing them all to jump. He gestured at Jack. "This is my brother, Jackson Merrick."

There was an astonished silence as they evaluated Jamie—and obviously found him lacking. Slowly, they rose, but no one curtsied or bowed, and the moment grew awkward.

Fat, sluggish Percy slithered forward, feigning amity and support, but his malice was transparent and couldn't be fully disguised. Jamie felt as if they were two cocks in the ring, about to fight. Unfortunately for Percy, he would lose any confrontation, though he didn't seem to fathom that he would.

As usual when Jamie bumped into Percy, he was astounded by the strong Merrick bloodline. Their kinship was undeniable. They were the exact same height, had the same startling blue eyes and facial features, but Percy was bloated from sloth and indolence, his body flaccid, his hands soft. If Percy had ever worked a day in his life, if he'd ever known an instant of adversity, he'd have slimmed down and they could have been triplets, but for the fact that Percy's hair was blond while Jamie's and Jack's was black.

"Welcome, Jamie!" Percy struggled to keep his smile in place. "I see you've arrived. Where is your

entourage? What? No company of soldiers? No pha-
lanx of guards?" He chortled as if he'd been making a
joke. "With all my money flowing into your pockets, I
know you could afford to bring them."

"I have no need of a battalion to take possession of
my own property. And it's *Lord* Gladstone to you."

The gibe was too much for Percy, and he could
barely contain his rage. "Don't push your luck."

"Why shouldn't I?" Jamie goaded. "I'm the luckiest
man alive. By the way, you've allowed a poacher to
roam about in my woods."

"A poacher? Oh my. What makes you think so?"

"He shot at me."

"I take it he missed."

"Pity, isn't it?" Jamie chided. "He should have
aimed a little more carefully. From now on, I'll be
more vigilant, so he'll never have another chance."

Percy was innocence itself. "Why are you so convinced he was shooting at *you*? Couldn't it have been a
regrettable error?"

"Is there a reason you're still here?" Jamie countered. "If I didn't know better, I might suspect you of
trying to kill me."

"Dearest long-lost brother, how could you raise such
a dreadful accusation?"

"I can't abide your foolishness. Even if you do away
with me, Jack is next in line. We were born nearly a
year before you were. Will you slay us both? Have you
the nerve?"

A muscle ticked in Percy's cheek. "I wish you no
harm."

"You've become a third son. Perhaps you should
join the church or the army. If it would guarantee I'd

be shed of you forever, I'd pay for your commission myself."

With the taunt, Jamie could see that Percy's motives were revealed, their cards on the table. Percy had arranged to have him murdered—either by his own hand or by hiring another—and Jamie wouldn't underestimate his half brother again.

Rudely, Jamie spun away from Percy, dismissing him, and focused on the others in the room—all female. Aging, senile Edith Merrick, the Dowager Countess of Gladstone, studied him vaguely, clearly not understanding who he was or what was happening.

Her daughter, Ophelia—Percy's twin and Jamie's half sister—understood completely, and her loathing wafted out. Sarah Carstairs looked as if she'd like to be rendered invisible, while Anne Carstairs was about to collapse in a stunned heap.

Where she was concerned, he seemed to have a second sense, and the sight of her blushing and squirming was so enjoyable. She was sincerely wondering if she could tiptoe to the door and sneak out undetected, but he wanted her to know that he was in charge of her and she had no secrets.

He grinned, and her embarrassment was so thorough that if she'd burst into flames he wouldn't have been surprised.

"Hello, ladies," he began. "Here is my plan. It matters not to me if you like it or no, and I won't hear any argument. You may concur and acquiesce—or you may leave my home at once."

They rippled with fury, but none dared berate him. The papers regarding the transfer of title had been signed so recently that there'd been no opportunity to discuss their fates. They had to be terrified, and he hated to have them fretting, but at the same juncture, he couldn't have them harboring any illusions about his intentions.

"Tomorrow morning," he continued, "I shall marry one of you."

"You can't be serious," Ophelia huffed.

"Oh, but I am. I have a Special License with me, and whichever woman I select, she will be my countess. The running of the household will fall on her shoulders, and whether the rest of you are permitted to stay at Gladstone will be up to her." He glared at Percy. "You're excluded, though. Despite what my wife may decree, *you* will not remain."

"I have no desire to remain," Percy lied.

"Fine. I expect you to be good as your word. You may attend the wedding; then you'll go."

Percy yearned to storm across the floor and initiate a brawl, but Ophelia stopped him with a subtle shake of her head. Her rapport with Percy was interesting— were they as attuned as Jamie and Jack?—and Jamie tucked away the information for later dissection.

He glanced over at Jack. "Look at my choices, Jack. A blonde, a brunette, and a redhead. How will I ever decide?"

"You've always been partial to blondes," Jack replied, referring to Ophelia but aware that the verdict had already been rendered. "Of course, brunettes are nice. And a redhead, well, you know what they say about redheads."

"Hot in life and hot in . . . other places, too."

They shared a laugh, and the ladies were incensed, but Jamie controlled their futures, so they couldn't antagonize him.

"Now then"—Jamie pretended to mull his options—"which one should I pick?"

He stepped to Edith, Percy's mother, a scrawny, older matron who had supplanted Jamie's mother. Edith was thin as a rail, as if she never ate, and her face was covered with frown lines, evidence of decades of misery. Had it been difficult, being wed to Jamie's father? Jamie was certain it had been.

"Countess." Jamie was polite, bowing in respect. He had no quarrel with her. She was slowly going mad, and she seemed as muddled as had been reported.

"Charles?" Apparently, she thought Jamie to be her deceased spouse. "Is it time for church?"

"I'm not Charles, Countess. I'm Jamie. I'm the new earl."

The cloud faded, and as lucidity flowed in, she soured. "Are you finally here, you interloper?"

"Would you like to marry again? You could be my bride, but you're a tad old for me."

"Yes, I am. Besides, one bad husband is enough for any woman."

"You won't mind if I move on to someone younger?"

"Be my guest," she said acidly.

He shifted to Ophelia. She was thirty, as were Jamie, Jack, and Percy. Since she thrived on excess, she'd put on a few pounds, as Percy had, so she was a bit pudgy around the middle. She didn't seem to recognize that she was growing chubby, and in spite of it, she was still quite beautiful, shapely and buxom, with thick, gorgeous blond hair and the Merrick blue eyes. She'd never wed, had remained single, and Jamie was curious as to why.

"What about you, Ophelia?" he needled.

She was his half sister, so his inquiry wasn't genuine, but he'd been told that she was extremely vain about her appearance, about her position as Percy's sister. She lorded herself over everyone in a cruel fashion, and Jamie would love to bring her down a peg or two.

"How do you know my name?" she queried.

"I know all about Gladstone. I made it a point to find out before I came. Considering that I was entering a den of enemies, why wouldn't I learn of you? Did you take me for a fool?"

He could read in her gaze that it was precisely what she'd assumed. She'd believed him stupid, coarse, and illiterate, and at having been so wrong in her calculations she was livid.

"No," she muttered, "I can see you're not a fool."

"She's our sister," Jack interjected. "Marrying her would be quite contemptible—even by your low standards."

"But if I was partial to her," Jamie responded, "do you suppose the church would give me a dispensation?"

"I wouldn't want one!" Ophelia insisted.

"Really?" Jamie pressed. "You wouldn't like to be my countess?"

Obviously, the prospect hadn't occurred to her, and for the briefest second, her greed shone through. Then she and Percy had another furtive exchange, and almost with regret, she declined.

"I'm sure we wouldn't suit."

"I'm sure we wouldn't, either," Jamie concurred. Having her in his bed would be like having a venomous snake.

He continued on to his true prey, Sarah and Anne Carstairs.

They'd come to Gladstone as orphaned toddlers,

taken in by their aunt Edith, but for most of their lives
Percy had been their guardian. They were his first
cousins, with his mother and theirs being sisters, but
they weren't exalted Merricks by blood, so he'd never
displayed the appropriate attention to them, had never
arranged for suitors, let alone coughed up the money
for dowries.

With the exception of a fleeting romance Anne had
had at age seventeen, the two sisters had puttered about
the estate with no means to alter their circumstances.

Sarah was twenty-six and the elder of the two. She
was also a beauty, with lush brown hair, big green eyes,
and a curvaceous body. She was quiet and restrained,
the pragmatic sister, the no-nonsense sister, and she
looked very sad, as if she'd never experienced anything but heartache. If she hadn't been so patently unhappy, she'd have been the logical choice.

"What say you, Sarah Carstairs? Would you like to
be my bride?"

"No, and I have no idea why you'd ask."

"Don't you? If I don't let you stay, where will you
and your sister go? What will you do?"

"We're not even related. How could our plight possibly matter to you?"

"It doesn't. I'm merely allowing my benevolent side
to poke through."

"Which is exactly what I expected your answer
to be."

"I'm not much for flowers and poetry, so this is as
chivalrous as I get. Haven't I swayed you?"

"No, but thank you for the offer."

"I'm afraid it has to be your sister, then."

He turned to Anne Carstairs, who had been his destination all along. Her pretty green eyes were wide with

terror, like a frightened fawn about to bolt. At the notion of marrying him, she was horrified, and on viewing her dismay, he was incredibly annoyed.

Who was she to spurn him?

He wasn't too keen on marrying, himself, but the Prince Regent had demanded it as the price for Jamie reclaiming his heritage. The King had once been friendly with the Carstairses' father, and he'd often worried over their situation.

Jamie was a proud man with few loyalties, but he was and always had been a British subject, so he hadn't been able to refuse the royal request. Nor would he have jeopardized his chance to regain his title by saying no.

The Prince hadn't wanted Jamie to join the ranks of the aristocracy, and Jamie had had no doubt that if he'd ignored the Prince's stipulation, His Highness would have found a way to keep Jamie's future from being realized.

Marriage to Anne Carstairs—to any woman—was a small price for Jamie to pay to get what he deserved.

"You shall be my bride," he advised. "We'll wed in the morning—at eleven o'clock. I presume you'll be ready?"

He was being a complete ass, but he couldn't help himself. There was something about her that made him want to misbehave simply to see how she'd react. Besides, it wasn't every day that a fellow tied the knot. He ought to be permitted to have a spot of fun before the drudgery set in.

"Miss Carstairs?" he badgered. "Has the cat got your tongue? Or are you struck dumb by my magnificent self? I guess I'll have to take your silence as consent."

She'd been gaping at him as if he were a ghostly apparition, and the remark spurred her out of her trance.

"Marry you?" she hissed. "Are you insane?"

"People say that I am, but I'm not. Although I must admit that, if the situation warrants, I can be a beast. Such as now."

Frantically, she assessed him, appraising his disheveled state, his unshorn hair and worn clothes. Her disdain was evident, and it rankled. While he'd learned many things about her, he hadn't heard that she was a snob.

"No, no, no!" She shook her head. "I absolutely will not marry you."

"Excellent! I'm delighted," he gushed as if she hadn't just curtly rebuffed him. "We'll discuss the details over supper."

"Aren't you listening? I won't do it. Not tomorrow, not the next day, not the day after that. I *never* will."

"And why is that?"

"Because I don't like you."

"So?"

"So! You're rude and overbearing, and I won't have a husband who's an arrogant lout."

"A lout?" He rolled the word on his tongue as if testing its flavor; then he chuckled. "I've been called worse. And I *will* be called worse, once you get to know me better. You don't throw things when you're angry, do you? I hate women who throw things."

"Are you deaf?" she snapped, exasperated. "I won't marry you!"

She appeared mutinous, and her surging temper flushed her cheeks and deepened the emerald color of her eyes. Her breathing was elevated, drawing his

attention to her bosom. Her pert nipples were en-
livened and visible against the bodice of her gown.

He vividly recollected how those nipples had been
pressed to his chest after he'd rescued her from the
stream. As he thought of how soft and sweet she'd been,
he was amazed to feel his cock stir between his legs.

His wedding night would be no chore, at all!

She was actually quite spectacular, and if he weren't
so adamantly opposed to matrimony, he'd have been
thrilled by how affairs had played out. If he had to
marry a stranger, and in a hurry to boot, she was definitely a fine choice.

Sarah Carstairs stepped forward, positioning herself
between him and Anne.

"She's said no, Lord Gladstone. As her elder sister, I
insist that you respect her wishes."

"Why would you deem it appropriate to butt in?"

She blanched as if she'd been slapped. "It's my duty
to watch over her."

"Well, you haven't done a very good job of it so far.
She's a twenty-five-year-old, poverty-stricken spinster.
Unless the two of you can prevail on my charity, she's
about to be tossed out on the road. Yet you dare to suppose she should refuse me?"

He studied her casually—as if he hadn't a care in
the world. And he didn't really. His life had wended its
way around till it was just about perfect. The only nag-
ging remnant that remained unresolved was his burning need to know who had aided his father in sending
them away when they were defenseless children. He
was also anxious to discover who'd finally felt guilty
enough to tell the truth about what had happened.

He wouldn't rest till he had the answer to both questions.

He turned away from the two Carstairs sisters to face the others.

"The ceremony is tomorrow at eleven," he explained, "in this parlor. Ophelia, I trust you to handle the arrangements so that it's an event my bride will never forget."

He spun on his heel and walked out, Jack bringing up the rear.

In Jamie's wake, the family was shocked to speechlessness, and as he made it to the stairs and started to climb, he heard Anne say, "Would you all excuse me?"

Then, she was chasing after him, and he was tickled to note that she had the backbone for a confrontation, though he wasn't about to quarrel with her, so he kept going.

He'd been captain of his own ship for fifteen years, and now he was Earl of Gladstone. He was never denied. His orders were always obeyed.

She would be his wife. No matter what.

Chapter
THREE

L ord Gladstone! There you are! I've been looking
everywhere."

Anne hovered in the threshold of the master
suite. She was anxious to appear meek, so she bit down
on all the furious remarks she'd like to add.

After his absurd demand for a marriage, she'd
wasted the afternoon trying to catch up with him. He'd
deftly evaded her till it was so late that the entire house
was abed. Except for him. And her.

She was frazzled.

"Hello, Miss Carstairs."

"I'm returning your coat."

She extended it like a peace offering, but when he
didn't rise to take it, she felt foolish and she laid it on a
table next to her.

"Thank you. Come in."

At the invitation, she hesitated. He was grinning as if
he were the cat and she the canary, as if she'd cornered
him precisely where and when he'd wanted her to.

His room was a mess, with Percy's belongings
only half-removed, but Jamieson Merrick had been

determined to spend his first night at Gladstone in the earl's chamber. He'd definitely made himself comfortable. He was sipping on some of Percy's finest whiskey, and he was lounged in a chair by the hearth. Even though it was a warm June evening, a huge fire blazed in the grate.

"What's it to be, Miss Carstairs? In or out?"

"In." She took a few halting steps, but she dawdled, unable to begin with what she'd intended to say.

"Well . . . ?"

"Today in the woods . . . why were you up on the ridge?"

"Why do you think? I was surveying all I own and gloating."

"Why would someone shoot at you?"

"I'm not wanted here."

"But who would do such a thing?"

"Percy. Or some miscreant Percy hired. Aren't you glad he missed?"

"Percy has many faults, but he's not a killer."

Jamie shrugged, indicating that her opinion was irrelevant. "Shut the door."

"I most certainly will not."

"Why? Are you afraid I'll bite?"

"No. I simply refuse to be in here alone with you. I won't have the servants gossiping."

"Who cares if they gossip? We're getting married in a few hours."

"We are not."

"Yes, we are. Shut the door."

"No."

"Do you ever do as you're told?"

"I'm a perfectly reasonable person—when I'm dealing with *reasonable* people."

No doubt, he was used to being blindly obeyed. She'd heard the stories, about his daring, about his bravery and treachery. He'd been a ship's captain for many years, but he had no qualms as to who hired him. Supposedly, he worked for the highest bidders, robbing and pillaging on their behalf and taking his share of what was stolen.

Others catered to his whims. They fawned over him and groveled to please, so in dealing with her he was in for a surprise.

She wasn't in awe of him, nor did he frighten her. His attitude was all bluster, meant to intimidate, so he could snipe and bark to no avail. The very worst thing he could do was kick her out of her home, but that's what she'd been expecting to have happen. He had no hold over her; he had no way to coerce her.

He uncurled from his chair, like a cobra about to strike, and he sauntered over but walked right past her. He closed the door himself and spun the key in the lock. She was stunned, and her mouth fell open in dismay.

"Give me that key!"

"No."

He placed it atop the door frame, putting it so far above her that he might have set it on the moon.

"Let me out!"

"No," he said again. "Now then, you had something to say to me . . . ?"

He leaned back, arms folded over his chest, making it clear that she couldn't leave until he was ready for her to go. Her temper flared.

"Yes, I have something to say. As a matter of fact, there are several topics I'd like to address."

"Where would you like to start?"

There was a twinkle in his eye, a galling sign that he was humored by her, and she grew even more irate.

How dare he laugh at her! How dare he poke fun! Her world was crashing down around her, the only existence she'd ever known destroyed by a few pieces of paper she'd never even seen, and all he could do was snicker and tease.

"I won't marry you."

"Yes, you will. At eleven tomorrow morning."

"Who are you to strut into Gladstone and command me in my private affairs?"

"I am the new earl. And as you are here in my residence, eating my food, and living off my bounty, you'll do as I bid you—and you'll do it gladly."

"I won't do it, I tell you! I won't! I won't!"

"You're acting like a spoiled child."

He was correct. She was carrying on like a toddler having a tantrum, and she took a deep breath, struggling for calm. There had to be a way to make him see reason. She just needed to stumble on it.

"Why on earth would you wed me?" she asked more levelly. "And so suddenly, too! When you've so recently reclaimed your heritage, there must be a thousand women who would beg to be your bride. Why not pick one of them?"

"I don't want one of them. I want you."

"But you don't know anything about me!"

"I know enough."

The comment sounded like a threat, or a censure, and she wondered what he'd heard, who had spoken of her. Before traveling to Gladstone, he'd been in London. Who in the city had been so familiar that they were competent to discuss her?

"And with this vast store of information you've gleaned, you're content to forge ahead?"

"Yes. Will that be all? If there's nothing else, I'd like to return to my warm fire and my whiskey."

He was dismissing her! Just like that! As if she were a lowly scullery maid or a stranger on the street! In his authoritative universe, was this the sort of one-sided dialogue that passed for conversation? If he actually ended up pressuring her into matrimony, he'd drive her mad the first week!

"This isn't the Middle Ages," she tersely reminded him. "You can't force me."

"No, I can't, and I wouldn't presume to try."

"Then how will you gain my agreement?"

"Once you're countess, you'll decide who stays and who doesn't."

"So?"

"Your sister can stay—for her entire life. She can remain single and benefit from my charity, or if she ultimately chooses to wed, I'll dower her so she can find a husband."

"And if I'm not willing to sacrifice myself for her?"

"Then you and she will pack your bags and depart."

"Where would we go?"

"Wherever you wish. You'll no longer be my responsibility."

He was silent, letting the import of his cruel words sink in; then he grinned his devil's grin. He'd trapped her, and he knew it.

She would do anything for Sarah. He'd learned Anne's greatest weakness, and he planned to exploit it. How could she fight him and win?

"So you see," he stated, "I won't have to bully you, at all. You'll consent of your own accord."

"But I don't even like you."

"So? Why would your personal feelings toward me matter?"

"If I were ever to wed, I'd want to love my husband." He gaped at her as if she were babbling in a foreign language, and she stupidly added, "I could never love you."

The bounder chuckled. "Well, I'm glad we got that out on the table."

"What about you? Doesn't it bother you that you'd have a wife who doesn't like you?"

"Not particularly."

"What if you eventually discover that you hate me? You'd be stuck with me forever."

"I certainly would be."

"I might annoy you with my frivolity."

"All women do."

"Or I might be rude to your friends."

"I don't have any."

"What if I have atrocious manners or laugh like a donkey?"

"Do you?"

"I often talk too much. What if I chatter like a magpie until your ears are full?"

"Then I'll order you to be quiet."

"And if I don't heed you?"

"Then I'll bind you and gag you and throw you in a closet till I feel it's safe to let you out."

"You would not."

"I might. If you were sufficiently irritating."

"Would you be serious?"

He chuckled again. "You might be right. Maybe I'd merely gag you, but we'd skip the closet."

She shook her head in consternation. "I don't understand you."

"You don't need to *understand* me. You just need to marry me. Tomorrow morning."

Her shoulders slumped with defeat. Why couldn't she make him listen?

She'd nearly been engaged once, at age seventeen, but her beau had run off with a rich heiress, instead. Anne's heart had been broken, her confidence shattered, and it had taken years to recover from the sting of his rejection.

Afterward, she'd sworn off men, and she wouldn't be so vulnerable ever again. She couldn't bear the wild swings from giddy joy to pitiful misery. She yearned to continue on as a staid, sedate spinster, where each day was the same as the next.

Jamieson Merrick was volatile and unpredictable. He'd bring havoc and change, and she didn't want what he was offering.

"Would you really put us out on the road?" she inquired, not quite able to imagine him doing it to her.

"It will be difficult for me to establish myself as master here. People will remain on my terms, or they'll leave."

She stared at the rug, her cheeks flaming with embarrassment. "Would you . . . would you at least give me some money, so Sarah and I can support ourselves while we figure out what to do?"

He didn't speak, but she could feel him studying her. The silence grew, and it underscored how pathetically she'd begged. Had he any compassion for her plight?

"Anne," he started, inappropriately using her Christian name, "would marriage to me really be so terrible? You'll live at Gladstone, and you'll be a countess. You'll be mistress of this grand house and several others. You and your sister will have everything you desire. You'll never go without. I swear it to you."

"It's not about the *things* you can give me."

"Then what is it? Why are you so reluctant? Are you scared of me? Do I disgust you? Are you pledged to another? What is it?"

She knew her reservations were silly, but with the exception of Sarah, she'd always been alone. No one had ever loved her. No one had ever cared about her. And she was so lonely. Was it too much to ask that any potential husband possess a shred of affection?

"It doesn't matter," she mumbled. "I just can't do it."

He sighed with resignation, or perhaps aggravation.

"You're sure?"

"Yes."

He reached out and took her hand.

"Come with me."

"To where?"

"I want to show you something."

"What?"

"You'll see."

He spun and led her toward the inner chamber where his bed was located, and it loomed up at her, hinting at behaviors about which she'd always been curious but couldn't unravel. It was large and wide, fit for a king, situated on a pedestal and positioned so the exalted occupant could gaze out the window on the land below.

She was such an innocent that she'd never peered this far down the matrimonial road to where it would end, and the mysterious possibilities frightened her. She dragged her feet, trying to slow their forward progress, but to no avail. He was bigger and stronger, and he was clasping her hand so tightly. She couldn't pull away.

"I'm not going in there with you," she insisted.

"You keep telling me all the things you *won't* do, and I hate being denied. It annoys me."

She yanked away and sprinted for the door, but she'd forgotten it was locked. She whipped around and glared at him, but he merely grinned, delighted by her predicament.

"You're not afraid of me, are you, Anne?"

"Of course I'm not. Don't be absurd."

"Then prove it. Come into my bedchamber with me."

He took a step, then another, and she extended her arm, palm out, to ward him off.

"You stay right where you are, you scapegrace."

"No."

"Lord Gladstone!"

"Call me Jamie."

"No."

"Call me Jamie!"

He swooped in and scooped her off her feet, and though she kicked and hissed, she couldn't wrestle away. In a few fleet strides, they were in the other room. He walked over to the massive bed and dropped her onto the mattress.

"Lord Gladstone! Stop it!" He climbed after her, panicking her as to his intentions. "Mr. Merrick! Jamieson! Jamie!"

At her capitulation, he was very smug. "I love it when I get my way. And so soon, too."

He lunged, grabbing her and hauling her under him, his body weighing her down.

"Get off me!" She pushed at his shoulders, but the oaf wouldn't budge.

"You're very pretty when you're angry."

The comment flummoxed her. He'd said much the

same when they'd been out in the forest, and his compliment had the same effect now as it had had then. She was thrilled that he found her attractive, but why would she be? Was she desperate for male attention?

"Get off me!" she repeated. "Don't touch me; don't maul me. Just let me out of this asylum."

"In our dickering over my marriage proposal"—he ignored her protest—"I've been remiss in clarifying some of the more *intimate* benefits you'll enjoy on becoming my wife."

"There aren't enough benefits in the world to convince me to marry you."

"When I was lying with you in the grass, in the woods—"

"I was not *lying* with you. You tackled me to the ground. Against my will, I might add. You're a brigand who has lunatics shooting at you."

He kept on as if she hadn't spoken. "It dawned on me that you're precisely the sort of female who ought to have a husband."

She scoffed. "What would I do with a husband?"

"You'd be surprised. Have you ever been kissed before?"

She blushed and glanced away. "Just this afternoon. By you."

"Did I kiss you this afternoon? I don't recall."

Their brief kiss had been wonderful, stupendous, amazing. He didn't recall it?

"You forgot? How could you?"

"I was teasing you. I didn't forget." The swine laughed, then sobered. "Close your eyes."

"Why?"

"I'm going to kiss you again, and this time, I'm going to do it properly."

"I don't want to kiss you," she insisted, but the breathy quaver in her voice belied her words.

"I don't care what you want. I'm going to do it anyway. Now close your eyes."

She should have argued, should have refused, but he looked so beguiling, as if he might possess some fondness for her, after all. The protective wall around her heart started to melt, and suddenly she wanted to be kissed by him more than she'd ever wanted anything.

Her eyelids fluttered shut, and she braced, expecting to be manhandled, but he didn't move, and she grew impatient. She was about to tell him to hurry when his lips brushed hers, the caress light as a butterfly's wings.

Their mouths were barely joined, and it was the sweetest, most enchanting interval of her life. She couldn't have said how long they lingered—perhaps a few seconds, perhaps an eternity—but when he drew away, she was bereft at the loss.

Gradually, she floated out of her sensual malaise and murmured, "Oh my . . ."

"Oh my, indeed."

"I want to do it again."

"I think I do, too."

As he began again, there was none of the tenderness he'd exhibited prior. He claimed her in a torrid, exotic manner that was beyond her realm of experience. With his arms wrapped around her, she was crushed to him, her feminine spots pressed to his, and her breasts in particular were elated with the naughty placement. Her nipples swelled and ached.

His fingers were busy, tangled in her hair, yanking at the pins and combs so that it fell in an auburn wave. He massaged her everywhere, as he continued to plunder her mouth, and the feelings he stirred were so powerful that she was glad she was prone. If she'd been standing, she might have collapsed to the rug in a stunned heap.

His tongue flicked against her lips, asking, asking again, and she recognized what he was seeking. She opened for him, and they engaged in a merry dance that had her reeling with sensation.

He shifted so he was more fully on top of her, his torso wedged between her thighs, and of their own accord her legs widened to provide him greater access. He fit perfectly, and she reveled in the odd positioning.

To her surprise, she had an incredible knack for wicked behavior. When he clutched her hips and flexed his loins, she instantly grasped what was required and met him thrust for thrust.

What did it portend? Where were they headed?

His hand was drifting to her chest, and without warning, he slipped it under dress and corset to stroke her bosom. The agitation he created was electrifying, and she moaned with excitement. She was on fire, burning with a strange flame that was about to incinerate her with pleasure. She struggled toward it, anxious to reach its heat, when he halted and pulled away.

He glared at her as if he was angry, as if she'd done something awful, when she couldn't imagine what it might have been. He was a skilled roué, while she was a sheltered spinster. How was she supposed to know what to do? If he made one derogatory remark, she couldn't predict how she'd react.

"What is it?" she demanded. "What's wrong?"

"Nothing's wrong." He appeared smug again. "Everything's very, very right. Let's get you back to your own bed."

"To my bed! Are you insane?"

"Tomorrow will be hectic, and you should rest."

"But I . . . but we . . ."

She hadn't the vocabulary for libidinous discussion, so she couldn't inform him of how ragged she felt on the inside. His ministrations had rattled loose her innards so that it seemed as if she were perched on a high cliff and about to jump off. He'd ignited a blaze, and she was eager for him to extinguish it.

He sat up, and she was irked to note that he was composed and completely unaffected, while she was frantic, confused, and thoroughly undone.

"You need to go," he said.

He tugged her up, her feet dangling over the edge of the mattress. He stood, and she should have stood, too, but her legs were rubbery and too weak to hold her.

"Why must I?" she inquired.

"Because, my little vixen, if you stay another second, I shall be overwhelmed by passion, and I'll do something I oughtn't."

"What do you mean?"

"I *mean* that a man can become aroused to where he can't control himself."

"And you are there?"

"Yes, and despite what you may have heard about me, I intend for you to have a wonderful wedding night. So let's get you out of here, while I still have the strength of will to let you leave."

She considered quarreling over his certainty that they would marry in the morning, but at the moment her head was spinning, her body in a dreadful state, and she couldn't put two coherent sentences together.

He guided her to the floor and steadied her. Then he escorted her to the door, finally opening it when she didn't wish to go.

"Would you like me to walk you to your room?" He sounded like a gallant swain.

"No, I can find my way."

They stared and stared, a thousand comments swirling between them that couldn't be voiced aloud.

"We'll get on just fine," he murmured. "Don't worry so much. It will all work out."

"But I don't want to—"

He laid a finger on her lips, silencing her; then he leaned down and kissed her very sweetly, very tenderly.

"You don't ever have to be afraid of me," he whispered, and he urged her into the hall.

She dawdled, unable to depart. It seemed wrong to go, wrong to spend the night without him, but his calm expression indicated that the encounter was concluded.

Not knowing what else to say, she whirled away and went to the stairs. All the way up, his keen gaze followed her until she vanished from sight and she was all alone.

Chapter
FOUR

We have to kill him."

"The bastard is like a cat. He has nine lives."

Ophelia glared at Percy, furious that he had no knack for homicide when she could have slain Jamieson Merrick a dozen times over. She'd offered to pull the trigger out in the forest, but Percy had insisted that *he* should have the satisfaction of dispatching Merrick to the great beyond. Yet Percy had botched it.

How difficult could it be to murder one lone man?

"Father taught you to shoot when you were three years old," Ophelia nagged. "How could you have missed?"

"Anne was there with him. She was in the way."

"So? What has she to do with your failing to rid us of Merrick?"

"I didn't want to hit her by accident."

"Oh, for pity's sake. Who cares about her?"

"You don't understand."

"No, I don't. Why don't you explain it to me?"

"It wasn't as easy as I thought it would be. I'm still getting used to the notion."

Ophelia rolled her eyes in disgust. "Why don't you get *used* to it a tad faster? The filthy swine is here, and the first night out he's sleeping in your bed!"

"Don't remind me."

"He's stolen your title, your fortune, and your property, and he's had you moved to a closet that's tiny enough to be a chambermaid's. In the morning, you're to leave Gladstone forever. What will it take to shame you into action?"

"Did you see how he lords it over me?"

"Yes, and how you can tolerate his still breathing is a mystery I can't solve."

"You heard him. He knows I'm the one who attacked him."

"So? How can that paltry fact keep you from trying again?"

"But I can't fathom why he's leery of me. Aside from our initial meeting, I've been courtesy, itself. I followed your advice to be as accommodating as possible, and it had to have put him off guard."

"Obviously, my plan didn't work. He blamed you immediately."

"We must be more cautious. Now that he's made a public accusation, if he were to suddenly perish, fingers would point directly at me."

She stalked over to her jewelry box and retrieved a very small, very sharp knife. "I'll go to his room and stab him to death this very second. Just give me the word, and it's done."

She stared Percy down, daring him, challenging him, but knowing he wouldn't consent. Not right away anyway. He'd need to be cajoled, but in the end, once she'd sufficiently goaded him, he'd be more vicious than she could have imagined.

It had always been thus between them. She was the wicked one, the depraved one, and she enjoyed coaxing him to mischief he didn't wish to attempt. Ultimately, he would relent, eager to prove that he was tougher and stronger than she.

She waved the knife, pretending she was ready to march down the hall and commence the assault. Simmering with rage, Percy stomped over and yanked it away.

"Give me that thing before you hurt yourself."

"You won't use it on him. Why shouldn't I?"

"I won't have him murdered inside this house. If he is, the investigations will never stop, and I'll be the prime suspect."

"I want him to die here—where he's caused so much trouble."

"Not in the mansion. Or anywhere close to the mansion. It has to be somewhere where he won't expect it. Out in the woods or along the road."

Percy leaned in, so that she was pressed to her dressing table, the edge cutting into her buttock. She could feel his hard cock against her thigh. When they quarreled, he grew aroused, and the more she enticed him, the quicker he'd be incited to do as she demanded.

Their incestuous lust for each other had sparked when they were very young. After their nanny tucked them in at night, Ophelia would sneak to Percy's bed, would slip under the covers and touch him all over. As they became adolescents, the attraction only increased.

Ophelia had never wasted any effort fretting over their abnormal passion. Their amour seemed normal and destined to occur, so it had been a huge surprise when their mother, Edith, had caught them and objected so vehemently. Their deviance was the reason for her mental decline, but Ophelia couldn't care less.

Percy was her love. Percy was her life. Percy was her lump of clay to mold and form so that he behaved exactly as required.

Her world had been perfect. She'd had a husband, without the bother of one. She'd had the acclaim of being a countess without having to suffer an earl's male dominion. *She* ruled Percy. She'd made the decisions and managed the estate; then, like an evil curse, Jamie Merrick had appeared on her horizon.

He was taking everything from her, and to top it off, he was intending to marry Anne! Anne would be placed above Ophelia. Merrick was piling on humiliations faster than Ophelia could tabulate them, and the affronts couldn't be allowed to stand.

Percy leaned nearer, titillated by her sheer red negligee. He shoved the thin straps off her shoulders, revealing her two spectacular breasts. His gaze heated; his nostrils flared.

"I'll kill Merrick for you," he vowed.

"You haven't the nerve."

"I do. You'll see."

Ophelia couldn't guess if Percy was sincere, but she wouldn't worry about it. Merrick was set to evict Percy in the morning, after the wedding, and if Percy gave up and left without a fight, Ophelia didn't want him.

Merrick's overture, where he'd suggested Ophelia be his bride, was fascinating, and she was considering his proposal. She could scare Anne into fleeing, then Ophelia would be the next logical choice, and now that she'd met Merrick, she wasn't so sure she'd mind being his wife. He looked so much like Percy—as Percy had been before dissipation had made him soft and portly—and possessed a dangerous, assertive air that Percy lacked.

She arched up, urging Percy to feast. She'd shut her eyes, would ride him and make believe he was Merrick, that the filthy pirate was taking her against her will.

Percy had just dipped to suck on her nipple when someone burst into her boudoir.

"Fornicators!" a familiar, croaking voice charged. "Fornicators!"

Percy lurched away as if Ophelia had the plague. She glared over to where aging, crazy Edith was quivering with indignation.

"Oh, for God's sake," Ophelia barked at Percy. "I thought you locked the door."

"I thought I had, too," he barked back.

"I can't deal with this. Get her out of here."

Despite his unholy proclivities, Percy was one of the few people who could still persuade Edith to do anything. With her wits so addled, she frequently assumed that Percy was her deceased husband, and she'd meekly obey his dictates, which was the only reason Ophelia hadn't smothered Edith in her sleep. Once Percy lost the ability to control her, she was a dead woman.

"Edith!" Percy said. "Why are you out of bed? You know you're not permitted to wander."

"You must listen to me! It's a sin, I tell you. A sin!"

"Edith!" he snapped more testily. He grabbed her by the elbow and escorted her out.

As he stepped into the corridor, he peered at Ophelia over his shoulder, his exasperation clear, his lust unassuaged. He was visually promising to return, and Ophelia nodded her assent, though she didn't mean it.

Edith's ranting would keep him occupied for hours, and Ophelia wouldn't wait for him.

The second he walked off, Ophelia raced to the mirror to check her hair and straighten herself. Jamieson Merrick was in the adjoining bedchamber, and it was high time she paid him a visit.

§

H ello, Miss Carstairs."
        At hearing a male speaking from so close by, Sarah Carstairs jumped in alarm. When Jack Merrick emerged from the shadows, she calmed a bit, but not much.

With all the changes in the house, it had been impossible to relax, and she'd finally given up and strolled outside. Apparently, she wasn't the only one who couldn't sleep.

He'd been quiet as a prowling cat, leaned against the balustrade and watching her from farther down the verandah, and he neared till he was right next to her. He was tall, six feet, and broad shouldered, and with her being just five foot six, he seemed incredibly large and manly in a fashion she enjoyed.

His size and stature flustered her, as did his attractive looks. With his black hair and piercing blue eyes, he had a rough, menacing manner that intrigued her, and she hated that she'd noticed him in such a physical way. It had been an eternity since a man had drawn her attention, and she knew she should spin around and go in, but she didn't.

"Hello, Mr. Merrick," she greeted.

"I see your insomnia is as bad as mine," he said.

"Who could rest with all this drama?"

He chuckled. "Jamie has a knack for theatrics, doesn't he?"

"He definitely does. Was he always this way?"

She was fishing for details, but too polite to come right out and ask what she was dying to know: Would Jamieson Merrick actually force Anne to marry? And what would happen both if she did and if she didn't?

"Yes, he's always had a flair for arrogance," Merrick admitted. "When we learned that he'd been born an earl, I wasn't surprised in the least. The title fit him exactly."

"There have been so many awful stories," she said. "Is he a good man?"

"As good as can be expected."

It was an enigmatic response and did nothing to ease her anxiety.

"If he marries my sister, will he be kind to her?"

"As kind as can be expected."

She scowled. "You're not being very helpful."

"This is new territory for me. If we were on a ship's deck and pillaging another pirate's bounty, I could tell you precisely what he'd do. But in this situation, I haven't a clue."

"But you know his character. It wouldn't alter merely because he's in a different location."

"No, it wouldn't."

It was the perfect opening for him to expound, but he was silent as stone, and she could barely resist the urge to reach over and shake some answers out of him.

He sat on the rail, his hips on the edge, his arms and ankles casually crossed, and he stared up at the mansion, its shape outlined in the moonlight.

"Have you always lived here?" he inquired.

"Since I was a baby. Our parents died, and my aunt Edith brought us to stay with them."

"You're so lucky," he murmured with a great deal of envy.

"Yes, I am," she agreed, not meaning it.

She didn't feel lucky. It was difficult, having to grovel to her Merrick cousins. They were selfish and cruel, and Ophelia in particular was overbearing. She relished tormenting Sarah and had wielded Sarah's painful secrets like an executioner's axe, constantly threatening to tell if Sarah didn't do as Ophelia bid her.

Sarah often felt that she was little more than Ophelia's slave, so for the most part, she tried to be unobtrusive and inconspicuous, to never bother her cousins or yearn for more than she'd been given. Years earlier, she'd been terribly greedy, but that sort of covetousness could drive a person insane.

She was older now—and much wiser. The consequences for insatiable conduct were exceedingly dire, so she'd convinced herself that she was contented with her lot. She would never again crave more than what she had.

"And how about you?" she queried, still delving for information. "Where was your home before you returned to Gladstone?"

"I didn't have one."

"Everyone has *one,* Mr. Merrick."

"Not me. I grew up at sea. With Jamie. I'm a nomad. I'd give anything to have a spot like this to call my own."

"Will you and Mr. Merrick—that is, Lord Gladstone—reside here full-time?"

"I doubt it."

"But why wouldn't you?"

"I suppose we're not the type to settle down. We never learned how."

"Why would your brother fight so hard to regain this place if he doesn't care about it?"

Jack shrugged. "It's his, and he's entitled to it, but he doesn't have to like it."

"What will become of Anne? Will he take her away?"

"I don't know his plans."

The comment was a bald-faced lie, Sarah was sure. She'd seen Mr. Merrick and his brother together. They were thick as thieves. When one of them inhaled, the other exhaled, their entire existence bound as if by invisible threads. Jack Merrick would have been apprised—down to the most minute detail—of what Jamieson Merrick intended to do, and the fact that he couldn't say, or *wouldn't* say, was extremely worrying.

It boded ill for Anne; it boded ill for herself.

"I spoke to Anne a while ago," Sarah told him. "She's discussed matters with your brother. He claims that if she weds him, he will let me remain on the property for as long as I wish."

"Did he?" Merrick was completely noncommittal.

"Is he a man of his word?"

"Occasionally."

She snorted. "You're an obnoxious tease, and I have no idea why I'm talking to you."

"What would you have me say?"

"I want you to enlighten me as to what will happen in the morning."

"How would I know? I'm not a fortune-teller."

"Will your brother keep his promise?"

"Will your sister do as he's demanded and wed him?"

"How would I know?" Sarah tossed back, and he was the one who snorted.

"Now who's being a tease?"

She was peering out across the garden, while he was still studying the house. He turned toward her, and it was the strangest impression, but suddenly she felt a powerful urge to fall into his arms and cast caution to the wind.

He felt it, too, the sense of connection flowing between them, and she could perceive his shocked awareness. She was no sheltered virgin like Anne, and she recognized what was occurring. He desired her, and the realization made her heart pound.

A dangerous and blazing need swept through her, and she was desperate to be touched by him, which stunned her to the marrow of her bones.

Her prior scandalous behavior had proven that she was possessed of a weak moral constitution and, given the slightest encouragement, she would do any reprehensible thing. She'd once been a virtual cauldron of smoldering lust, and she continually battled the scurrilous impulses. Yet a man had merely smiled at her again, and she was eager to leap to iniquity.

What was wrong with her? Had she no honor? No strength of will?

"What would it be worth to you," he asked, "to have Jamie's oath that you could remain at Gladstone?"

"Why? Could you get him to promise and mean it?"

"If I wanted to. If the price was right."

"That's the most sordid proposition any man's ever made to me."

"It was horrid, wasn't it?"

"I'm going to pretend that you had too much brandy after supper."

"It's more likely that I'm too exhausted to be circumspect." He scrutinized her, his interested gaze roving down her torso. "I notice that I didn't drive you into a maidenly swoon."

"I'm a bit beyond swooning."

"I'm glad to hear it. I can't abide a timid woman."

He shifted, narrowing the distance between them as she hadn't dared. She could feel his heat, could smell his skin.

"Are you ever lonely, Miss Carstairs?"

"No," she lied.

"Well, I'm lonely—every minute of every day. And I'll be here for weeks, maybe months."

It was the very worst thing he could have said to her. She rippled with anticipation, already conjuring how they could arrange a few trysts.

"Good night, Mr. Merrick."

"Call me Jack."

He leaned in and kissed her, and at the feel of him, so warm and solid and masculine, her knees buckled. Instantly, he caught her and dragged her to him, her body wedged between his thighs, a hand fisted in her hair.

He was hard for her, his phallus igniting a flash fire of wanton desire she'd never been able to control. For a mad, wild moment, she joined in the fray, kissing him back with all the passion an unloved, untended spinster could exhibit.

She pulled and scratched and clawed. But as he reached for her breast, as he fondled the soft mound, she yanked away with a moan of anguish.

"I can't do this," she wailed. "I can't. Not again. Not ever again."

She whirled away and hurried into the house.

❧

Jamie was awakened by the outer door to his suite being opened. As a female tiptoed toward him, he suffered a brief glimmer of hope that it might be Anne.

When he'd agreed to wed her, he'd scarcely considered what sort of person she'd be. He didn't plan to tarry at Gladstone, so the wife he'd leave behind had mattered very little. It could have been Anne or anyone.

But now that he'd met her, he was intrigued, thinking about her when he oughtn't, and stupidly anxious for her to consent of her own accord.

He knew her stride, though, and it wasn't her sneaking in. He'd left a candle burning, so he could see perfectly well that it was Ophelia.

Her fabulous blond hair was down and brushed out, the golden locks hanging to her waist. She was dressed in a slinky red negligee that outlined every lush curve and valley, and she'd reddened her lips to match her garment. The cosmetic enhancement made her look like a whore, but a very, very sexy one.

"Hello, Ophelia."

He scooted to a sitting position, propping the pillows against the massive headboard. Her interest piqued as she saw his bare chest and realized he'd be naked under the covers.

"Hello, Jamie," she said in a throaty, lusty way. "You don't mind if I call you Jamie, do you?"

"Not at all."

He remembered how cozy she was with Percy. He didn't trust Percy, and he trusted her even less. Had she come to shoot him? To stab him? To poison him?

"It's rather late, Ophelia. What can I do for you?"

"I've been in my room, trying to answer that very same question. What *can* you do for me?"

She sauntered over, her intentions clear, and he struggled to unravel her scheme. She and Percy were thirty years old, as Jamie was himself. By all accounts, she was a spinster who'd never had a single suitor, but from how she was advancing on him, she was no virgin.

How many lovers had she had? Who had they been?

She perched a hip on the mattress, a palm braced on either side of his lap. The front of her nightgown was loose, and he could see to her navel.

In a practiced move, she licked her bottom lip, by the simple gesture guaranteeing many courtesan's tricks. He was disgusted to find himself pondering how far he'd let her go before he stopped her. And he *would* stop her.

His standards regarding women were very low. He had no moral qualms, belonged to no church, worshiped no God, but he wasn't about to fornicate with his sister. It was a deed more depraved than he cared to attempt.

"When you initially arrived," she started, "you were throwing around marriage proposals."

"Yes, I was."

"You can't seriously mean to wed Anne."

He shrugged. "She's the best choice. Sarah Carstairs is too sad, and you're too old."

"I'm the same age as you," she bristled.

"Every man likes a young, innocent bride. You know that."

"But *Anne*!"

"What about her? She's sweet; she's biddable. She'll be ideal."

"She's a timid rabbit! You'll eat her alive. You need a wife who possesses your same zest for life."

"And you presume that would be you."

"Of course it would be me. Have you forgotten"—she

laid a hand on his belly and rubbed in slow circles—
"that your roving eye landed on me first?"

"No, I haven't, but you're my sister."

"So? Affinity be damned. You're lord and master
here now. You can make your own rules."

"That's my plan."

"I could be your countess," she purred. "I'd be so
good at it. You'd never want for anything."

"Wouldn't I?"

"No. I swear it to you." She was spectacular, oozing
sexual promise and coaxing him to misbehave. "I know
what you want, Jamie. I know what you need."

"Do you?"

"Oh yes."

"I'm very selfish. Whoever becomes my countess,
she'll have to please me however I demand. I never
permit a woman to refuse me."

"I'm sure you don't. That's why *I* should be by your
side."

"Anne is so pretty and so amiable. I'm not certain I
can be dissuaded."

"You'll let me try to change your mind, won't you?"

She crawled across his lap and tugged at the straps
on her negligee.

❧

Anne gave up trying to sleep and kicked off the
tangled blankets. She was hot and sweaty, careening between despair and excitement. She
was on fire with strange yearnings she didn't understand.

She slid to the floor and went to the window to stare

out. The night was rapidly passing, and in a few hours she'd marry Jamieson Merrick. Or not.

"Oh, what should I do?" she wailed to the stars, but they had no answer.

If she accepted, Sarah would be safe forever. Anne would be a countess and as much in charge of her destiny as any female ever was.

What woman wouldn't kill for such a chance? Was she crazy to dither and debate?

She'd heard horrid stories about Lord Gladstone, but they weren't true. He could be domineering, but he was also smart and shrewd and kind and funny. He had a wry sense of humor and a wicked wit that she enjoyed very much. He was unique in every way, a handsome, dynamic, and brave individual who could be hers if she dared make him her own.

She didn't know the secrets of wifely duty, but it was clear that *he* grasped what was necessary. He'd ignited a spark that had her craving what he'd provide as her husband. Would it be so bad to revel in the pleasure he'd lavish on her?

"Safe forever," she murmured. "Sarah and I . . . safe forever." She closed her eyes and rested her forehead on the cool glass of the window. "Oh, how can I do anything else?"

With her decision rendered, she was eager to inform him right away, and she wondered if he was still awake. She tiptoed into the corridor and raced down the stairs.

If she had a more devious, more salaciously personal reason for returning to the master suite, she wasn't about to admit it. Perhaps—just perhaps—he might deign to rollick with her again, and if he suggested a dalliance, she wouldn't complain.

The door to his room was ajar, and she pushed it open and entered.

"Lord Gladstone?" she whispered. When she received no reply, she called more loudly, "Jamie?"

There was a candle lit in his bedchamber, and bold as brass, she marched over and peeked in, but the sight that greeted her was so shocking she couldn't comprehend what she was seeing.

"Ophelia?" she said, the name thick on her tongue.

Her cousin glanced over and chuckled as if she and Lord Gladstone had shared a joke; then she raised up so that her naked breasts were fully visible. Gladstone was naked, too, their nude flesh pressed together. Even the most sheltered of virgins could figure out what was transpiring.

"Anne, what are you doing here?" Ophelia smiled a sultry, malicious smile, intended to humiliate and wound. "Isn't it a little late to be roaming the halls?"

"Ophelia?" she naively repeated.

She was very hurt, very angry, and a surge of potent jealousy rushed through vein and pore. Her accusing gaze shifted to Lord Gladstone, letting him witness how he'd betrayed her, how he'd broken her heart.

"Dammit!" he cursed.

Anne whipped away and fled.

Chapter
FIVE

W"here is your sister?"

"I don't have any idea."

Jamie glared at Sarah Carstairs, as the clock chimed the half hour, taunting him with how many minutes it had ticked past eleven.

Jack's boots pounded down the hall, and shortly he entered the parlor where the family was assembled for the ceremony.

"Well?" Jamie asked.

"She's gone. I questioned the maids and had them search her bedchamber. They say a satchel and some of her clothes are gone, too."

"Did she leave a note?"

"If she did, it wasn't in her room."

"Was she observed sneaking out?"

"One of the grooms believes he saw her, about seven o'clock this morning, walking down the road to the village."

Jamie's expression became lethal, and he focused it on Sarah Carstairs.

"I repeat: Where is your sister?"

"It sounds as if she left," Miss Carstairs replied, calm as you please.

"What was her destination?"

"I haven't a clue."

Her pretty green eyes were guileless, open wide, brimming with candor, but she was absolutely lying.

He towered over her, but she wasn't intimidated, which made him even more irate. He couldn't abide obstinate females.

"Can the two of you actually presume to best me?" he hissed. "Have you any notion of what I can do to you? To her?"

"I'm not afraid of you."

He was humored by her bravado, but it was so pitifully misplaced. Here on his estate, he could behave in any foul manner he chose, and no one would gainsay him.

"You have managed to incur my wrath. I haven't the slightest concern over you or why you would deem it appropriate to intervene in my personal affairs, but pray tell, why would she dare defy me?"

"In light of your monstrous ego, I'm sure this will come as a huge shock, but she doesn't care to have you as her husband. She wasn't overly impressed by the company you keep."

Her gaze drifted to Ophelia, letting Jamie know that Anne had informed her of the debacle in his bedchamber. Under Sarah's hot scrutiny, Ophelia preened, looking smug, as if she and Jamie had intentionally set out to hurt Anne, which had been the furthest thing from his mind.

Who could have predicted that Anne would return in the middle of the night? What had she wanted? Why had she done it?

She'd seen him with Ophelia! They'd been mostly naked, and though Jamie hadn't planned on any serious mischief, and would never have dabbled with Ophelia in any way that mattered, it had appeared as if they were about to engage in a sordid session of incestuous sex.

Was it any wonder Anne had fled? Considering what she'd witnessed, what woman would have stayed?

Percy stepped forward, determined to butt his nose into the mess. "Jamie, I'm so sorry about this. I counseled her to accept the match. I can't imagine what she was thinking."

"Can't you?" Jamie sharply retorted.

"I've advised her that I can no longer support her. She understood the enormous boon you'd extended."

"Obviously, she failed to grasp a few of the finer points." He spun to Sarah Carstairs. "Pack your bags and get out of my house."

There was a stunned inhalation of breath from everyone, but no one was brave enough to speak against his harsh command, save for his brother.

"Jamie!" Jack chided, a hint of warning in his voice.

"Be silent, Jack," Jamie barked.

Sarah Carstairs peeked over to where Jack lurked like a berserker. A glance flickered between them that Jamie didn't comprehend. Then she curtsied politely.

"As you wish, *Lord* Gladstone."

If she was frightened about being tossed out without a penny, she gave no sign.

Insolently, she strolled by him, and as she passed, Jamie said, "Jack, before she departs, search her. Make sure she doesn't take anything of mine."

She scoffed. "Don't worry. I wouldn't sully myself."

He recognized that he was being a beast, but he

couldn't remember when he'd last been so angry, and he couldn't stop lashing out.

He'd been ready to marry Anne Carstairs, to make her Countess of Gladstone, one of the most respected and wealthy women in the land. He'd been ready to provide for Sarah Carstairs—a female who wasn't even a blood relation—merely so Anne would be happy.

He'd never exhibited such kindness to anyone prior, yet the two sisters had flung his generosity in his face as if it had no value.

They were a pair of ungrateful, thankless curs!

Regal as a queen, Sarah sauntered out, but Jamie ignored her, and instead, stared at Percy, Ophelia, and Edith. They'd observed how Anne had humiliated him, and when he was surrounded by the Merricks he was standing in a nest of vipers. He couldn't let them see the smallest weakness.

"The rest of you will go, first thing in the morning."

Percy frowned, oozing feigned sincerity. "But you wanted us to attend the wedding."

"There will be no wedding."

"I could locate Anne for you," he cajoled. "I could talk to her again."

"There's no need," Jamie said. "She will be cast out, as her sister has been."

Ophelia piped up. "But Jamie, you can't mean to be rid of me. I thought . . ."

"Thought what?" His eyes were cold and hard.

"Wouldn't it be beneficial if I remained to aid you in the transition?"

"*All* of you are to go." He swept his hand, indicating mother, brother, and sister. "By tomorrow noon at the very latest."

He stormed into the hall and headed for the front door. Sarah Carstairs was in the foyer, huddled with Jack and whispering animatedly.

"Where are you off to?" Jack asked.

"I'm going to fetch Anne back to Gladstone."

"I thought you didn't know where she is."

"Oh, I *know* where she is, all right."

"And where is that?"

"The time is eleven forty. Do you see the vicar anywhere? He was supposed to arrive an hour ago to perform the ceremony."

"She's at the church?"

As Jack posed the question, Sarah trembled, proving that Jamie's deduction was correct.

"If not there, then somewhere close by."

"Would you like me to accompany you?"

"No. Stay here and escort Miss Carstairs off the property."

"Can't she at least wait for her sister?"

By arguing with a direct order, Jack was risking much. They were brothers, but captain and first mate, too. Usually, Jack was aware of what parts they were playing.

Apparently, Sarah Carstairs had rattled his wits—as Anne had rattled Jamie's.

"No. She had her chance to revel in my largesse, and she wasn't interested."

"But—"

"Just do it, Jack," Jamie snapped, "and be quick about it or you can return to the ship immediately. If you can't assist me in my endeavors here, then what good are you?"

"They're simply two anxious, poverty-stricken women who need your help."

"No, they don't. They've been very clear, and it's bad enough to have one of them plaguing me. I won't have two. I want her gone."

He marched out, and behind him, Sarah spoke to Jack.

"Will he hurt her?" she said.

"I don't know," Jack replied. "I've never seen him so enraged."

Jamie smirked, wondering himself what he might do. If Anne had been a man, he'd be loading his pistols, sharpening his sword, and checking the dagger in his boot.

No one refused him! No one! From the day he'd told the Prince Regent that he'd wed her, he'd felt that she was his—his charge, his chattel, his responsibility. Her skewed point of view was completely irrelevant, as Anne was about to learn to her peril.

He saddled his own horse in the stables and cantered off, the animal's hooves swiftly eating up the road to the village. Within minutes, he was dismounting outside the rectory. He proceeded to the door, rapped twice, then threw it open without his knock being answered.

They'd obviously been watching for him. He could hear frantic footsteps, hissing, and murmurs. Momentarily, the weasel of a vicar slithered in. He was all smiles and fawning courtesy, the precise sort of individual who aggravated Jamie the most.

"May I help you?" he inquired, pretending he didn't know who Jamie was.

"I am Jamieson Merrick, Lord Gladstone. You're late for my wedding. So is my fiancée. Where is she hiding?"

"Are you referring to Miss Carstairs?"

"Where is she?" Jamie demanded again, out of patience.

"I'm sure we can resolve this situation in a civilized fashion. If you would be so kind as to join me in the parlor . . . ?"

The vicar gestured to the room off the vestibule, a salon crammed with fussy furniture and objects. Evidently, he enjoyed having money to treat himself in frivolous ways.

"As I am now the earl at Gladstone," Jamie threatened, "the vicar's living in this parish is mine to dole out. I can keep you, or I can give it to another."

The vicar blanched with alarm. "You wouldn't."

"I would. Where is Miss Carstairs?"

The man was no fool. He didn't hesitate. "Second door on the right, at the top of the stairs."

"Thank you."

Jamie pushed past him and stalked up. He could sense Anne listening to his approach, could practically feel her consternation. She'd been positive the vicar would be able to reason with him.

What a ninny she was! Jamie had been raised in a world where there were no rules, where only the fittest and most brutal survived.

What force, what power, could one such as she—an indigent female, with no name or family—hope to wield?

Without pausing, without missing a stride, he entered the room, as she stood—mute and mutinous—and stared him down.

In her straw bonnet and worn traveling cloak, she looked so young, so lost, and he steeled himself against any tender feelings.

"Have you something to say to me?" he inquired.

She bit her lip, struggling as to what her response should be. His fury was palpable, and she didn't want to further antagonize him. At the same time, she wasn't sorry for running off, so she wouldn't display any meekness or contrition.

"Spit it out," he pressed, and he stomped across the floor till they were toe-to-toe.

"I can't marry you."

"Why would you presume your opinion in the matter to be requested or welcome?"

"I saw you with Ophelia!" she accused. "On the very night before my wedding! I won't have a husband who is so . . . so . . ."

She couldn't finish the sentence, so he finished it for her. "Who's so what? Dissolute? Reprehensible? Foul in his habits?"

"If you insist on putting it that way . . . yes."

"Miss Carstairs, I am a blatant fornicator. I admit it, but my personal associations are not—and never will be—any of your affair. If I choose to copulate with a dozen women, with a thousand women, it's none of your business."

To his amazement, the atrocious comment appeared to wound her.

"You care so little about me. You could be marrying anyone."

"You're correct, I could be, but in order to stabilize your life and your sister's, I agreed to have you over all others. However, it recently occurred to me that I have no idea why I sought to exhibit any compassion when it is so unwarranted and so unappreciated. Now let's go."

"Go?" She was incensed. "To where?"

"To Gladstone Manor."

"I'm not going anywhere with you."

"It's not up to you, Miss Carstairs. And you need to realize that it will never be up to you."

He wrapped his hands around her slender waist and, in a smooth, brisk move hoisted her onto his shoulder as if she were a sack of potatoes. Her head dangled down his back, her feet down his front, her shapely bottom hovering next to his ear. Amid much outraged screeching and pounding, he carted her out.

"Vicar!" she cried as they passed him in the foyer. "Vicar! Help me! Stop him!"

Jamie glared at the vicar, flashing a warning.

"Ah, I think this is for the best, Miss Carstairs," the sleazy preacher said, easily selling her out to the fattest purse. "I really do. You'll see. It will all work out in the end. I'll call on you in a few days to check how you're getting on. . . ."

He continued to prattle, but Jamie ignored him and proceeded out to his horse. He tossed Anne over the saddle and jumped on behind her. Within seconds, they were galloping to Gladstone, and she spent the short journey casting aspersions on his mother's character and hurling curses he was surprised she knew.

Once they drew up in the yard, he leapt down and pulled her down, too, and though she fought and complained, he wrestled her up to the master suite. She was like a slippery eel, all arms and legs, and her determination to escape was very intense, but his determination to prevent her was even more strident.

He slammed the door, spun the key, and stuffed it in his pocket.

"Let me out!" she seethed.

"No."

"You can't keep me here against my will."

"Yes, I can."

"You're a bully, and I hate you."

She stormed to the door, rattled the knob, and banged on the wood, begging for assistance, but the corridors were suspiciously empty, and no one rushed to her aid.

She whirled around, her eyes blazing. She was spitting mad, a ferocious sight, and he could only marvel at her foolishness.

The pins were gone from her hair so that it was falling. Her bonnet and cloak were lost in the fray. The sleeve of her dress was ripped, as was some of the stitching along the waist, and he couldn't remember how the fabric had been torn.

He'd never been acquainted with a female who spurred him to such pinnacles of temper, and he couldn't decipher what it meant. She was lucky he wasn't holding a switch. If he had been, he'd have thrown her over his knee and given her a good paddling.

"I'm tired of fussing with you," he advised.

"I'm not too keen on having to deal with you, either."

"Get your ass into my bedchamber."

"What?"

"You heard me."

"What are you going to do to me?"

He hadn't decided, but he threatened, "I'll let you know when we arrive."

"Tell me first."

"Walk in there on your own, or I shall carry you."

"No." She didn't budge.

"Go!" he shouted with such vehemence that she skirted by him and raced into the other room.

He followed her, and as he entered, he was annoyed

to note that she was trembling with terror. He wasn't an ogre unless driven to act like one, and she seemed to have no clue that his current ill humor was all her fault. She'd humiliated him in front of his enemies, yet she hadn't the vaguest notion of how he'd been wronged.

The woman was a menace!

When the Prince had insisted they wed, he'd obviously never met her. What rational man—royal or no—would deliberately burden a husband with such a fickle, ridiculous wife?

"I demand to speak with my sister," she bravely said.

"*You* demand?" Jamie bellowed, causing her to cringe. "By what gall do you *demand* of me?"

"She's my only family, and I . . . I wish to see her."

"Sarah has left."

"Left?"

"The terms of our bargain, Miss Carstairs, were that your sister would stay if you married me. Your chance to secure her future passed at eleven o'clock. She was evicted thirty minutes later."

"You sent her away?"

"Why wouldn't I? Do you think this a game? Do you think we play for jest? For sport?"

She was horror-stricken, on the verge of weeping. He felt as if he were kicking a puppy.

"But where will she go? What will she do?"

"What concern is it of mine?" he heartlessly asked, shamed by his ruthlessness.

He was a hard taskmaster, but he strutted and blustered for the benefit of recalcitrant men. At having reduced her to tears, he was disgusted with himself. What was the matter with him? Why did he allow her to goad him to insanity?

"Have you any idea of where she is?"

"No, I don't. Perhaps you should have thought of her plight a tad more carefully prior to your sneaking off."

"Oh, Jamie, how could you?"

At her use of his Christian name, he was thoroughly chastened, and his cheeks reddened with chagrin. His wrist began to ache, the old memory suddenly plaguing him, and he could barely keep from rubbing it to soothe himself.

She collapsed onto a chair, her head bowed, her hands clasped in her lap. She looked so beautiful, so forlorn, like a Madonna in a painting.

He fidgeted with dismay, trying to deduce what his next move should be. He spent such a small amount of time around women, deigning to fraternize mainly for carnal purposes, most of his encounters having been with whores in port towns. His exchanges were strictly business, money paid for services rendered.

At witnessing her anguish, he was so far out of his element that he might have been standing on the moon.

He was prepared to bestow a life of wealth and ease. Why would she reject such a boon? Why wasn't it enough?

He walked over to where she was sitting, and he reached out, as if he might comfortingly stroke her back or shoulder, but he let his arm fall away.

"We'll wed tomorrow, instead," he gently told her. "I'll have Jack find your sister and bring her home."

It was the largest stab at an apology Jamie had ever taken, yet she peered up at him and said, "Why won't you listen to me? I can't marry you."

"Can't? Can't?"

Rage made his voice shrill. His gaze narrowed till

her saw her through a red haze. A vein pounded so violently at his temple that he wondered if he was about to suffer an apoplexy.

"We'd have to speak vows before God," she explained. "You'd have to promise to be true to me, but we both know you never would be. I can't let you lie to God."

He was offering her the world, yet she balked over petty details like infidelity and God's displeasure! Was she deranged?

Appearing dignified and insulted, she rose. "I'd like to leave now. If I may?"

"If you may . . ."

Like a half-wit, he was repeating every word she uttered. He studied her, bewildered and speechless and positive that her absurd feminine hysterics had driven him to imbecility.

When he'd dragged her home, he hadn't known what he'd do with her. He'd simply wanted her back where she belonged. But the fog had cleared, and his motives were gradually growing defined and imperative.

"Take off your dress," he commanded.

"I most certainly will not."

"You will remove it on your own." He grinned wickedly. "Or I will remove it for you."

"You wouldn't dare!"

"Wouldn't I?"

As if an alien creature had slithered inside him and seized control, he clutched the neckline of her gown and ripped it down the center. The material dropped away and pooled at her feet.

She stood before him, clad in her undergarments, and at being so rudely bared she squealed with affront and crossed her arms over her torso.

"My dress! My dress!" she wailed.

"I'll buy you a dozen more—after the wedding."

He turned and started out.

"Where are you going? You can't leave me like this."

"That's where you're wrong, Anne. I am lord and master at Gladstone, and I can do anything I like—to anyone. At this moment, I'd *like* you to remain here, and remain you shall."

"But I'm trapped in your bedchamber, and I don't have any clothes!"

"Precisely. I doubt you'll hie yourself off to your precious vicar in corset and drawers."

He started out again, when she snapped, "Lord Gladstone!" When he didn't halt, she implored, "Jamie!"

He stalked over and pulled her to him. At feeling her so exposed and so vulnerable, he was inundated by a wave of lust so potent that he was amazed it didn't knock him over.

"You have tried my patience," he fumed, "beyond what any normal person should have to endure."

"I've done nothing but what I felt was right, which is to keep both of us from making a terrible mistake."

At having her describe their pending union as a *mistake*, he saw red all over again.

"I am struggling to honor you as I should—when I am not an honorable man." He gripped her shoulders and gave her a slight shake. "I've sworn to myself that I will wait for our wedding night, when you will be my respected and esteemed bride, but I am in such a state that if you continue defying me, I will shed my vow and proceed at once as if you were the lowest sort of harlot. Trust me: You won't enjoy it."

"You would . . . would . . . ravish me?"

"To force this marriage? Absolutely." He stepped away from her. "Stop fighting me, Anne. You can't win."

He strutted out, slamming numerous doors and spinning several keys, sealing her in like a dangerous prisoner, but attired only in her unmentionables.

He tarried a few seconds, then a few more. As her shock abated, she began hammering with her fists, yelling and cursing him again, but it wouldn't do her any good. She wouldn't be able to escape, but if she somehow managed it, he'd make sure the staff knew not to aid her in her folly.

He would not fail in what the Prince had ordered, and she would not foil him in his matrimonial plan.

In the morning, they would be wed, and he would have the chance to fornicate with her as he was burning to attempt. After seeing her, with her hair down and her clothes off, the notion sounded more exciting by the minute.

He left her to her fury, and he hurried down the stairs, eager to find Jack and have him fetch Sarah Carstairs back to the manor.

Chapter
SIX

Anne slowly came awake.

She was so warm and cozy that she couldn't open her eyes, but she knew she had to rouse herself. There was something important she was supposed to do, but she was too comfortable to remember what it was.

She sighed and smiled, wanting her drowsy malaise to go on just a while longer.

Suddenly, she jerked to full consciousness as she recollected that she was locked in Jamieson Merrick's bedchamber without any clothes.

The man was a demented fiend!

After he'd stomped off and left her, she'd pounded on the door till her limbs grew tired and her voice raw. Finally, exhausted and disheartened, she'd fallen onto his bed and dozed, but from the sunlight streaming in the window she'd slept all night—when she hadn't intended to.

She was about to sneak over and try the door again when it occurred to her that she wasn't alone. Someone was stretched out on the mattress behind her. Their bodies were spooned together, her back, bottom, and thighs touching where they had no business touching. An arm was lazily draped across her waist, a hand firmly planted on her belly.

She peered over her shoulder, and as she might have guessed, Jamieson Merrick was snuggled with her, but she had no idea of when he'd returned. She attempted to ease away, but he scowled and dragged her to him, as if—even in slumber—he refused to relinquish the slightest authority over her.

She was determined to escape, though, and she shifted away, but the second she moved he was alert and grinning as if he'd played a wicked joke.

She was ready to scold and berate, but he flummoxed her when he murmured, "Good morning, my beautiful Anne."

"Lord Gladstone."

"You call me Jamie when you're angry."

"Then I'm sure I'll be calling you *Jamie* very soon."

He chuckled and snuggled nearer.

"Can I go now?"

"No."

She was curious if cajoling would work where arguing never had. "Please?"

"No."

She could have started another quarrel, could have harangued about Ophelia, about his arrogance and conceit, but she was weary of their constant bickering.

"Have you found my sister? Is she all right?"

"She's fine. Jack was with her; she never left the house."

"Don't send her away again."

"It's up to you, Anne. Not me. Whether she stays or not is completely your decision."

She yearned to tell him what a lying swine he was. She had no actual control over Sarah's fate. Anne could do everything he asked and he might still renege on his promise not to evict Sarah, but any dispute was lost in the fog of their burgeoning intimacy.

Their bitter feud of the previous day had ended with him as the winner, but it wasn't a fair fight. Anne hadn't any weapons with which to battle him, and it was draining, going up against all that masculine certitude. He was bigger and stronger, and he wanted events to happen much more than she did.

His plans for her seemed inevitable. Wasn't it better to simply relent?

He came over her, his torso pressing her down. His naughty fingers caressed her hip. His lips were mere inches from her own.

Down below he was wearing his trousers, but the upper half of his body was bare. Instantly, she was awash in too much male flesh, but she wasn't alarmed. When he tucked away the bluster, he could be very charming.

"You smell good," he sweetly told her.

"Do I?"

"Yes, and you look so pretty, with your hair down and the sun shining on your skin."

He dipped under her chin and nuzzled her nape. He hadn't shaved, so his face was rough and scratchy, and it tickled, causing goose bumps to cascade down her arms.

He positioned himself between her thighs, and he flexed his loins, the odd gesture making him groan with what could have been pain or a strange sort of ecstasy.

"I'm always filled with lust first thing in the morning," he said.

"So it's a common condition that has nothing to do with me personally?"

"Oh, it has everything to do with you, my dear scamp."

She smiled, a glutton for his compliments.

"After we're wed," he continued, "there'll be no separate beds for us. We'll sleep together every night—so that I can wake up with you just like this."

He kissed her, one of those long, lush embraces he was quickly teaching her to relish. With his anatomy crushed to hers in several delectable spots, she should have pushed him away or at least pretended maidenly outrage, but she didn't want to object. The moment was incredibly precious, and even though he was a bully and she was furious with him, she was bowled over.

He was fussing with the laces on her corset, and as he yanked it away without her protesting, she wondered where her moral fortitude had gone. Whenever she was with him, he swiftly goaded her to iniquity, and he was so clever at tempting her that she forgot to complain or resist.

The thin fabric of her chemise was scarcely a barrier to any advance, and his hand easily drifted to her breast. He fondled the soft mound, gently squeezing the rigid nipple.

She couldn't understand how she'd failed to note that the rosy tip was so sensitive. It seemed to be directly connected to her womb, and with each pinch and tug her insides wrenched in an enchanting way.

"You've never had a lover, have you, Anne?" he asked.

"Of course not. When would I have?"

"So no man has ever touched you here but me?"

"No."

"Not even your beau, when you were seventeen?"

She scowled. "How do you know about him?"

"I know all about you. I made it a point to know."

"But . . . why?"

"I had to find out if I was getting a shrew."

"And since I'm not a shrew, you must have been relieved." When he didn't jump in to agree, she added, "I'm not a shrew. Right?"

"Right." His reply was hesitant, and he sounded as if he hadn't quite decided.

"Could you be a tad more certain?"

He laughed, redeeming himself. "You're definitely not a shrew."

"Would it have made any difference to you if I was?"

"I don't think so."

The comment was ominous, as if there'd been negotiations over her, and she wasn't too keen on his having private information to which she wasn't privy. She'd meant to inquire as to how he'd learned of her, who had investigated, and why, but he grinned again, and she was swept up, unable to pull away or fight his potent allure.

He was smug with his possession of her, and as he shoved away the bodice of her chemise, baring her bosom, she was lost. Any argument or discussion was incinerated by the heat he generated.

He gazed at her, rippling with male appreciation.

"My, my, Anne, you are so lovely."

He bent to her inflamed nipple and sucked it into his mouth, and he nursed as a babe would its mother, but with none of the tenderness. He was rough and demanding, his tongue and teeth nipping and laving her.

He played with both nipples, his lips tormenting one while his fingers worked at the other. He shifted back and forth, back and forth, driving her to such a fevered pitch that she was dizzy, and she started to fret. It had to be dangerous for something to feel so good.

"Jamie, stop. Oh, do stop."

"No."

"You never listen to me."

"I would—if you ever said anything worth hearing."

"Someone might come in. They'll see."

"No one will see," he insisted. "Besides, you spent the entire evening in my bedchamber, so you're thoroughly ruined. If a maid walked in just now, you'd be doing precisely what she'd expect."

"Ruined," she muttered with dismay. In the quiet ambiance of the lazy morning, she hadn't thought about the consequences of her being imprisoned in his room. By locking her in, he'd effectively quashed any refusal to wed.

If she spurned him now, she'd be tarred and feathered and run out of the neighborhood by an angry mob.

"There's no fixing the past, my little soiled dove. You'll have to marry me."

"You're a beast, Gladstone."

"Yes, I am, and don't you forget it. And you're to call me Jamie when we're alone. Don't forget that, either."

"I hate you."

"No, you don't."

"I do. I absolutely do."

"I can't abide a surly woman. Don't pout."

He commenced again, and for a brief second she imagined herself rearing up, tossing him off, and strutting out in a huff. But with her downfall complete, it seemed so futile. His mouth was at her breast, and every inch of her—down to bone and pore—was elated.

Though she was loathe to admit it, she was possessed of a previously unobserved licentious character, and he knew that she was. He'd lured it to the fore, had teased and cajoled until she wished to do nothing but lounge in his bed and romp with abandon.

With resignation, and a bit of petulance, she joined in, drawing him close and beginning to explore. She'd never viewed a man's body before, and she was intrigued by the differences. He was so firm and muscled, so strong and solid. She wanted to touch him all over, and she glided her hands over his shoulders and arms, excited by the feel of his hot skin.

To her amazement, he had hair on his chest. It was thick across the top, but it narrowed to a thin line and disappeared into his trousers. She kept riffling through it, never tiring of how soft and springy it was. He enjoyed having her massage him, and occasionally he'd tremble with delight. The realization—that she had the power to titillate him—made her more bold, which spurred him on, too.

His hand was moving down in slow circles, dropping lower and lower. She was too overwhelmed to fully focus on his destination, and before she could clearly discern his intent, he'd eased up the hem of her chemise so that her privates were bared.

He caressed her between her legs, his fingers tangled in her womanly hair. She tried to protest, tried to wiggle out from under him, but he merely held her more tightly.

"Jamie?" She felt as if she were standing on a cliff and he was about to hurl her over. "What are you doing?"

"I'm making love to you, as a husband does to his wife."

"I don't like it."

"You will."

"But . . . but . . . are you sure this is how it's done?"

"Very sure."

"It seems awfully . . . physical."

"It is that."

"But . . ."

"Hush."

He slid two crafty fingers inside her, and they fit perfectly, as if they'd been created for just that purpose and no other. To her ultimate chagrin, her loins flexed, eagerly trying to drag him deeper.

He smirked. "You are so right for me."

"What do you mean?"

He started pushing in all the way, then withdrawing. The tempo quickened, his gestures more precise.

"Let me show you something."

She was terrified about what it might be. "No. Don't show me anything. Whatever it is, I don't need to know."

He dabbed at a spot she'd never noticed prior, and it set off such a maelstrom of sensation that she arched up, hissing and spitting at him to desist, but he pinned her down and kept on. His thumb flicked out, again, again, until she shattered into a thousand pieces.

She cried out in wonderment and spiraled to the heavens, while he cradled her throughout the tumult. As she reached the peak and floated down, he was smug and chuckling again.

"What was that?" she asked when she could speak.

"Female sexual pleasure."

She glared at him. "Did I scream?"

He considered for a moment. "Yes, I would say that definitely qualified as a scream."

"Do you suppose anyone heard me?"

"Just the entire household—and maybe a few folks down in the village, too."

"Aah! What will they think?"

"They'll assume either that I'm beating you or that you're loose."

She blanched in horror. "I'll never be able to leave this room!"

"Poor me."

She gazed at the ceiling, mortified, but already secretly wishing they could do it again. Was it addicting? Could she become obsessed?

"Can it happen more than once?"

"Yes. Whenever you're in the mood. But only with your husband."

"We're not married."

"A minor technicality, I assure you."

"So . . . we could do it in the marital bed?"

"All the time." He nestled close and whispered, "Wouldn't such bliss be worth any price?"

At the carnal promise in his voice, she shivered.

She had a vision of herself, locked in his bedchamber—unwashed, unfed, unclothed—content to loaf and wait for him to inflict his base amusements. She saw herself chasing after him, begging him to proceed. She'd offer anything, would relinquish anything, would *do* anything, if he'd give her more of the same.

"You're going to kill me, aren't you?" she complained. "That's your plan. For some reason, you've been sent here to drive me crazy, and if that doesn't work, you'll slay me with ecstasy, instead."

"What a way to go." He sighed like the arrogant man he was.

"I hate you," she said again, which made him laugh.

Disgusted with him, with herself, she rolled onto her side and curled into a ball. He rolled, too, and spooned himself to her. With her ardor waning, the air was cold, and he pulled a blanket over them.

She yawned. "I'm so tired."

"Why don't you nap for a bit?"

"I just might."

"When you awaken, if you're very, very nice to me, I'll do it to you again."

"I'll never survive it."

He snuggled himself to her bottom, and as he took a slow, languid flex, he shuddered as if he was in pain.

"Tonight, after the wedding," he murmured, "I'll show you the rest."

Despite her lethargy, her body rippled with greedy anticipation.

Chapter
SEVEN

Jack Merrick stared out the window toward the park that sprawled behind the mansion. Sarah Carstairs had just walked by, headed into the woods with a basket slung over her arm. Without pausing to wonder what he was about, he hurried outside to follow her.

Their encounter on the verandah had been one of the more peculiar episodes of his long and sordid life, and he was fascinated by her.

She was beautiful and educated, serious and proper, her background the total opposite from his own, so he wasn't certain how he'd ended up kissing her with such wild abandon, yet he wasn't sorry.

The taciturn, pragmatic woman was no aging spinster, whiling away at her cousin's country estate. She was hot-blooded and eager. Jack had dabbled with whores who hadn't been as adept as she, and he was extremely curious as to how she'd come by her carnal experience.

If she was a virgin, he'd eat his hat!

Where was she going? Was she off to meet a lover

for a clandestine romp? The prospect disturbed him in ways he didn't care to acknowledge.

What sort of fellow would tickle her fancy? Probably some urbane, snooty aristocrat. He'd have persnickety manners and an annoying, upper-crust lilt to his words.

Jack hated the man already.

He hastened after her, keen to keep her in view. If he stumbled on her with a paramour, he wasn't sure what he'd do. He couldn't imagine spying like a pathetic voyeur, but he had to know what she was about.

The path meandered by a dilapidated cottage. The roof sagged; the window glass was missing, the holes covered with old boards. Sarah stopped in the weed-strewn yard and called out to someone. The door opened.

Jack had been expecting a grown man, so when a boy of nine or ten years emerged, he couldn't make sense of the sight. The lad was slim as a rail, half-starved, and dressed in clothes that were little more than rags.

His insolent expression was the same one Jack had observed on children throughout his youth. It was a look of accusation and distrust. He and Jamie had gazed at adults with the same sullen, bitter rage.

Sarah approached the boy, moving cautiously, as if he were a rabbit that might bolt down a hole. Chatting quietly, she set her basket on the ground, and it appeared to be loaded with food.

Jack crept nearer. He couldn't hear them, but he could see them clearly, and he was stunned to note the obvious: Sarah was talking to her son. She had to be. With his thick brown hair and big green eyes, he couldn't be anybody else.

A thousand questions spiraled through Jack's mind. When had this happened? *How* had it happened? Where was the lad's father? And most important, why was the child living in a hovel and being regarded as a dirty secret? Had Sarah been too ashamed to claim him?

The possibility incensed Jack. Every injustice he'd ever suffered from his own father rose up to torment Jack till he felt as if he were choking on the boy's appalling circumstance. It too closely resembled his own, and he lurched away, too disconcerted to continue watching.

He rushed to the manor, his temper at a slow boil. He'd kissed her once, and for some stupid reason he'd convinced himself that he understood her character. On learning that he didn't know her at all, he was so angry that he couldn't think straight.

Like a deranged lunatic, he proceeded directly to her bedchamber and stormed inside. He pulled up a chair and sat down to wait for her. It was wrong to enter, wrong to accost her over such a private matter, so he couldn't decide on the exact purpose of his mission.

Eventually, she trudged down the hall and slipped into the room. She collapsed against the door, pressed to it as though she might fall if she didn't have its sturdy support. She sighed with dismay and rubbed a weary hand over her eyes.

"Hello, *Miss* Carstairs."

At the sound of his voice, she glared at him but didn't seem particularly alarmed.

"What are you doing in here, Mr. Merrick?"

"I wanted to speak with you."

"What? You couldn't do it down in the front parlor?"

"No."

"Well, just because your brother abducted my sister

and is holding her hostage, don't presume that I'll stand for the same disgraceful treatment." She reached for the doorknob. "Get out, or I'll shout the house down."

"I'll go when I'm damned good and ready."

"Don't curse at me. I've had enough of you Merricks to last a lifetime. Where is my sister?"

"Still locked in my brother's suite."

"What is he doing to her?"

"I wouldn't hazard a guess."

When it came to females, Jamie had no scruples. Any wicked conduct was likely.

"When will he let her out?"

"When the vicar arrives to perform the ceremony. Not a moment before."

"So the wedding is on?"

"Of course it is. Why wouldn't it be?"

"I won't permit that womanizing reprobate to marry my sister. I don't care how high-and-mighty he's turned out to be. I'll never agree."

"It isn't up to you." Jack was tired of discussing Jamie, tired of having his older brother be the only topic on anyone's lips. He switched to the sole subject that interested him.

"What is your son's name?"

Panic flared, but she shielded it by tugging off her bonnet and hanging it on a hook in the wardrobe. She dawdled, straightening clothes that didn't need straightening.

"I have no idea who you mean," she contended.

"Don't you?"

"No."

"I saw you, Sarah. Out in the forest."

"You were following me? How crass."

"What's his name?"

"Oh, you must be referring to Tim." She'd sufficiently composed herself that she could face Jack, and she tried to be nonchalant, but she couldn't quite manage it. She went to her dresser and pretended to search for something in the drawer. "His mother died recently, and he doesn't have any other family, so he's all alone. I take him food occasionally."

"Liar," Jack hissed, and he uncurled from the chair and stalked over to her.

He leaned in, trapping her against the dresser.

He should have known she'd had a child. While she looked very much like slender, willowy Anne, Sarah had a mother's body. She was pleasingly rounded, with the type of lush bosom and curvaceous hips that only came after childbirth.

"How could you abandon him like that?" Jack charged.

She shoved him off. "If you're caught in here, there'll be a big ruckus. I'm not in the mood for it."

"Tell me about him!" he bellowed.

"Leave it be, Jack. It's none of your affair."

She skirted by him and flitted to the other side of the room, the bed between them as if it were a barrier that could keep him from asking the questions he was desperate to have answered.

"How old is he?"

"Nine."

"So you were sixteen when you became pregnant. Where is his father? Why wouldn't he marry you?"

"I have no details about his parentage. He was a foundling, given to a widow to raise."

With each volley, Jack was advancing on her, and she'd wedged herself into the space between the mattress and the wall. Her only escape would be to crawl across the bed.

"Who is his father!"

"How would I know?" she insisted through clenched teeth, her temper spiking in direct proportion to his own.

"And why is that?" Jack cruelly taunted. "Have you had too many lovers to count?"

She slapped him so hard that he staggered. His ears rang; his eyes watered. He stood like a fool, rubbing his burning cheek, clearing his muddled head.

"Go away," she said with a quiet dignity that shamed him.

"I'm sorry; I'm sorry. I'm being an ass. Forgive me."

He reached out to lay a comforting hand on her shoulder, but she batted it away.

"Go!" she repeated, tears threatening to fall.

"Who forced you to renounce him? Your aunt? Your cousin Percy?"

She was stoically mute, but he could see in her expression that he'd hit close to the mark. Her aristocratic relatives had been scandalized, had coerced her disavowal, and from her distraught state it was obvious the situation was eating away at her.

He couldn't fathom the attitudes of the wealthy and privileged. He'd come from a rough world, where babies were the natural result of illicit deeds. A child wasn't forsaken simply because the parents had behaved badly. An unwed mother wasn't shunned or cast out. It was the affluent who punished their pretty girls for doing what was normal, for having base drives that were impossible to ignore.

"Sarah," he said, reining in his fury, "Jamie wouldn't

give two figs about that boy's pedigree. Let's talk to him. You can publicly claim Tim, and bring him into the house."

"Are you mad?" she responded, dropping the pretense. "I could never claim him."

"But . . . why? Who cares what others would say?"

"I care! Me! I've lived here all my life, and the only thing I have to show for it is my good name."

"So Tim should continue to suffer merely because your neighbors might gossip about you?"

"You don't understand anything," she wailed, and she spun away from Jack, but the only place she could go was farther into the corner. She burrowed herself against the wall as if she yearned to become part of it and disappear.

"Then make me understand," he coaxed, and he stepped in and snuggled himself to her.

"Anne never knew," she whispered miserably. "They sent me away for a whole year, and they told her I was at finishing school. She believed I was off on a lark, having a holiday. She'd write me these chatty letters, and I'd have to write back and pretend that . . . that . . ." Her voice trailed off. "If she found out now, I'd die of shame."

"Is Tim aware that you're his mother?"

"No, and I could never tell him. How would I explain that I reside in this grand mansion, but he's not welcome in it with me? How could I admit that I dumped him off on a stranger as if he were a pile of rubbish?"

"You can't leave him out in the woods to fend for himself."

"Oh, I don't know what to do."

The yoke of her secret was too much to bear, and

she started to cry. Jack hated that she was so sad, and he turned her so he could take her in his arms.

He stroked her hair and murmured soothingly. Gradually, her tears slowed, and he reclined on the bed and brought her down with him. They stretched out together, as if it were the most ordinary thing in the world.

For a long time, he held her, and she was so still that he wondered if she was asleep, so she surprised him when she mumbled, "I'm not a whore—if that's what you're thinking."

"The prospect never occurred to me," he fibbed.

"I was young and foolish. He said he loved me, that we'd wed."

"Why didn't you?"

"He was engaged!"

"What a cad."

"I certainly thought so."

"Did he marry her?"

"Oh yes. She was very rich."

"Couldn't Percy have provided you with a dowry so he'd have had you instead?"

"I'd never have dared ask for one. Besides, even if Percy had agreed, it could never have been enough money."

"She was *that* rich, was she?"

"That rich," Sarah echoed, sighing, as if it had happened the previous morning rather than a decade earlier. "Do you ever wish you were someone else? That you could utter a few magic words and change who you are?"

"I've wished it every day of my life."

"So have I."

She peered at him, her beautiful green eyes poignant and glum, and he felt as if he were drowning, as if she'd bewitched him so that he could never do anything but exactly what she wanted.

"Lean on me, Sarah. I have wide shoulders. I can carry your load for a while. I don't mind."

The room grew very quiet, the interval terribly intimate, and he had to kiss her. It seemed that he had no other choice.

While there were now papers that said he was son and brother of an earl, the pesky detail couldn't alter who he was. He'd been orphaned, then kidnapped onto a ship where he'd been beaten and starved and worse. He'd seen and done things that were so foul the average human being would have perished just from witnessing them. He'd fought and won and survived.

He wasn't—and never would be—the type of man a lady like Sarah Carstairs could esteem, but he couldn't ignore the passion that sizzled between them, nor could he ignore the connection he felt.

At the moment, she was hurting, so her defenses were at a low ebb. It was inexcusable to take advantage, but he decided to proceed anyway. He'd dally with her for as long and as often as she'd permit, though he wouldn't behave as reprehensibly as Tim's father. Jack knew how to revel without her ending up pregnant.

He started in kissing her, and she was too weary to complain or quarrel. He was on top of her, his tongue in her mouth, his fingers busy at her bosom. As he caressed her, she moaned with resignation and delight, but when he slipped under the bodice of her gown to clasp her nipple, she stopped him.

"I can't, Mr. Merrick."

"I have my hand on your breast, Sarah. You should probably call me Jack."

She chuckled, but woefully. "I can't, Jack. I don't want this from you."

"It's not a matter of wanting, Sarah. It's a matter of *needing*. Let me please you. You'll feel better."

There was nothing to distract a person from his troubles like a raucous bout of fornication, so he began again, being forceful and insistent. She clutched at him as if she were dying, as if only he could save her. She pulled and hugged and rasped, digging her nails into his scalp, into his skin, but he didn't care. He wanted her to be heedless of her conduct.

Almost against her will, her hips responded, meeting his in an even tempo that seduced and promised. His cock was so hard, pushing into the soft cushion of her skirt, that he was amazed he didn't spill himself in his trousers like a callow boy.

He reached under her dress, fumbling up her leg like an uncouth oaf. He couldn't delay, couldn't woo her or display any finesse. He was simply desperate to touch her in her most private places.

He shoved two fingers inside her, being rough, being demanding, and with no more stimulation than that, she came in a potent orgasm. She spiraled up and up, until he wondered if her pleasure would ever end, but as soon as she finished, she was crying again. She squirmed away and showed him her back.

"My God," she muttered, "what's wrong with me?"

"There's naught wrong with you, Sarah. You're very fine."

"I should have been born a harlot," she said. "It's the only thing I'm good for. Just lust and lust and more lust."

Suddenly and without warning, they were swimming through some very deep waters, and he didn't understand what direction they were headed. He couldn't remember when he'd last had a partner who was so quick to find her release, but he didn't suppose he ought to mention it.

"You have a sexual temperament," he cautiously ventured. "There's nothing the matter with it."

"Nothing!"

"The people who say a female shouldn't enjoy mating are a bunch of pious idiots."

"But wouldn't you think I'd have learned something from the past?" She rose up on an elbow and glared at him over her shoulder. "You're the first man who's looked at me in an amorous way in an entire decade, and I fell into bed with you before I'd even gleaned permission to use your given name."

"And I didn't mind a whit."

"Well, *I* mind. I must be mad."

Wretched and furious, she flopped down.

Their brief foray had left him aching. He nestled himself to her bottom, taking a slow, leisurely flex, but she moved away, making sure there was plenty of space between them and indicating—at least in her opinion—that the tryst was concluded.

"Would you go?" she urged.

He didn't budge, and he thought about arguing, but he could tell that words would be pointless.

"Don't be sad," he said.

"I'm not sad," she claimed. "I'm mortified at my degenerate nature. Now I'd appreciate it if you'd let me fume in peace."

He climbed to the floor, and he stood, staring at her, dawdling like an imbecile, then gave up and sneaked out. His phallus was in terrible shape, and he hoped there was a competent whore in the village. In light of Sarah's fickle disposition, he imagined a throbbing rod would become a constant, so he'd best get acquainted with every trollop in the county.

Chapter
EIGHT

I t's for the best, Anne."

"How can you say that?"

Percy Merrick gazed at his cousin and bit down a caustic retort. Didn't she comprehend that she *had* to marry Jamieson Merrick? How could she think Percy would let her refuse?

Stupid girl.

He liked Anne much more than was wise, but it wasn't in a brotherly manner. No, his interest was purely carnal. He'd often considered sinister behavior toward her, and he couldn't understand why he hadn't forced the issue. She was completely beholden to him, and he should have demanded a higher price for his benevolence.

"Won't you help me, Percy?" she begged.

"No, Anne, I won't."

"But you've always been my friend, and you're my only male relative. Why won't you intervene?"

"You're being absurd to spurn him—especially when you've spent the night in his room."

"I didn't do anything!" She threw up her hands in exasperation. "How many times must I tell you? I tried to run away, so he locked me in to keep me in the house. That's all there was to it."

"He was in there with you! Am I to assume that the two of you were merely playing cards and drinking tea?"

"We were sleeping! At least, I was! I don't have a clue what he was doing."

The moment the words left her mouth, she blushed bright red as she realized that many dastardly things could have been done to her as she'd slumbered, and Percy fumed as he speculated as to what some of them might have been.

Jamie was notorious for his rampant fornications. In London, he'd cut a swath through the female members of High Society. No man's wife had been safe.

Had he already raped Anne? Had he taken her virginity as he'd taken everything else from Percy?

"The maids advise me that he ripped your gown from your body and they had to deliver new clothes."

Idiotically, she contended, "It was an accident. My dress . . . tore."

He laughed in a snide way, indicating she had no secrets. "What were you required to do that convinced him to let you out?"

"Nothing! I had to swear that I wouldn't sneak off again before the ceremony."

"And will you?"

"Well . . ."

"Do you imagine the servants haven't started talking? Do you suppose the neighbors haven't heard of your shame?"

She studied the rug and fiddled with her skirt. "I hadn't thought."

"No, you hadn't. You must listen to me, Anne. We tried to bring the vicar back this morning, but he can't come till tomorrow. You have a reprieve for today."

"I don't want a reprieve; I want a rescue."

"You're being silly. Any woman in the land would give her right arm to be in your shoes. You're marrying an earl; you'll be a countess."

"I don't want to be a countess. I've never wanted that."

"Jamie could have searched for years for a bride, but he chose you. You should be grateful."

"I am grateful, but it's all happening too fast. I hardly know him, and I . . . I . . . don't love him."

"Bah! Love has nothing to do with marriage. He's offering you a home and a fine position here at the estate. You should go to your room and reflect on your fortunate situation."

"He scares me. I'm afraid of him."

"Your fears are unfounded. I recognize that he's a bit rough around the edges, but you'll get used to his odd habits. Every bride feels the same doubts before her wedding."

"Really?"

She oozed sarcasm, and she was glaring at him so haughtily that she was lucky he didn't slap her. Where had she come by such temerity? Why couldn't she sympathize with *his* predicament? Did she presume she was the only one with problems?

Though it infuriated him, Percy agreed with Ophelia that he should pretend to be a gracious loser. It kept people off guard. Should a diabolical mishap befall Jamie, the finger of blame had to point in other directions, but Percy was sick with all the unctuous courtesy that was necessary in order to deflect suspicion.

"Yes, really," he sneered. "An approaching wedding is cause for jitters."

"And you know so much about it because . . . ?"

"I know so much about it because—as you said yourself—I'm your only male relative, which means I decide for you. And I've *decided* that you shall wed the new earl." He leaned in, menacing her with his greater size, with the authority he'd always had over her. "Am I being clear enough for you?"

She shrank away, looking very frightened, and he reveled in her anxiety. He'd never been sufficiently stern with her, and at seeing how easily she was intimidated he rippled with an excitement that was almost sexual.

"I understand perfectly," she sulked.

"Good. Now I'm weary of your complaints. Leave me be."

She hovered, aggrieved and wanting to persist with her pleading, but at viewing his stony expression she scampered off in a snit, and he frowned at her retreating form.

He might have temporarily lost the status of being an earl, but he'd been in charge of her for most of his life, and despite what Jamie assumed to the contrary, Percy would continue to command her in any fashion he desired. In fact, he'd do more than *command.*

Anne had never known her place, had never acknowledged the power Percy wielded over her, but she needed to be reminded. It would be so satisfying to creep into her bed, to steal her virginity—if Jamie hadn't already taken it. Jamie would get a ruined bride, which would be a little wedding gift from Percy.

Percy might even impregnate her, so that she'd give

birth to Jamie's heir, but the babe would be Percy's. It was such a sweet picture to ponder.

If Jamie had actually proceeded, if he'd actually lain with Anne, then Percy would betray him in other ways.

Jamie wouldn't stay at Gladstone. Eventually, he'd go back to London, to his mistresses and his ship and his obscene parties. His brother would go, too, and Anne would be left behind. She'd be responsible for the house and accounts, and she wouldn't dare deny Percy access to what had been his. She hadn't the nerve.

No matter how futile the lawyers declared his case to be, Percy didn't ever intend to relinquish Gladstone. He would regain his position; then he'd avenge the humiliations Jamie had inflicted.

Anne was the key. If she tried to refuse Percy anything, she would finally learn how ruthless he could be. With Jamie in London, she'd be alone and unprotected. Percy could do whatever he wished to her, and she'd be too terrified to inform Jamie of what was occurring. Jamie was such a hothead that he might murder Anne for any cuckold.

His smile grim, he realized that he was aroused just from contemplating how he'd ultimately best Jamie. Desperate for immediate tending, Percy went to locate his sister.

❦

"Sarah, come here," Ophelia ordered as Sarah tiptoed by, obviously hoping to be invisible.

She trudged to a halt. "What do you want, Ophelia?"

"I left some mending for you in your room. I need it by tomorrow."

There were a dozen maids who could complete the task faster and better than Sarah, and Sarah hated sewing. They both knew it.

"I'm busy, Ophelia."

Ophelia chuckled, relishing the game Sarah occasionally played but could never win. "How is Tim? I haven't seen him around lately."

It was a subtle threat, one that Ophelia used constantly and to great effect. She could and would do anything to Tim without a moment's hesitation, and Sarah had no doubt as to whether Ophelia was vindictive enough to follow through.

For an entire decade, Ophelia had taunted Sarah with the prospect of the *accidents* that could befall her son, and Ophelia was so humored by Sarah's pathetic bond to the little bastard. Her fondness had allowed Ophelia to garner ceaseless boons, with Sarah unable to decline or fight back.

"The mending, Sarah," Ophelia urged. "When can you have it ready?"

Sarah gnawed on her lip, a thousand rude retorts festering, begging to be spewed; then, like an obedient slave, she nodded. "I'll see to it right away."

"You do that."

Sarah slithered off, and Ophelia smirked, enjoying her petty torment.

Feigning nonchalance, she sauntered down the hall to wait near the salon where Anne was sequestered with Percy. As Anne emerged, looking distraught and furious, Ophelia was simpering with fake sympathy.

"Anne, what is it?"

"Nothing."

Ophelia stepped in, blocking Anne's access to the stairs. Before Ophelia talked to her brother she had to hear Anne's side of the story.

With so much at stake, Ophelia had to ensure she was in the middle of all the intrigue. If she wasn't, how would she ever orchestrate the conclusion she sought?

"Tell me," she demanded.

"It wouldn't interest you, and I'd rather not discuss it."

Anne was still smarting over her catching Ophelia in bed with Jamie. Not that there'd been time for anything relevant to transpire. Anne's inopportune appearance had seen to that, but she wasn't aware of how rapidly Jamie had ended the tryst after she'd fled.

His behavior was enough to make Ophelia suspect he had some scruples.

"You might as well spill it," Ophelia needled, "or I'll go ask Percy and find out his version. I can side with him—or not."

Ophelia could be an ally or an enemy, and her relationship with Percy could be used to benefit or harm. Though Anne was loathe to parley, she considered her options, then tucked away her sour attitude.

"I tried to convince him that I can't marry Lord Gladstone."

"Don't call that pirate *Lord* Gladstone to my face or I'll rip your tongue out."

"Fine then. He insists that I have to marry Jamie."

"But you don't want to?"

"No."

Ophelia shielded her livid reaction. She wouldn't openly work against Percy, but she'd cut out Anne's heart and feed it to the chickens in the yard before she'd let Anne become countess.

"Did Percy say why you should proceed?"

"He thinks that I'm lucky Jamie picked me and that I should be glad."

"He would," Ophelia falsely commiserated. "He's not the one who will have to live with that barbarian after the ceremony."

"Precisely, but he couldn't fathom why I'd have reservations. Since I was . . . ah . . ." Embarrassed, Anne cleared her throat. "Since I was forced to spend the night in Jamie's bedchamber, I suppose there's no other result that's possible."

"I can't believe Merrick locked you in like that! I begged him to release you," Ophelia lied, "but the man is insane. He listens to no one."

"I know. I'm scared of him. He chose me, but it should have been you, instead. You're much better suited to be his wife."

Ophelia scowled. Had she just been insulted? She studied Anne, trying to decide, but Anne looked innocent as a cherub painted on a church ceiling.

"Have you spoken with your sister?" Ophelia inquired.

"I was about to."

"I noticed that she's friendly with Jack Merrick. Perhaps she could persuade him to reason with his brother on your behalf."

"That's a marvelous idea."

Anne flitted off, and Ophelia tarried, wondering how the universe could have conspired against her so completely. Was there no justice in the world?

Ophelia had plotted and planned, had managed and directed, while Percy had reveled in his London pursuits. She'd never been able to make him grasp how the estate paid for his amusements. He only wanted to play—and to have money available when he needed it.

She had kept the coffers full of cash, and now Anne might wind up in charge of everything! It was a tonic so bitter that Ophelia couldn't swallow it.

She went to the stairs and climbed, eager to fret and fume in the privacy of her boudoir. She'd occupied the countess's suite for nearly two decades, having evicted her mother from it at the earliest opportunity. It was her sanctuary, her haven, and she hastened toward it, lost in thought, when her mother leapt out from the shadows.

Ophelia jumped a foot.

"Mother, what are you doing?"

"I'm watching you," the demented shrew said. "I'm watching you and him."

"You're crazy as a loon," Ophelia hissed. In case there was a servant lurking who might overhear, she leaned closer and whispered, "As soon as this mess with Merrick is resolved, I'm sending you to an asylum. I intend to select the most disgusting one I can find. Do you understand me, Mother?"

"The Lord will protect me, you spawn of Satan."

Ophelia laughed. "Satan didn't spawn me, Edith. You did. It's all your fault."

"Not my fault," Edith declared. "I knew nothing! Nothing!"

"Are there any bats left in your belfry?"

Ophelia walked on, and Edith began spewing Bible verses, which set Ophelia's teeth on edge. Edith had always been peculiar, but she hadn't really fallen into the abyss of madness till the day she'd stumbled on Ophelia and Percy immersed in a particularly raucous session of fellatio.

She hadn't been the same since.

The old lunatic was growing more deranged by the second, and she should have been committed eons ago. Ophelia had no idea why she was delaying the inevitable, but something had to be done.

She slipped into her bedchamber and was about to lock the door to keep Edith out, but she stopped, stunned to discover a bevy of maids packing her belongings.

"What is the meaning of this?" she demanded.

Appearing guilty and terrified, the group curtsied as the most senior among them stepped forward to explain, "It's Jamieson Merrick, Lady Ophelia. He commanded us to prepare the suite for Miss Carstairs."

"He what?" Ophelia was so enraged that she was surprised she didn't collapse in a swoon.

"He made us do it, milady," another added. "He told us, himself. We didn't see as how we could refuse."

"Was the impertinent swine kind enough to clarify where he's moving me *to*?"

"Off to the other wing, to the room next to your brother's."

She was being demoted to a spot reserved for the lowliest, most unimportant guests.

"He said you'll be leaving shortly anyway," the maid continued, "so we should keep out some things for tomorrow but pack the rest. We picked out several gowns for you, but if milady would like to . . . to—"

The woman recognized that there was no proper way to end the sentence, and mercifully, her idiotic voice screeched to a halt.

Ophelia stared them down, worried that the top of her head might simply blow off. Then she spun and stormed into the hall, bellowing, "Percy! Percy! Where are you? I need you!"

Her mother was still fluttering about. "Damnation, Ophelia! Damnation! The fires of Hell are nipping at your heels."

"Shut up, Edith!"

Ophelia swept by, looming like a Valkyrie, shouting and carrying on till someone pointed her toward Percy's tiny bedroom located on the far side of the house.

How had this happened to them? Was there no humiliation Jamieson Merrick would fail to inflict? Was there no limit to the indignities Percy would tolerate?

She stalked in like a tempest on the wind, only to find him brooding in a chair and feeling sorry for himself. She slammed the door so hard that the windows rattled.

"I want him dead!" she seethed.

"What's he done now?" Percy's tone was placating, as if he were speaking to a bothersome child.

"He's taken away my boudoir and given it to Anne!"

"Without asking me first?" he stupidly said. He couldn't accept that he no longer had any authority.

"It was my room! Mine! You gave it to me, and he's taken it away."

He chuckled meanly. "Are you finally riled? If he's seized something you cherish, then you know how I've felt for months. You've lost a petty bedchamber, but I've lost everything else."

"I want him dead," she repeated. "Today!"

"And how am I to accomplish it? Have you a magic gun that will automatically hit its mark?"

"I don't care how you do it, just do it."

"Don't order me about, Ophelia. I've told you I won't slay him anywhere near the manor."

"Then I'll deal with it myself," she wildly vowed. "I'll stab him or pour some poison into his soup."

"You won't. *I* shall have the pleasure of murdering him—but in my own good time."

"You've persuaded Anne to proceed with the wedding!" she accused.

"Of course I have."

"I won't have her as countess. I won't! I won't!"

"Darling, Ophelia, I believe the matter is out of your hands."

"If she becomes countess, I'll kill you. I swear it."

"Your threats are tiresome, and I'm weary of listening to you. Why don't you put your mouth to better use?"

"You wish to fornicate? Now?"

"Yes. Lie down on the bed."

"No."

"I command you to lie down."

"No," she said again.

His passions were inflamed, and his gaze dropped to her bosom. After her race through the house, her pulse was elevated, and her breasts strained against her corset. Their sex was most enjoyable when he was enraged, so as he grabbed her arm and threw her onto the mattress, she fought just enough to make it difficult for him.

They'd been lovers for so many years that she often felt they were naught more than an old married couple, and their wrestling brought a rough edge to their ardor that pushed it to new heights.

He held her down, but she scratched and clawed at him, so he captured her wrists and pinned them over her head.

"If you won't murder him," she taunted, "then I'll marry him, myself. I'll never let Anne wed him and rise above me."

"You would marry my bastard half brother?"

"Yes—if that's what it will take to keep Anne in her place."

He was aghast, and she was tickled to have astounded him. He always thought he knew best, always thought he had all the answers. Well, if he didn't make a move, and soon, she would make some moves of her own. And they wouldn't include him!

Her remarks pitched him to a higher level of ferocity. He yanked at her skirt, and impaled himself, and he took her like a harlot, like a scullery maid caught in the kitchen late at night.

He loosed her wrists to clasp his hand around her throat, and as he thrust, he began to squeeze, tighter and tighter, so that she struggled to breathe. It was the most dangerous, most erotic thing they'd ever done, and as his lust spiraled, she grew frightened, worried that—for once—he might not stop, and her fear enhanced the excitement.

He came with a bellow of fury, his seed shooting into her, and as his flexing ceased, he lifted his palm from her neck. She sputtered and gasped, drawing air into her lungs.

"You'll never have him as your husband," he vowed.

"Then you'd better kill him for me, hadn't you?"

She shoved him off and stood, disgusted and seriously questioning why she kept on with him. Had she finally goaded him sufficiently that he'd respond as she wanted? Would he prove his mettle?

If he didn't buck up and assume control, she knew how to spur him on. She'd dabble with Jamie until Percy was provoked into a jealous, homicidal frenzy, which would solve all their problems.

She grinned, deciding that the prospect of seducing Jamie again wasn't repugnant in the least.

❧

E dith watched Ophelia storm into the hall, swaying her hips like the whore she was. Ophelia couldn't have been more sinful if she'd worked in a brothel.

Edith smirked, relishing Ophelia's distress at losing the bedchamber she'd stolen from Edith so many years earlier. Edith had suffered constant disregard from her dreadful children, and it was her deceased, loathed husband who'd entrapped her.

In his Last Will, he'd granted total authority to her wicked son, leaving Edith unprotected and at Ophelia's mercy.

She'd never had any power or influence, and she'd endured her horrid plight for three decades. Was it any wonder everyone deemed her mad?

But silent revenge was so sweet.

Ophelia was gradually realizing that her whoring days were coming to an end. Percy had been brought low, too, rendered as insignificant as a man ever could be, and Edith gloated over every degradation Jamie Merrick imposed.

Unnoticed and unobserved, she sneaked after her daughter, aware of where Ophelia had gone and what she'd do when she arrived.

Edith halted outside Percy's door, and she pressed her ear to the wood, eavesdropping as her two children argued, then copulated. She usually let them finish, humored to have them add to their list of sins. The more they transgressed, the greater their damnation, the more potent God's ultimate wrath would be.

"You'd better kill him for me, hadn't you," Ophelia nagged, and Edith had had enough of their antics.

She flung the door open. Her daughter was over by the window, her breasts bared, her gown askew. Edith's slothful, evil son was on the bed, his clothing messy, too, his wormy little phallus hanging out of his trousers.

They both jumped to cover themselves so that she couldn't view what she'd seen a hundred times previous.

"Fornicators," Edith charged, using the taunt that angered them the most.

"Oh, for pity's sake!" Ophelia seethed.

"Will you be ready to meet your Maker? What lies will you tell Him? Do you think they'll save you?"

"Get her out of here," Ophelia hissed to Percy.

Percy sighed and rose. "Come, Mother. You know you're not allowed in my room."

"Fornicators," Edith hurled again as Percy led her out.

"I've had enough, Mother," Ophelia threatened. "Do you hear me?"

"I hear, but I am not afraid," Edith replied. "The Lord will look after me."

"I doubt it," Ophelia said. "He has to be as weary of your harangue as I am. He'll let me do whatever I want to you, and He'll be glad about it."

"Ophelia! Mother!" Percy snapped. "Shut up!"

He dragged Edith out, as Edith smiled, delighted with her afternoon's effort.

Chapter
NINE

W hat are our plans?"

"I don't know yet."

"Will we return to London?"

"I'm sure we will."

"How soon?"

"Probably directly after the wedding. Why?"

Jack studied his brother, wondering how he could be so cavalier about Gladstone. Jack was tired of traveling. He yearned to settle down, to give up his nomad's life, but Jamie couldn't wait to get moving again.

"When you go," Jack said, "I think I'd like to stay here."

Jamie gaped at him as if he'd pronounced that he enjoyed diving into shark-infested waters. They'd always been together, just the two of them against the world, and Jack couldn't imagine an existence where Jamie wasn't smack in the center of it. Maybe Jack would join him later, but for the moment, Jack wanted to hold still.

"Of course you won't stay at Gladstone," Jamie scoffed. "You'll come with me—as you always have in the past."

"To do what, Jamie? What's in London that's so bloody important?"

"My ship. The crew. The women, the food, the parties, the gambling. What would you suppose?"

"So what? You have all this now." Jack swept his hand from horizon to horizon. "Forget about the ship and the crew and the rest of it."

They were loafing on the verandah, talking and sipping whiskey. The sun had set, and the sky was an indigo blue, the green colors of the park so vibrant that it hurt to look at them. As far as the eye could see, the land was Jamie's. It was rich and fertile, the sort of place that represented the very bedrock of British wealth and class.

What more could he possibly want? What more could he possibly need?

"Forget about the ship! Are you insane?" Jamie asked. "What would our men do if we didn't come back? And the ship! You know what it means to me. Should I just abandon it?"

Jamie had never had anything to lose, so nothing scared him; nothing worried him. He was the luckiest individual Jack had ever met, and he was unafraid of any fate, even death, itself. He'd almost been killed so many times that the notion of him actually succumbing was laughable.

They didn't remember how they'd been spirited away from Gladstone or how they'd ended up at sea. Their first memories were as indentured boys, with no history, with just their names to link them to what might have been if they hadn't had a despicable, callous brute for a father.

The adults who'd populated their lives were blackguards with no ethics or scruples. Jack and Jamie had been beaten and starved and worked to the bone, betrayed, tricked, and abused. The few relationships they'd established were fleeting, so they'd stopped caring, had stopped reaching out, deeming it better to be alone.

After years of struggling to survive, Jamie had latched onto their ship like a drowning man. He'd been a brash, wild adolescent, and he'd won it with a toss of the dice. He'd cheated to be allowed in the game, then had wagered what he didn't have to steal it from a drunken captain.

The ship was their foundation, their only constant after a life of chaos and turmoil.

For their sailors, they'd hired the most ruthless criminals, picked for their ability to complete any task without balking. The men were unusually loyal, their allegiance purchased with the large amounts of money they made following Jamie, who would risk any dangerous venture if the price was right.

"Give them each a farewell stipend," Jack suggested, "and let them hire on with other crews. Then sell the ship. It would bring a pretty penny."

"Never."

Jack could read his brother's mind. Deep down, Jamie didn't believe he'd get to keep Gladstone. If they awoke some morning and discovered it had all been a peculiar whimsy, the ship would be all they had.

"Then have the crew carry on without us," Jack said. "We can remain here—where it's safe and easy—and they can send you your share of the loot."

"What fun would that be? Are you hoping I'll die of boredom?"

Jack stood and went to the balustrade, staring out at everything he'd ever wanted. As a cold and hungry boy, he'd dreamed of this very spot, though he was positive he hadn't seen it as a baby. So how could he have pictured it so vividly?

He couldn't have described where it was located, or how he'd ever get to it, but throughout his turbulent childhood, the vision had haunted him.

When he and Jamie had first turned off the lane and ridden up the drive to the manor, it had been the strangest impression, but Jack had recognized every fork in the road, every tree in the woods. Now that he'd arrived, he didn't wish to ever leave.

"Get down," Jamie suddenly murmured, cutting into Jack's reverie.

"What?"

"Get down!"

Jack ducked as he heard a loud bang, as a gun flashed out in the forest. In the increasing dusk, he'd resembled Jamie enough to make a good target, but the person who'd shot was too far away to do any damage. Still, it was disturbing to be fired upon.

Jack straightened and raised a wry brow. "You might have warned me a little sooner."

"That's the second attempt in a matter of days. Would it be remiss of me to point out that you're failing in your obligation to watch my back?"

Jack scrutinized the shrubbery, searching for movement. "Should I have a look?"

Jamie considered, then shook his head. "No. I'm sure he's gone. And it's too dark to see anyway. We'll check his tracks in the morning."

"Is it Percy?"

"Most likely." Jamie shrugged, casual as if they'd been discussing the weather.

"I wouldn't have thought he'd have the nerve."

"He might have hired a local miscreant."

"That sounds more like it." Jack gazed at Jamie over his shoulder. "How can you be so blasé? Don't these attacks bother you?"

"Yes, but what would you have me do? Shall I call him out? Beat him to a pulp? Have him whipped in the public square? What?"

"He's a pompous ass. Why not? What's stopping you?"

"It's all mine now, and he's about to lose it forever. Why not let him vent his wrath?"

"What if his aim improves? If he accidentally kills you, when you're not paying attention, it will really piss me off."

"If he manages it, you have my permission to avenge me."

"I will—if I'm not busy."

"Thank you, Brother. You're too, too kind."

They both laughed, a companionable silence growing.

"There's a young lad, about ten or so," Jack abruptly said, when he hadn't realized he was going to speak up. "He's living out in the woods in one of the shacks."

"And . . . ?"

"He's an orphan; he reminds me of you and me at that age. I'd like to invite him to the manor, maybe teach him to work in the stables. That way, I can be certain he's fed and clothed."

"Fine. I don't give a shit what you do around here. You know that."

Jamie's flip reply was typical of his slapdash attitude, so Jack was used to it, but on this occasion, he was uncharacteristically annoyed. He couldn't figure out if he was so touchy because the boy was Sarah's or because he hated to see another child suffer as they had suffered.

Jamie's nonchalance was so aggravating. When would something matter to him? Would there ever be anything in the world that he loved?

Jack understood that Jamie's detachment was a result of their wretched upbringing. They'd learned—early on—to establish no ties, but their destiny had changed. Jamie could afford to care and bond. It was all right for him to let down his guard.

That's what Jack intended. He would let down his guard, would trust and hope. He was excited to remain at Gladstone, where he had such a sense of belonging. How could Jamie fail to feel their powerful connection to the estate?

"I don't want to go back to London," Jack asserted.

"So you've said. But I've already decided, and I won't argue about it."

It was the tenor of their relationship that Jamie was the boss, that Jamie chose what they would do and when. Jack had never yearned for a path different from Jamie's, so they'd never bickered. When their existence had been so precarious, one place had been much the same as another, so it would have seemed silly to protest.

Jack would do anything for Jamie, even lay down his life, but he wouldn't do this.

"Not this time, Jamie. When you go, I'm staying behind."

Jamie was aghast, as if the spot were Hell on earth. "You're mad."

"No. I want this. I've always wanted this."

"You have not."

"I have," Jack insisted. He'd never told Jamie of his verdant dreams of Gladstone, hadn't mentioned how appropriate it had felt when they'd ridden up the lane.

"I belong here," Jack persisted.

"You might, but I don't, and I'm heading out as fast as I can."

"If you find it so distasteful, why did you fight so hard to claim it?"

"Because it's mine, and I wasn't about to let an ass like Percy keep it."

"And that's the only reason?"

"Yes. Besides, I like flaunting myself in London as the earl. I like forcing our father's snooty friends to see me every day. I like having them fume over the fact that I've returned and they can't make me disappear as they did when I was a baby."

"I don't care about any of that. Neither do those horrid old men."

"Well, *I* care!" Jamie's near shout rang out across the yard, his words echoing off the hills, magnifying the depth of his outrage.

"It's such a waste of energy, Jamie," Jack murmured quietly. "You can't fix what they did to us."

"And your plan is better? You want to lie to yourself and pretend that these despicable people will eventually accept you. Do you actually think they weren't aware that our mother was pregnant with us? You think they didn't comprehend what had happened when we were sent away? They were silent for three decades! I say: To hell with them and this stupid property! They can all rot!"

"I want to get married," Jack blurted, surprising himself with the declaration. He hadn't known that he craved it so desperately.

"Married! What's come over you?"

"I want to settle down. I want to quit traveling."

Jamie stared at him, pondering whether to continue the quarrel or switch to persuasion and coaxing.

"Stay then," he finally conceded, "if that's what you wish."

"It is."

"I'm thirty years old. I guess I can go on alone. It won't kill me. I don't need you tagging after me as if you're my nanny."

"I'll run the place for you. I'll keep it solvent."

"You do that. You be my gentleman farmer."

"And I'll be here, waiting for you, if you want to come home."

"I have no home, and if I started to assume I might like one, it wouldn't be at Gladstone, where such treachery was inflicted on me."

"What about Miss Carstairs?" Jack asked.

"What about her?" Jamie replied.

"She'll expect to build a life with you, to have you be a real husband. She'll want babies to mother."

"What would I do with a gaggle of brats?"

"Once you speak the vows, you'll owe her children," Jack pressed. "Last I heard, it's impossible to sire them from London. I'm quite sure you have to be in the same location as your bride."

"I don't care about her or what she wants. Why would she have any impact on what I choose to do?"

"She'll be your wife!"

"So?"

"Jamie! What a thing to say!"

Jack threw up his hands, his exasperation beyond bearing.

His brother was vain and self-centered, callous

conduct his normal condition, so his heartlessness was nothing out of the ordinary. But Jack liked Anne Carstairs very much. She'd be a fine spouse for Jamie. With her calm, cool demeanor, she might be able to curb some of his wilder tendencies. Jamie might even grow fond of her, might form an attachment for a change.

"You know I'm only doing it because the Prince made me," Jamie said.

"And if he hadn't?"

"I'd never have picked her."

Jack winced. Jamie meant that he hadn't wanted to ever marry. He thought he'd be a terrible husband, and Jack agreed, but Jamie could be so harsh in his manner.

"Swear to me that you'll never tell her your true opinion."

"How can it matter? She'll be my wife, so she'll simply have to get over it."

"For a man who supposedly knows everything there is to know about women, you're an idiot."

"Why? Merely because I won't pretend to be a romantic fool?"

"Precisely. I just hope to God she never learns what a cold bastard you are."

❧

Anne stood in her room, brushing her hair, when movement out in the forest caught her eye. A distant bang sounded, and she saw a flash. It was eerily reminiscent of the first day Jamie had come to Gladstone, and it was so late in the evening. No one would be hunting.

Was someone shooting at him again?

While she would have happily strangled him with her own two hands, she couldn't imagine him actually being killed, and she was aggravated that the assailant had tried again.

Jamie claimed it was Percy. Could it be? Would Percy dare?

She wondered if, from her vantage point, she might see who it had been. She walked over to the window and leaned out, when she realized that Jamie and Jack Merrick were on the verandah below, their voices drifting up.

If it had been another crack at an assassination, they didn't seem bothered in the least. They were the strangest men she'd ever met. Nothing fazed them. Not even attempted murder.

They were such a magnetic duo, both so tall and dark and handsome. They exuded power and authority, but with a rough edge honed through decades of struggle. She couldn't help watching them, especially when she'd had so few chances to observe them together.

Jack Merrick asked, "What about Miss Carstairs?"

She grinned, delighted that they were talking about her and curious as to what Jamie might say. She was certain she'd hear if not something romantic, then something pragmatic and reasonable as to why they'd be a good match. But of course, as soon as Jamie opened his mouth, she remembered why eavesdropping was such a bad idea.

"What about her?" Jamie answered, his tone dismissive and cruel.

The conversation went downhill from there. Anne was barraged by snippets of it—*gaggle of brats* . . .

I don't care about her or what she wants . . . the Prince made me—and she nearly plugged her ears to shut out the awful remarks, but she couldn't quit listening.

"I'd never have picked her," Jamie said, and the brutal comment cut her to the quick.

While she hadn't expected much from the marriage, she'd assumed fondness would grow, that friendship would blossom. If she bore him his *gaggle* of children, would he even stay around to be a father to any of them?

A vision of Ophelia, naked and in his bed, blazed in Anne's mind, and she saw years of misery stretching ahead. If he was truly repulsed by her, then he'd never develop any regard for her feelings. There'd be a line of strumpets to humiliate her, and he'd be gone for lengthy periods when she would worry about where he was and what he was doing.

Neighbors would titter behind her back. The servants would assess her with veiled pity. She'd be a laughingstock, the lowly girl who'd put on airs to wed the new earl who'd never wanted her.

Devastated, she collapsed against the sill, and she'd forgotten she was still holding her brush. It slipped from her fingers and tumbled down to the verandah, where it bounced across the smooth stones.

The twins were jumpy, ready to fend off an assault. Jack whipped around with fists clenched, and Jamie leapt to his feet, gripping the hilt of a knife he carried strapped to his waist.

They glared up the wall to where she was staring down on them. As they grasped that she'd overheard every vile word of their discussion, she was mute and horrified. For an eternity, they were all three frozen in place.

Ultimately, Jack Merrick muttered, "Dammit!"

Jamie said nothing but continued to study her, his expression wiped of any emotion. If he was chagrined, if he was embarrassed, if he was feeling anything, at all, not a trace of it showed.

Eventually, a corner of his mouth lifted in a smirk or a smile, and he shrugged as if he couldn't figure out what the fuss was about. Casually, slowly, he turned from her, sat in his chair, and reached for his whiskey.

His brother whispered something, and Jamie responded just as softly. As if she'd ceased to exist, neither of them looked at her again, and she lurched away from the window, desperate to be hidden by the shadows in her room.

Chapter
TEN

Anne slipped a note under Sarah's door, explaining where she'd gone and why, then tiptoed out of the house and headed for the stables. She knew how to saddle a horse, how to ride one, and she was delighted to have the chance to steal one of Jamieson Merrick's prized animals.

It was very late, but she'd have many hours to travel before anyone discovered she'd fled again. It was stupid to leave. Stupid and dangerous and pointless, but she was leaving anyway, and she wouldn't seek refuge with that idiotic vicar, either.

Despite how it often seemed, she and her sister weren't alone in the world. Their mother's childhood friend still resided in Rudwick. The moon was up, and Anne could be there by morning, safely concealed where no one would think to look. She'd be able to reflect and plan, and she'd have an older woman's guidance as to what she should do.

She was scarcely acquainted with Lord Gladstone, and he'd already broken her heart a dozen times over. If she wed him, what would become of her after a month? After a year? She was too gentle a soul to marry him. He'd kill her with despondency. It would be a horrible death, too, and she refused to suffer it.

She reached the edge of the verandah and had nearly made it to the stairs when the smell of a burning cheroot gave him away.

"Hello, Anne. Fancy meeting you here."

She sighed with resignation. "Hello, Lord Gladstone."

As he moved to block her path, she envisioned herself knocking him down, running like a deer, leaping on a horse, and galloping away, but it would never happen. *He* wouldn't let it happen.

"You've packed a bag. Are you going somewhere?"

"No," she said, dejected. "I'm not going anywhere, at all."

"Good. I'd hate to have you miss our wedding tomorrow."

He took her satchel, and she relinquished it without a fight.

"How did you know I'd be here?" she inquired.

"It's the funniest thing, but I told my brother you'd sneak off again—most likely in the middle of the night—but he insisted that you'd never be that foolish." He paused, his words sinking in so she would recollect that she had no power. "Isn't it interesting how quickly I've figured out how your mind works?"

"You know me well."

"I certainly do. Where were you hoping to hide?"

"It doesn't matter now."

"Yes, it does. You must inform me, so that when you next try something this ridiculous, I'll have some idea of where to start searching."

Silent and furious, she glared at him, and he shrugged off her pique.

"Fine then. I'll just ask your sister. She's not as stubborn as you are." He turned her toward the house. "It's chilly out. Let's get you back to your room."

She didn't bother to argue. Like a felon, marching to the gallows, each step conveyed her to the inevitable end of the line.

She trudged into her new, grand bedchamber, the one from which he'd evicted Ophelia without considering the ruckus it would cause. He'd simply pronounced that it was the countess's boudoir and since Ophelia wasn't the countess, it would no longer be hers.

Ophelia was in a snit about the change, and Anne hadn't been too keen on it, herself, but she hadn't been able to dissuade him. She was ensconced in the huge suite, located far from her sister, and feeling like an impostor.

He strutted in behind her, and she didn't attempt to keep him out. If he wanted to enter, he would. If he wanted to lock her in, or stay and guard her, he would, and there'd be nothing she could do about it.

In her haste to depart, she'd left a candle burning, so she could easily see her way to the dressing room. The large space was designed for a countess to use, and Ophelia—with her fashionable and extensive wardrobe—had filled it to bursting.

In comparison, Anne's four gowns looked lonely and ragged.

She hung her bonnet and shawl on a hook, then spun to him. He was over by the door, feet braced, his cheeks dark with stubble, his eyes impossibly blue. He appeared devilish, or maybe like a fallen angel who'd come to earth to entice and torment her.

"Are you even sorry?" she queried.

He was as oblivious as she might have predicted he'd be.

"Sorry for what?"

"For hurting me! You don't care about me, and you don't wish to marry me. At least have the courage to say so aloud, and I won't continue harboring these absurd delusions."

"You imagined I . . . I . . . cared for you?"

"Silly of me, I know."

"I've never cared for anyone—except my brother."

"I'm sure that's true."

He crossed to her so that he was close enough to touch her, the tips of his boots slipping under the hem of her skirt, and he studied her as if he'd never seen her before.

"I don't understand you," he finally muttered. "I'm giving you everything a woman could ever want—for no reason, at all—yet you're so miserable."

"Why did the Prince make you marry me?"

"The King was a friend of your father's."

"Was he? I wasn't aware of any connection."

"He's always been worried about your plight."

"If I don't wed you, will you still get to keep the estate? Was the transfer contingent on our union?"

"No. It's mine no matter what I choose to do."

He said it with a straight face, so she couldn't discern if he was lying or not. No doubt, he was adept at fabrication. A man couldn't rise as he had without being ruthless and untrustworthy.

"Then why would you agree?"

"It was important to the Prince, and it won't kill me. There seemed no basis to refuse."

It was such a cold remark, and it made her feel so

insignificant, so absolutely ordinary. Couldn't he have left her with the illusion that he'd found something about her to be special?

"If we wed—," she began.

"*When* we wed," he interrupted.

"Have it your way," she replied, capitulating. "When we wed, what kind of life do you expect we'll have?"

"What kind of *life*?"

"Yes. Have you given any thought as to how we'll carry on? Does it concern you in the slightest?"

"No."

She chuckled, but wretchedly. "You are so brutally frank, which isn't what I need at the moment. Couldn't you humor me? Couldn't you pretend we can make it work?"

"Of course it will *work*. I'll tell you what to do, and you'll do it. We'll get on fine."

"Is that how you run your ship?"

"Yes."

"So that's how you'll run our marriage?"

"I never learned any other way. It's easier when everyone knows who's in charge."

"You're such a bully. I hate that about you."

"What would you have me say, Anne? I'm not the sort to court you with flowers and poetry."

"No, you're not."

"But I swear to you that you'll never want for anything, that you'll be safe, that you'll be fed and sheltered. Why can't that be enough for you?"

"I just always assumed my husband would love me. It's a dream that's dying very hard."

He sighed and took her hand, their fingers linked as if they were sweethearts.

"Come with me."

"To where?"

"Does it matter?"

"I guess not."

He led her into the earl's suite and proceeded directly to his bedchamber, where the king's bed sat in the middle of the floor.

"Has anyone ever explained to you what happens in the marital bed?"

"No."

"Then some of what we're about to do may seem very strange."

"Why? What are you planning?"

"I'm going to bind you to me, so you can never leave."

"How?"

"How would you suppose?"

"Can I talk to my sister first?"

"No."

"Please?"

"She can't help you."

"But I don't want to do this."

"I don't care," he said, though gently. "I have to put an end to all your nonsense. We're to speak the vows tomorrow anyway, so we're just pushing ahead with the inevitable."

"You'd take me against my will?"

"If you wish to look at it like that, you're entitled. I'd rather have you disposed and amenable. It will be more enjoyable for you."

"I'll resist," she bravely contended.

"Will you, Anne? Will you really?"

She never would, and as he'd mentioned, their marriage was inevitable. He was determined to have it transpire, and he always got his way. She would have to submit now, or she would have to submit the following evening after the ceremony. She had no power to alter events.

"If I fought you," she asked, "could I ever win?"

"No. Turn around," he commanded, and like a puppet on a string, she obeyed.

He fussed with her hair, pulling at the pins and combs, so that it fell to her hips in an auburn wave; then he unbuttoned her dress and stripped her. Her garments dropped away, piece by piece.

In a thrice, she was bared to her chemise, and he snuggled himself to her back, his arms encircling her, his palms flat on her belly. He nibbled at her nape, taking soft bites along her neck and shoulder.

She shivered, goose bumps cascading across her skin, and he smirked.

"Are you cold?" he inquired.

"No."

"Do you know what I think?"

"What?"

"I think perhaps you like me a tad more than you can admit."

He was probably correct, but she'd never fan his inflated ego by agreeing. He was too vain by half, and if he thought she was infatuated, he'd be more unbearable than he already was.

"You were worried about how we'll carry on," he said. "Well, this is how. Every day and every night, we'll be together like this. It's not so terribly bad, is it?"

"Not so far," she allowed, refusing to be anything but surly.

He laughed and urged her onto the mattress. She didn't hesitate, for if she defied him, he'd simply lift her and toss her where he wanted her to be.

She lay on her stomach, her face buried in the pillows, listening as he removed some of his clothes, then climbed up, too. He stretched out on top of her and clasped her flanks. He flexed his loins against her bottom, taking several slow thrusts that made her stomach flutter with butterflies.

"Will it hurt?" she asked.

"Will what *hurt*?"

"I heard some women gossiping once. They said it hurt."

"They were wrong. It feels very, very good."

He slid to the side and drew her to him. His shirt was off, and the front of his trousers was loose, a few buttons undone, the placard dangling lazily.

At the sight of so much exposed male flesh, she was giddy and reckless. Her body was goading her to try things she'd never imagined, things she couldn't comprehend. She wanted to touch him all over, wanted to lick him and kiss him all over. She was frantic with the need of it.

"There will always be one rule between us," he murmured, dipping to nuzzle under her chin.

"What is that?"

"When we are alone like this, anything is permitted."

"Anything?"

"Yes. Whatever you say or do, it's all right. Do you understand?"

"No."

He smiled. "You will. This endeavor takes some getting used to, so this will seem awkward, but we'll practice till you get the hang of it."

"You sound as if I'm a skittish mare and you're breaking me to saddle."

"In a way, I guess I am."

His gaze drifted down her torso, lingering at each delectable spot. His rapt focus made her throb and burn, made her desperate to try any deed he suggested.

"You're very fine, Anne," he said. "Very beautiful. Have I ever told you that?"

"No."

"Despite what you assume, I'm delighted in my choice of bride. I couldn't be more pleased."

He kissed her so tenderly, so sweetly. A silly flood of tears surged into her eyes, and she was beyond speech. She moaned a sort of pathetic wail and pulled him nearer, deepening the kiss, anxious to halt his compliments. She had no defense against them.

The embrace intensified, his tongue in her mouth, his fingers at her bosom. They'd been down this track on the carnal road before, so she knew what was coming, and her anatomy was disgusting in its eager welcome.

He trailed down her chest, rooting at her cleavage, and he tugged on the thin straps of her chemise, baring her breasts so he could feast. He suckled her, pushing her up and up into the spiral of ecstasy, and she was so disordered that she didn't realize he'd continued ridding her of her chemise, that he was working it down her belly, her legs.

Shortly, she'd be nude, and she grabbed at it, needing the scant protection it provided.

"Let it go, Anne." He appeared tense and annoyed. "I want you naked."

"No, not naked," she protested.

"Yes."

She held on to it as if it were the last wall around the castle, and he the invading army, but he ripped it away.

"This is how I want you," he said, "and how you shall be for me whenever I demand it of you."

"But . . . why?"

"Because I am your husband and it's what I enjoy more than anything in the world."

"It's too much, too soon."

"If we went slower, we'd still arrive at the same conclusion, and I can't bear to delay. I want you too badly."

"You do?"

"Yes. I always have. From the very first day."

Could that be true? She didn't think so. He'd been complaining about her to his brother.

His hand was between her legs and probing her sheath, making her wet, making her ache. His thumb dabbed at the sensitive nub he'd previously located, and she easily soared to the heavens. With this second demonstration of passion, the ending came more quickly and was much more powerful, and she could only wonder if it grew more potent with each attempt. If so, she'd likely expire from lust.

As the commotion waned, he hovered over her, strained and keeping a firm rein on his control. The ferocious gleam in his eye was terrifying, and it boded ill for whatever was coming next.

Nervously, she licked her lip, the gesture galvanizing his attention.

"What are you going to do to me?" she asked.

He was fumbling with his trousers. "This is the wifely obligation you've heard about, Anne. All women learn it eventually. In the beginning, it might seem peculiar—or even a little scary—so relax as much as you can."

Relax! Was he insane? She was so rigid with alarm

that she felt as if she might shatter. "Tell me what will occur."

"We're about to mate, Anne. I'll join myself to you in a special way."

"What does that mean?"

"I'll show you."

He clutched her thighs and widened them, his torso dropping between them as if he was created to fit there perfectly. Suddenly, he was pressing something into her, and she panicked and started to struggle.

"What are you doing?"

"Hold still."

"Not till you tell me what's happening."

"You trust me, don't you?"

"I absolutely don't. You're a fiend and a bully."

He chuckled, but it was a tortured sound. "If I'm not inside you immediately, I can't predict what I'll do."

"You're talking in riddles."

He flexed against her, again, again. The pressure was extreme, the exploit too odd to be described or believed.

"Jamie, you're frightening me."

"I'm almost done."

"Stop it. It's too big."

"No, it's not. It's exactly the right size. You're a virgin, so your body is fighting its fate. It's a natural reaction."

It didn't feel *natural,* and she wrestled in earnest, but he scarcely noticed.

He yanked her thighs even wider, and with a particularly vicious thrust the object he'd wielded burst into her. She reared up and cried out in agony, but he swallowed down her anguish with a delicious kiss. He was very still, cradling her in his arms.

"Hush," he soothed.

"What was that?" A few tears seeped from the corners of her eyes. Her respirations came in short gasps.

"I've finally made you mine in the only way that counts."

"You said it wouldn't hurt," she accused.

"I lied." He wasn't contrite in the least. "But this is the only time it will. After tonight, it won't bother you."

"I'm not a virgin anymore, am I?"

"No."

She now understood why maidens were kept in the dark about matrimonial duty! What female would willingly submit to such a humiliation?

"What did you push into me?"

"A piece of myself, Anne. We're built differently. I've bonded with you as no other man ever will."

She was trembling with shock, but he wasn't in such a great condition, either. Obviously, he was restraining himself, every muscle taut with anticipation. She took a deep breath and let it out, the simple motion calming her slightly, and she seemed to pull him into her even farther.

He shuddered with what appeared to be pain. Was he suffering as she was suffering? Males were purported to relish the endeavor, but why would they?

"I can't wait," he said. "I have to finish it."

"What should I do?"

"Hug me as tight as you can."

He eased into her over and over, and he was being very careful, trying not to injure her more than he just had. To her amazement, the ache was lessening, the position seeming more normal by the moment.

He growled low in his throat, and he drove in all the way, his anatomy quaking with his attempts at control, then it was ended, and he slumped down onto her. She could feel his heart hammering under his ribs.

They were frozen in place, the rod he'd inserted remaining hard, and he sighed with satisfaction. But as he grew more composed, he glared down at her, almost as if he were angry.

"I want you again," he peculiarly claimed. "Already, I want you again!"

He voiced the comment as if it was a complaint, and he began, once more, but with none of the moderation he'd exhibited prior.

She'd acclimated to the strange coupling, and while she'd found the initial experience unpleasant, the second one was very interesting—as he'd promised it could be. As he kissed and fondled, coaxed and praised, she was stunned to find herself responding quite vigorously.

Her hips adopted the tempo he'd set, meeting him thrust for thrust. He became more focused, more wild, his penetrations working her across the mattress till her head was banging into the headboard.

The tension escalated, and as he reached down and touched the special spot at the center of her torso, she shattered with ecstasy, and he did, too, both of them shouting out with an excitement that was shamefully thrilling.

They soared to the peak together; then they floated down, until they landed—tangled and sweating—in the middle of their marital bed.

"Oh my," she murmured. "Is it always like that?"

"It definitely can be, my little strumpet."

He laughed and slapped her on the rear; then he drew away. As their bodies separated, she winced, her feminine flesh protesting its new state.

He turned her onto her side so that he was spooned to her. As if he cherished her, as if she was his dear bride in truth, he brushed a tender kiss on her bare shoulder.

"That wasn't so bad, was it, Mrs. Merrick?"

"No," she said, her tummy tickling at hearing how he'd referred to her. "Not bad, at all."

"Let's rest a bit; then we'll do it again." He paused. "Unless you're too sore?"

"I'm sore," she admitted, "but if you're game, so am I."

"That's my girl."

He tucked a blanket over them, sealing them in a snug cocoon, and she closed her eyes. In an instant, she was asleep.

Chapter
ELEVEN

Jamie awakened next to Anne. She was snuggled to him and sleeping like a babe, as if they'd been wed for an eternity.

He'd been a beast, and he understood that he had been, but his crude behavior couldn't be helped. He wasn't a calm or patient man, wasn't prone to verbal discussions or romantic wooing. He was a man of action, of few words and plenty of authority.

It was growing painfully obvious that being married to her would never be boring. She had a temper, and she had some backbone, and while he'd always presumed he liked his women to be meek and submissive, he was slowly changing his mind.

He liked her just fine, when he didn't want to like her, and his elevated sentiment scared the hell out of him.

He simply wanted to wed her and get his line of heirs established. His sons and their sons would rule at Gladstone for a thousand years and a thousand years after that. Whenever a new boy was birthed, Jamie's father would roll in his grave, the thought of which tickled Jamie enormously.

Anne stirred, cuddling closer. They were both naked, her lush, shapely body pressed to his all the way down. He was hard as a rock, his cock keen with arousal and demanding a bit of morning delight.

It would be easy to coax her to consciousness, but he wouldn't. He'd had her several times during the night, and she had to be sore as the dickens. After he'd rutted with such reckless abandon, she'd probably need a month to recover, and he'd be lucky if she let him near her ever again.

He couldn't describe what had driven him to such excess. He never lost control with a paramour, yet he'd been randy as a sixteen-year-old lad.

There were so many willing women in the world, and so many of them had drifted through his worthless life. He viewed sex as a physical release, and he'd always deemed one female to be much the same as the next, especially after he blew out the candle.

Why was Anne so different?

He studied her, thinking how beautiful she looked, how sweet she was, and the strangest sensation swept through him. His heart began to ache, and it seemed to swell, as if it didn't fit under his ribs anymore.

She was so perfect, so young and innocent, and she was his. His!

Shortly, he'd marry her true. He'd be expected and entitled to watch over her and keep her safe, and the notion created a possessive wave of excitement so foreign to his character that he was terrified.

What was the matter with him? He was carrying on like a virginal girl with her first swain, and he wouldn't allow himself to be inundated by affection.

He was marrying Anne because the Prince had asked it, because Jamie would have done anything to secure his place at Gladstone. She was a means to an end, very much like a brood mare he might have purchased at an auction.

If he was unsettled, it was merely because he'd been under so much pressure. The stakes were very high, and she was part of the resolution. Plus, he'd been extremely busy and too distracted by events to locate a good whore. The combination of abstinence and tension must have made their fornication seem more refreshing than it actually had been.

She was pretty and interesting, but not unique by any stretch of the imagination. He wouldn't let her be. Nor would he wallow in bed with her like a besotted bridegroom who was too infatuated to leave her side.

Very carefully, he slipped from her arms and eased off the mattress. For the longest while, he stared down at her in a smitten stupor, massaging his wrist and rippling with unfulfilled yearning, but once he realized how pitiful he was acting, he lurched away and hurried to his room. He washed and dressed, then raced downstairs. Briefly, he considered stopping for breakfast, but he was so overwrought that if she waltzed in while he was eating, he'd gape at her like a love-struck fool, which he refused to do.

The chances were great that there'd be no wedding that day, and maybe not for a few days after that. They couldn't possibly proceed until he'd gained some control over his careening, absurd emotions.

He marched out to the stables, saddled his horse, and galloped away, quickly putting as much distance as he could between himself and the manor, and he couldn't predict when he'd return.

H ello, Jack. You don't mind if I call you Jack, do
you?"

"No, I don't mind."

Jack glared at Ophelia. She resembled a deadly spider, one that would sneak up and bite without warning. No doubt, her sting would be lethal.

He was perched on a log behind the stables, taking a break in the shade from an afternoon of chores. As she sauntered over, she was very fetching, the bodice of her gown tugged extra low to reveal her large breasts, her bonnet tilted at just the right angle to flatter her winsome face.

He couldn't move beyond the impression that she'd intentionally tracked him down, so instantly he was on guard. He was aware of how she'd crawled into Jamie's bed, which was one of the more bizarre occurrences since their arrival, so Jack wouldn't put anything past her.

She sat next to him, and she took an inordinate amount of time fussing with her skirt so that it was perfectly arranged. Then she shifted and leaned in, surprising him with how much of her body rested against his own.

Her pose had to have been rehearsed for maximum effect, and he almost laughed aloud but didn't. Obviously, she wanted something from him, and whatever it was, his response would be *no*, but he was humored to have her beg so charmingly.

"I need to ask you a question." She was practically batting her lashes.

"I hope I have an answer."

"Oh, I'm sure you will. I noted that there's a new boy working in the barn."

"Yes, there is."

"But no one sought my permission for the change to be implemented."

"Really?"

"I've always given the orders as to the house and grounds."

"Have you?"

She gave a credible pout, the sort that pursed her lips in an appealing way and would have spurred a more imprudent man to kiss them.

"You're making me feel positively unnecessary."

"We can't have that, can we?"

"Will you promise to consult with me from now on?"

"Why, yes," he lied. She was the last person on earth from whom he'd solicit an opinion. "I don't see why not—if it will make you happy."

She smiled her thanks, and she placed her palm on the middle of his chest, rubbing it in slow, calculated circles.

"I've been watching you around the estate," she said. "You and your brother are so much alike."

"We certainly are."

"But you seem so much more manly than him."

She simpered in not-so-subtle invitation. Her nipple was poking into his forearm like a shard of glass.

"I can't believe you noticed," he replied, toying with her. "Everyone thinks he's the best and brightest, simply because he's a few minutes older."

"Who would presume such nonsense? Only an idiot would fail to observe your vigor."

"That's what I've always thought."

"You should have been earl. Not him. It's written in

your character as plain as day. Oh, how can you bear it? How can you stand by as he runs amok with all our lives?"

"I can't. It drives me mad."

"It's such an injustice."

"If I was earl," he boasted, "I'd do things differently."

"I just knew you would!" she gushed. "That's why I decided to speak with you."

"On what topic?"

Matters were getting interesting. She'd turned so that the front of her torso was flattened to his, and with how her corset was pushing her breasts up and out, his view was intoxicating. Pathetic as it sounded, his cock grew hard merely from pondering the possibilities.

"If you were the earl," she said, "you wouldn't send me away, would you?"

"Definitely not."

"I knew it! I knew you'd be kinder than your brother. This is my home. I shouldn't have to leave it, should I? Will you talk to him for me? Will you convince him to let me remain? I'd be ever so grateful."

She raised up and brushed her lips to his, and if he hadn't detested her so much—if she hadn't been his sister!—he'd have considered her proposition. Unfortunately, he had a few scruples in his sexual affairs. Not many, but a few. More than Jamie had anyway.

Call him crazy, but he wouldn't fornicate with a female he loathed, and when he slid between a woman's thighs he liked to pretend he was the only one who'd been there in a while.

His dear sister failed on both counts.

Who was she fucking to have gleaned such carnal experience? Unless she wallowed with the hired help, which he couldn't envision, the only other man who was constantly underfoot was Percy. The notion would have been funny if it hadn't been so distasteful.

"There's just one problem," Jack murmured, drawing away.

"What is it?"

"Jamie is marrying Miss Carstairs, so it will be up to her to determine who is to stay and who is to go."

At his mentioning Anne Carstairs, Ophelia's flirtatious mask slipped, and she scrambled to keep it from vanishing altogether. "But you can't mean for it to be me who goes. Not when we've just begun to get acquainted. We could become such good friends."

"It's out of my hands, I'm afraid."

"What if Anne sides with your brother? What if she demands my departure?"

"Then there'll be no hope for it. You'll have to leave."

"There must be something I could do to make it worth your while to intervene."

"I can't imagine what it might be."

"Are you certain?"

She flashed a wicked look of licentious promise that he felt clear down to his toes, and he could vividly picture the whore's tricks she might ultimately perform. It was such a diverting prospect that he nearly relented.

Instead, he clasped her arms and set her on her feet; then he stood, too. She frowned with fury, and suddenly she wasn't quite so attractive.

"You never had any intention of assisting me," she charged.

"No, I didn't."

"Bastard."

"Now, now, let's don't bring my poor mother into it. It's been well established that she married the old asshole."

At the insulting reference to their mutual sire, Ophelia was incensed, but she was anxious to sway him and bit down on any caustic retort.

"Anne hates me. She always has. She'll cast me out in a trice. I'm your sister. Don't you care what will happen to me?"

"You should have thought of that before you and Percy rejected Jamie's offer. It was more than generous."

She paused, murder in her gaze. "What *offer*?"

"Jamie's not without some empathy for your plight. He proposed that you be given one of the smaller estates and a liberal quarterly allowance."

"And . . . ?"

"Percy tossed it back in Jamie's face. He claimed he didn't need charity from his own coffers. So you get nothing."

"I was never consulted!"

Jack shrugged. "I guess you should take it up with Percy, next time there's a lull under the blankets."

She rippled with panic, indicating that her lover was Percy, after all, but she hastily tamped down her reaction.

"I have no idea what you mean," she insisted.

"Suit yourself, but you really should watch that temper of yours. In this instance, it's cost you a pretty penny."

She whirled away and stomped off, looming toward the manor like a thundercloud ready to rain mayhem on Percy's parade, and Jack almost felt sorry for the man.

He shook his head in disgust, wondering at the

crazed taint of Merrick blood that flowed in his veins. How could he be so closely related to the strange pair? He'd be glad when Percy and Ophelia left, and he wished Jamie would get on with the wedding so that there'd be no reason for them to dawdle.

Only disaster would come from their presence at Gladstone, but it wasn't Jack's province to send them packing. He had to observe from the sidelines and clean up whatever messes they caused.

He turned his mind to more pleasant subjects, like Sarah Carstairs and her son, Tim. Jack hadn't wanted to appear as if he was hovering, so he hadn't checked on Tim in several hours, but he was eager to make sure the boy was adjusting. Tim was working in the stables and sleeping there with the other grooms, but that situation would improve as matters resolved.

Jack hadn't spoken with Sarah about what he'd done, and he couldn't wait to hear how grateful she was for his intervening on Tim's behalf.

Smiling at the prospect, Jack spun and went inside.

❧

Anne was having the most splendid dream, where she was relaxed and aroused in the way only Jamie could make her, when it dawned on her that she wasn't dreaming.

Jamie was with her and slowly goading her to consciousness. He was nuzzling her bosom, his fingers on her nipples, the thin fabric of her summer nightgown providing a delightful friction.

She was so happy to see him that she could barely keep from making a fool of herself with silly pronunciations of relief.

After he'd stolen her virginity, he'd vanished. At first, she'd been pleased that he was gone, but as he'd stayed away for an entire day, then another and another, she'd been irate. How could he ravish her so spectacularly, then trot off as if the encounter had been insignificant? She wasn't some London doxy he could use and abuse!

But as his absence had continued, her fury had metamorphosed into mortification. Evidently, he'd pressed the issue of marital relations but had discovered that he didn't enjoy her in an amorous fashion. She hadn't satisfied him, but she hadn't a clue as to how or why she'd failed to entice.

Now, like an unexpected gift on Christmas morning, here he was! How could she be angry?

She sighed and stretched, loving the feel of his body on hers, and she reached down and ruffled his hair. He stopped what he was doing and grinned up at her.

"Hello, sleepyhead," he murmured. "I didn't think you'd ever wake up."

He looked wicked, unrepentant, a sin any woman would gladly commit.

"Where have you been?" she asked. "I was so worried."

"Really? I don't remember anyone ever worrying about me before."

"Then you should know that, with you as my husband, I'm positive I'll fret constantly. And I don't care for it, Jamie. It makes me grouchy."

He chuckled and rolled them so that she was on top of him, braced on an elbow and scowling at him as if he were a misbehaving schoolboy.

"I wasn't going to come back," he oddly admitted.

"Not ever?"

To her surprise, the notion had her catching her breath in panic. Apparently, she was growing accustomed to having him around, and life without him would be terribly dull.

"But . . . why?"

For a brief moment, it seemed as if he might explain; then he tugged at the strap of her nightgown. Her breast popped free, and he rooted down and sucked the nipple in his mouth.

"Are you still sore?" he inquired.

"No, why?"

"Because I want to make love to you. It's all I thought about the whole time I was away."

"So you're not upset with me?"

"Why would I be?"

"When you left, I assumed I did something wrong, so you changed your mind about marrying me."

"I didn't change my mind, and I could never be upset with you."

"Never?"

"Well, not about anything that happens in here when we're alone."

"So . . . I did everything correctly?"

"Of course. If you'd been any more *correct,* I'd have died and gone to Heaven. Now about your womanly parts . . ."

He was pulling her nightgown down and off, quickly stripping her, and he rolled them again, so that she was tucked beneath him.

"My womanly *parts* are fine," she insisted.

"They certainly are." He slid two fingers into her sheath, and he paused and gazed at her, his confusion plain, his consternation palpable.

"You make me happy," he said. "Why is that?"

She didn't know what sort of answer would be appropriate, so instead, she drew him into a kiss that he abruptly ended so that he could kneel to yank off his shirt. She came up on her knees, too, and boldly she rested her palm on the placard of his pants.

"The other night, you said we were built differently."

"We are."

"I want to see you."

She'd galvanized his attention. He was fixated on the naughty spot where her hand was positioned.

"Are you sure?" he queried. "You won't swoon with maidenly alarm?"

"No swooning. I promise."

"All right."

He started in on the buttons of his trousers, opening the front as if it was the most natural thing in the world. He jerked the fabric down to his flanks, and she was stunned to see the large rod protruding from his loins.

It was very big, very hard, all red and menacing, and it seemed alive, as if it was reaching out to her. How could she be twenty-five years old and not know such a disparity existed?

"My goodness!" she mused. "Would you look at that?"

She pushed him onto his back so that she could move closer for a thorough examination, and she hovered between his legs and explored every inch. The shaft was warm and rigid, but smooth and pliant, too, and she stroked across it, tightening the skin at the crown, letting it go.

Each touch had the most riveting effect on his anatomy. He would tense and relax, would hitch his breath, then exhale and mutter.

"What's it called?" she asked.

"A cock, usually. Or a phallus. When I'm feeling friendly, I refer to it as my John Thomas."

"You named it?"

He barked with laughter. "I guess I did."

She began again, and he couldn't bear to watch. He flung an arm over his eyes, so she was free to try whatever she liked.

Without thinking, she bent down and kissed the tip, and he lurched away as if he'd been burned.

He appeared horrified or shocked, which made her angry. *He* was the one who claimed everything was allowed.

"What is it?" she snapped. "What did I do?"

He was up on his knees again, advancing on her like a beast of prey. "Oh, I am going to have such fun teaching you how to use that mouth of yours."

"What do you mean?"

"I'll show you later."

"Show me now."

"No. At the moment, I'm busy."

"With what?"

"With you, my little strumpet. With you."

He tossed her onto the mattress and came down on top of her. He gripped her thighs, widened them, and in a thrice he was impaled and flexing into her with a raucous abandon.

There was a tenderness in his expression, as if— despite his protestations to the contrary—he might be developing fond feelings for her, and she tucked away the realization for subsequent dissection and analysis.

Could he learn to love her? Why couldn't it happen? Why not?

As she was quickly discovering, there was nothing finer than having Jamie Merrick's regard. He made her feel special and needed, and her heart raced with a foolish, giddy joy. For a woman who'd never believed she'd marry but who would get to spend her life rollicking with him, she'd done all right for herself, after all.

Chapter
TWELVE

H ow dare you!"

"What? What did I do?"

Sarah stormed into the dark, empty kitchen, as Jack Merrick whirled around.

It was very late, everyone asleep except for the two of them. The cook always heated bathing water after supper, leaving it in a basin behind the stove, and in Sarah's mad dash to locate him she hadn't paused to remember that if he'd come to the kitchen, he was intending to wash.

He'd already removed his shirt and boots, and he was just about to start in on his trousers. He stood before her, all that virile male flesh perfectly flaunted, and of course her harlot's body quivered with unrestrained glee at catching him so indisposed.

A single candle burned on the table, and it starkly outlined the planes of his face, making him look sexy and devilish, and she pulled up short. When she was away from him, she forgot how handsome he was, and she didn't care to be reminded.

She'd been searching for him ever since she'd gone

for her afternoon walk to visit Tim, only to find that he was missing and his hovel had been leveled. Her panic had been so great that she'd worried she might simply drop over dead.

She'd raced to the manor, wondering if Ophelia had sent Tim away. She'd often threatened that she would and had used the possibility as leverage to win concessions from Sarah so that, for the prior decade, Sarah had basically been Ophelia's slave.

Sarah would do anything to keep Tim safe. As a result, whatever Ophelia ordered, whatever Ophelia demanded, Sarah complied without complaint, groveling to Ophelia's petty whims like a drudge.

But while hurrying home, Sarah had seen Tim playing with some boys behind the stables. She'd been so relieved that it had taken a full hour to compose herself before she could saunter over and calmly question him about what had happened.

He'd explained how Jack had tracked him down, how Jack's brother, the new earl—the notorious pirate, himself!—had asked Tim to move to the house to learn a trade. At having the Merrick twins interested in him, Tim had been so proud that Sarah was extremely ashamed.

In all the years since his birth, she'd never aided him in any fashion that mattered, yet in the better part of an afternoon Jack had altered Tim's life forever.

Did Jack have to rub salt in her wounds? She was a disgusting coward, a woman so terrified of a bit of scandal that she'd let her only child wallow in poverty and despair. At Jack's forcing her to confront how pathetic she was, her temper was raging and she was eager to commit mayhem.

"It was none of your affair! None, I tell you."

"What wasn't?" he inquired, confused.

"Tim is *my* son. Mine!"

"Yes, Sarah, Tim is *your* son. Poor lad."

The insult had her rippling with fury. "You had no business interfering."

"I had every right. My brother is earl, and I am to be his estate manager."

On top of everything else she'd endured during the dreadful day, the news was too unsettling.

"You're staying?"

"Yes, so it's up to me to pick the employees who'll work the farm, and *I* have picked Tim. For now."

"What does that mean? For now?"

"It means for *now*," he said. "I haven't made any final decisions."

Was he saying Tim might be sent from Gladstone? For how long? On what grounds? Jack had the same blood running in his veins as Ophelia and their reprehensible father. He might do anything.

Dismissing Sarah, he turned and went to the table, where he unwrapped a towel. He'd brought a razor, soap, and a change of clothes, and the sight of his toiletries was unbearably intimate. She yanked her eyes away.

"I don't want you to stay here," she declared.

"It's not up to you. And if you must know, I'm not too keen on having you here, either, so I guess we're both stuck. Unless you'd like to hit the road . . . ? I can arrange to have you gone like that."

He snapped his fingers, the sound echoing off the walls, and it was frightening to recall her precarious position. Whether Anne married the earl or not, she and her sister would be at the mercy of the Merrick brothers for the rest of their lives, and Sarah abhorred the notion.

Her entire life had been one ordeal after the next,

due to her being constantly under the thumb of various males who were never concerned as to her fate. She yearned to be mistress of her own destiny, and she couldn't abide the thought of Jack remaining at Gladstone. She couldn't be bumping into him on the stairs or in the hall by her room, couldn't lie awake at night hoping he was about to sneak to her bedchamber again.

"Do you mind?" he queried. "I'd like to get on with my bath."

"I'm not leaving till we hash this out."

"I'm finished discussing it."

"Well, I'm not! Tim is my son, and I won't have you meddling."

"Now you claim him?" Jack laughed cruelly. "Why would you? You tossed him aside as if he was a mutt in a litter of puppies. He's nothing to you, and whatever I choose for him, your opinion is irrelevant."

"What a despicable thing to say to me."

"Name one thing you've ever done for him besides bring him a few scraps of dried bread."

"It wasn't like that!" she insisted.

"Wasn't it?"

"I love him! I've always loved him. I tried to do what was best for him."

"Every time you open your mouth, I like you less. Please go away before I end up despising you completely."

He grabbed the bar of soap and flung it into the washing tub, but she didn't budge.

"I've lived here at Percy's discretion," she tersely explained. "He and Ophelia wouldn't let me keep Tim. What could I have done?"

"First of all, Percy is an ass. And second of all, pardon me if I seem overly touchy on the subject, but

I have no sympathy for a parent who doesn't want his own child. If Tim had been mine, I'd have killed Percy before I'd have denied him."

"Bully for you!"

At that moment, she hated Jack Merrick as she'd never hated anyone, and if she'd been holding a pistol, she'd have shot him dead.

What did he know about anything?

She'd been a desperate sixteen-year-old girl, with no mother to guide her. The instant pregnancy was mentioned, her paramour had fled to London. Aunt Edith had offered no advice but had merely railed about sin and damnation. Ophelia had been the only one willing to grapple with the consequences, the only one willing to take charge, and Sarah had been more than happy to follow Ophelia's stern instructions.

It was later, when the enormity of Sarah's loss began to sink in, that she'd grieved over her decision, but by then she couldn't change the charade they'd set in motion. Tim had been ensconced with his new family, the situation accepted by all.

There'd been no way to renege on her devil's bargain, so she'd observed Tim from afar. She was heartsick and guilt ridden over her stupidity, yet Jack Merrick stood there smirking and condemning her as if he were some sort of wrathful god.

"You pompous blowhard!" she seethed. "You have no right to judge me!"

"Sticks and stones, Sarah. Sticks and stones. Now I'd appreciate it if I could have some privacy."

His flip attitude enraged her, and she resolved to tarry simply because he'd ordered her out. She was sick of men telling her what to do, sick of them controlling her every move so that she couldn't so much as swallow a crumb of food without one of them informing her that it was allowed.

"I resided at Gladstone long before you ever arrived," she said. "I'll be damned if I'll scurry off to my room on your say-so."

"Suit yourself."

He shrugged and, as if he hadn't a care in the world, he unbuttoned his trousers. His gaze was locked on hers, and with each flick of his wrist he bared more of his abdomen, until the placard was flopping loose.

He seemed to be daring her to remain, or taunting her with his nudity. Apparently, he was expecting to chase her out in a prudish snit, but he was in for a surprise. She was no squeamish miss who would quail at viewing a man's torso. No, she was Sarah Carstairs, the selfish, faithless woman who possessed the intellect of a ninny and the soul of a harlot.

Nothing would thrill her more than to watch him at his bath. Why, if he but asked, she'd waltz over and wash him. It would be the ultimate wicked pleasure.

With no concern for modesty, he tugged his pants down and off. Then he climbed into the tub, giving her plenty of opportunity to assess his masculine form.

He was a fine male specimen, all muscle and brawn, his chest broad, his waist and hips narrow. His body was that of a warrior, honed by rough living and battle. There were scars everywhere, evidence of prior stab wounds, of prior gunshot wounds, and he'd been flogged, the skin on his back crisscrossed with old injuries.

The sight made her queasy. Mentally, she'd comprehended that his time away from England had been difficult, but until that instant, the truth hadn't really hit home.

He glared over his shoulder. "Why don't you make yourself useful and scrub my back?"

"I don't want to."

"Liar."

He held out the washing cloth, dangling it like a talisman, but she refused to reach for it.

"You were flogged," she said, stating the obvious.

"I certainly was."

"Did it happen often?"

"Often enough."

"Why were you whipped?"

"On which occasion?"

"That's not funny."

"Who's being funny? I was a slave on a ship, and I wasn't very biddable. I'm contrary that way. Beatings were a common occurrence."

"How old were you when they started?"

"I don't know. Seven? Eight?"

"You were flogged when you were seven years old?"

"Were you thinking our absence from here was all High Tea and rose gardens? I used to curse my father because he hadn't had the courage to simply murder us outright." He hurled the washcloth at her, and it landed at her feet like an accusation. "Go away. You annoy me."

He spun and sank down in the water, sighing as it swirled around his tired torso. He closed his eyes and tipped his head against the rim, shutting her out as if he'd forgotten she was present, and his disregard made her unaccountably reckless.

He'd discovered all her secrets, and he loathed her for them, which was galling and humbling. She craved his esteem and his undivided attention. Frequently, she felt as if she were invisible, and she wanted him to treat her as if she mattered.

She snatched the cloth from the floor and went over to him, perching her hip on the edge of the tub. His reproachful eyes opened, and he stared at her as if he didn't know who she was.

Boldly, she grabbed the soap, and without a word being exchanged, she stroked it across his chest and shoulders. He didn't comment or request that she stop. He merely studied her, his expression mulish, as if he was curious to see how brave she'd actually be, how far she'd actually go, before sanity and morality returned with a vengeance.

She scrubbed him all over, and he let her try whatever she wished. The sensation of being in charge was arousing and exciting, and the longer she continued, the more risqué the encounter became.

Finally, she urged him to his knees, the water slapping at his thighs. His cock jutted out, his balls hanging heavy between his legs. Without hesitating, she caressed him as she'd been yearning to do, her fist clutching him and pumping him to a sturdy erection.

He dipped down to rinse; then, looking angry and irked, he clasped the front of her dress and pushed the fabric away, baring a breast. He leaned over and latched onto her nipple, biting it, sucking on it so hard that she cried out in delighted distress.

He rose and stepped to the rug, and she was kneeling before him, at eye level with his phallus. He brushed it against her lips, and she licked the crown over and over, then eagerly took him inside. Silent and stoic, he peered down at her, as he methodically thrust.

Clearly, he assumed she'd call a halt, but she couldn't imagine that she ever would. He was so hot and virile, and she'd been missing this decadence, where her base temperament could run free, where she didn't have to constantly rein it in.

His lust was at a fevered pitch, and vaguely she wondered if he'd spill himself, if *she* would take him all the way to the end. Just how depraved did she intend to be?

At the last moment, he yanked away and picked her off the floor, laying her on the baker's table. He wedged himself between her thighs, and with no wooing or delay, he shoved into her.

It had been an eternity since she'd had sex, so she was tight as a virgin. She moaned with agony, but he didn't care. Nor did she. He rammed into her again and again, and she reveled in the naughty pleasure, dragging him nearer, goading him on, and it never occurred to her to tell him to slow down or be cautious.

As she'd learned to her detriment, when she was fornicating it wasn't in her nature to exercise prudence, and for some reason, her attraction to him made her even more irresponsible.

He nursed at her breasts, shifting from one to the other. The torment was so delicious that the instant he reached down and touched her, she exploded into an orgasm. Through the tumult, he kept flexing until he, too, arrived at his own conclusion.

Luckily, he had the presence of mind to withdraw and spew his seed on her stomach. After, he retreated and walked to the washtub to swab his privates clean. He was very meticulous, as if he wanted to wipe away every trace of her; then he retrieved his clothes and tugged them on.

She was sprawled on the table, her skirt rucked up, her legs spread wide, as if she was hoping he'd saunter over and mount her again. She forced herself to sit up, and she straightened her garments and mutely observed as he packed his things and tidied up. Low on her belly, the wetness of his seed was soaking into her dress.

He scanned the room to be sure he hadn't forgotten anything; then he turned to go, his face a mask she couldn't read. He appeared cool and unaffected, while she felt like a whore, like a housemaid who'd copulated with him for the promise of a meager penny.

He came over and kissed her, and it was the only kiss he'd bestowed during the entire bizarre episode.

"Tim will be fine," he vowed. "I'll see to him."

"Swear it to me."

"Why should I have to swear for you to trust me? Isn't my word good enough?"

She trusted no man, and she wouldn't pretend he was doing her any favors. If he was acting kindly toward Tim, he had an ulterior motive. Men always did.

"Don't you dare hurt him," she warned. "Don't send him away from me."

Jack must have been expecting gratitude, for her remark angered him. He looked as if he might bite her head off, or plead his case, but instead, he scoffed with derision.

"Next time you put your mouth on me," he crudely said, "I won't hold back."

"I didn't ask you to hold back."

"No, you didn't, and you need to realize that—with me—it's all or nothing. Next time, I won't pull out."

He stomped off, and she dawdled—all alone—in the quiet.

Chapter
THIRTEEN

W hat's your name?" Jamie asked.

"Pegeen," the saucy housemaid replied, leaning her delectable bottom on the balustrade of the verandah. "But milord, you can call me Peg, if you'd like."

Jamie grinned. The girl was plump and buxom and pretty as a spring day in May. In blatant invitation, she tossed her hair over her shoulder, advising him—in no uncertain terms—that she was interested and available.

The front of her dress was damp, so the cloth clung to her large breasts. He couldn't decide if she'd intentionally moistened the fabric or if she'd spilled something by accident, but however it had happened, she'd definitely gotten his attention.

He was humored by her offer and wouldn't be averse to tumbling her occasionally. Women were always throwing themselves at him, and he usually caught them. Why deny himself? Especially now that he was an earl.

It was his prerogative to romp with the servants, and when such a lusty female was prancing about right under his nose, how could he be expected to resist?

For the briefest second, he thought of Anne, and instantly he felt guilty as hell, which annoyed him to infinity and back. He'd been spending entirely too much time with her, and he couldn't quash his incessant need to revel in her company.

He'd tried to stay away from her, but his attempts to create distance had failed miserably. He couldn't stop himself from crawling into her bed, and his fixation was putting them both in an untenable position.

She was the sort of person who would read too much meaning into their relationship. She'd think he was doting on her, and he was—in a way. With her being so sweet and wonderful, she was so different from the whores in port towns who'd made up the bulk of his amorous adventures.

He didn't want to hurt her, but if he continued trifling with her, she'd presume that a commitment was forming, when it never would.

He simply wasn't the type of man who grew attached. He didn't know how to care or bond, or perhaps the ability had been drummed out of him during his hard years as an abandoned little boy.

Whatever the reason, he didn't have it in him to cherish her as she deserved. So while he'd support and honor her, he would never fall in love with her, and he had to exert some control over his obsessive conduct.

Pegeen would be a great place to start, and if Jamie copulated with her, who would know? She would add spice to the boring intervals when duty forced him to Gladstone, and if she was particularly adept with that intriguing mouth of hers, she'd keep his mind off Anne and his foolish, unrelenting desire for her.

"Are you Irish, Pegeen?"

"On my mother's side, milord."

"I just love Irish women. They're so"—his gaze drifted to her bosom—"wholesome."

"It's the fresh air."

"Is it?"

"It's so *arousing*."

She waved toward the woods, indicating that she was eager to tryst. Any other time, he might have agreed, but it *was* his wedding day, and he just couldn't go. He wasn't such an ass that he'd roll around in the forest with another woman only moments before he lied and promised himself to Anne.

"I'm getting married," he told her. "In a few minutes."

"I heard. Congratulations."

"So I'm busy right now."

"But later . . ." She peered up the side of the house, to the windows of the earl's suite, where soon he and Anne would shut themselves in to commence their wedding night. She stepped closer, her pointy nipples poking his shirt. "A *real* man often finds that a virgin isn't what he requires, at all."

"He often does."

He chuckled, even as he was appalled to note that he didn't move away from her. Like the worst cad, he was leading her on, acting as if he might actually sneak from his marital bed to fornicate with her.

He was so disgusting!

All of a sudden, from inside the manor, an irate female shouted, "Pegeen Riley! Leave my fiancé alone!"

He and Peg froze, then leapt apart like guilty schoolchildren as Anne burst out the door and advanced on them.

"Run, Peg," he whispered. "I'll take care of this."

She flashed a thankful look and slipped down the stairs into the park, racing away like a thoroughbred.

On seeing her go, Jamie sighed, wishing he could have raced off with her.

He wasn't even married yet, and he was already in trouble with his bride. It was a sorry way to begin, and he hoped it wasn't a sign of how the rest of their life would go. Unfortunately, he doubted that he'd ever behave any better. He had no idea how to act like a husband, as Anne was swiftly learning.

She marched up, stopping when they were toe-to-toe, and she studied him as if he were a bug she'd like to squash.

"What was that?" she hissed.

"What was *what*?"

"Don't play dumb with me, Jamieson Merrick. Have you any notion of how long I've been watching you?"

"How long?"

"Long enough for you to make a public spectacle of yourself where the entire estate could see. Why do I feel that I'm living through the same despicable event over and over?"

"She's a silly young girl," he claimed. "Don't work yourself into a lather over it."

"Tell me one thing: If I hadn't come outside just now, how rapidly would you have been out in the woods with her?"

At being apprised of how much she'd truly observed, he could barely keep from wincing.

"Don't be ridiculous. I was teasing her. She's naught but a bit of fluff."

"And what am I in comparison?"

"Well . . . you're Anne."

He thought the comment said it all, but from the hurt expression that crossed her beautiful face, it was clear he'd missed the mark by a wide margin.

"Do you know what time it is?" she snapped.

"Ten thirty?"

"We're supposed to marry in half an hour! The vicar is about to arrive. How could you do this to me?"

"What did I *do* to you? I've merely been chatting with a servant."

Her jaw dropped; tears flooded her eyes. "You are a horse's ass, Mr. Merrick. An unrepentant, unlikable, unpleasant horse's ass."

"I've been called much worse, and if you're going to take that snotty tone with me, it's *Lord Gladstone.*"

"If you ever conducted yourself like a lord, maybe people would treat you like one."

It was the lowest remark she could have hurled, and it cut him to the quick. Not that he'd let her know.

Her attitude enraged him. He wasn't in the habit of permitting others to insult him, and he deemed it quite bold of her. If she'd been a man, he'd have pounded her into the ground. As it was, a muscle ticked in his cheek, his fists clenched with a fury he couldn't vent.

He was aware that he'd behaved badly, but he wouldn't apologize for his natural tendencies, and he refused to be gelded by her. He was who he was. Not a saint. Not a dandy. Not a blushing swain. But a terrible sinner, and she would have to get used to it, because he wasn't about to change. He didn't *want* to change.

"I won't dawdle out here in the yard, arguing with you," he quietly stated. "Go back in the house."

"You have no intention of being faithful to me, do you? Why am I such an idiot that I can't figure this out?"

"Anne!" he scolded. "I won't discuss such a topic."

"Are the vows irrelevant to you?"

"They will mean everything to me," he brazenly fibbed.

In truth, he believed in nothing and he trusted no one. Vows were inane, given frivolously and without consideration, and while they were uttered constantly, he'd never met a soul who stuck by what was promised.

She scrutinized him, then shook her head. "You are such a liar."

"Go back in the house," he repeated more sternly, nodding to the manor. "I'll join you shortly so we can get started."

"Do you understand how absurd you sound? You can't practice fidelity for a single day, and you think I'll still marry you?"

"I know you will, Anne. You're letting your temper run away with you over a trifle, and I have to tell you that I don't care for it."

"You don't?"

"No."

"Then let me tell you this, and see if you *care* for it: I wouldn't marry you if you were the last man on earth. You can chew on that bit of information while you're standing—alone—in the parlor with the vicar."

His cheeks reddened with ire, as she turned and hurried off, shouting, "Sarah! Sarah! Where are you?"

"Anne!" he commanded in his most authoritative, ship captain's voice, but she just kept going.

⚓

W hat time is it now?"
        "Eleven twenty."
        The wedding had been scheduled for eleven, but Anne had meant it when she'd said she wouldn't participate. A union between them was wrong, wrong, wrong! She knew it, but he was so good

at cajoling and demanding that she always ended up re-
lenting.

Well, not again. She wouldn't make such a dreadful
mistake, and despite how he nagged, she would stick to
her guns.

She gazed over at her sister, then at the locked door
that led to the hallway. They were huddled in Sarah's
room, sitting on the bed like two women about to be
stoned to death.

"How long will he wait before he realizes you were
serious?" Sarah inquired.

"For hours. He's so vain, it won't occur to him that I
didn't arrive. Then again, perhaps he's holding the ceremony without me. He probably hasn't noticed that
I'm not there."

"Are you sure about this, Anne?"

"Oh, Sarah, if you'd seen him with Pegeen!"

"It's a man's way," she gently counseled. "They're
like beasts in the field, so a dalliance is insignificant to
them. If you care for him—"

"That's the problem. I care for him too much. If I go
through with it, he'll break my heart on a daily basis. I
couldn't bear it; I'm not that strong, and I won't pretend to be blind to infidelity. I'm sorry."

"Don't be sorry. I simply want what's best for you. I
always had my doubts that it would be Jamie Merrick."

"He'll be so angry. I don't know what will happen to
us now."

"We'll figure it out. I'm acquainted with his brother.
He might help us."

"I wish Percy would intervene."

"He won't; he's been very clear."

"Yes, he has, the rat."

Sarah rose and walked to the window, and she stared out. She looked so sad, so weary.

"Are you all right?" Anne queried. "Anymore, you seem so . . . despondent."

Sarah snorted at that; then she peered over. "There's something I've been needing to tell you."

"What is it?"

As if Sarah hadn't the strength to stay on her feet, she collapsed against the windowsill, a palm braced on the wall, and on seeing her so beaten down Anne was frightened. She'd been so wrapped up in her own melodrama with Jamie that she'd scarcely spoken to Sarah in days.

"What is it, Sarah?" Anne soothed. "You can confide in me. It can't be that bad."

"You'd never hate me, would you, Anne? If I'd done something awful?"

Her expression was so bleak that Anne grew alarmed, and she rose, too, and rushed over.

"*Hate* you? Are you mad?"

"Oh, this is so difficult." Tears surged into Sarah's eyes.

"Go on," Anne urged. "Whatever is it, I won't swoon. You can't shock me."

"Do you remember the year I was sixteen, and I went away to finishing school?"

"Gad, yes. I was so jealous."

"Well . . . I . . . I . . ."

She swallowed twice, about to confess her secret when noise erupted in the hall.

"Anne Carstairs!" Jamie bellowed. "By God, when I find you, I will wring your pretty neck!"

He was marching toward them, checking every

bedchamber. A door slammed, then another and another, and soon he was directly outside. He tried the knob.

"Whose room is this?" he asked someone.

"Her sister's," his brother answered.

Jamie pounded on the wood so forcefully that it bowed with the blows. "Anne! You have five seconds to let me in, or I will kick my way in. Do you hear me?"

"Shall I open it?" Sarah whispered.

"No," Anne replied. "Let him make a fool of himself. He enjoys acting like a barbarian."

"Five seconds, Anne," Jamie counted. "Four, three, two, one." There was a pause; then he muttered, "Fine. Have it your way."

A hard jolt sent the knob flying, the wood shattering, and he stormed in, looking magnificent and livid and lethal. Anne imagined this was how his enemies saw him when he was boarding ships and plundering booty, and she had to admit that his reputation for menace was definitely deserved.

With all that visible fury focused on her, she was shaking. While she hadn't thought he'd ever hurt her physically, at that moment he appeared capable of any violence. He stomped over to her, and she flinched, as if expecting to be hit, but no strike landed. He simply towered over her, intimidating her with his size and presence, and it was certainly working.

In such an agitated state, he was fearsome and formidable.

"You're late," he seethed. "Everyone is awaiting you downstairs."

"I told you I wasn't coming."

"So you did. Silly me, I didn't believe you." He gestured to his brother. "Bind her hands behind her back."

Jack stepped forward and produced a length of

rope he'd brought for that very purpose. Sarah gasped and wedged herself as a shield between Anne and Jamie.

"What are you doing?" she demanded of Jack.

"She's getting married," Jack calmly responded, "and we won't hear any argument."

"Oh yes, you will!" Sarah hurled. "She's my only sister, and I won't have her miserably shackled to a gadabout roué."

"It's none of your affair, Sarah," Jack warned.

"If it's not my affair, then whose is it? Maybe if your brother could keep his trousers buttoned, we wouldn't be in this fix."

Jamie turned his deadly gaze on Sarah. "When I want to be insulted by you, Miss Carstairs, I'll let you know."

He grabbed Sarah by the waist, picked her up, and set her to the side; then he nodded at Jack to proceed.

"I'm weary of both of them," Jamie said. "Let's finish this."

It was over in a thrice. Jamie gripped Anne's arms and pinned them together as Jack twined the rope around her wrists. With a few quick knots, she was trussed like a Christmas goose. She was so stunned that she didn't even consider complaining. What could she say? The man was a lunatic!

"You can drag me to the altar," she bravely boasted, "but you'll never pry any vows out of me."

"We'll see." The retort sounded like a threat and a promise.

He spoke to Sarah. "After this nonsense, Miss Carstairs, you're not welcome at my wedding."

"That's all right," Sarah fumed. "I have no desire to attend a farce."

"Good. You'll remain up here until I inform you otherwise."

"Yes, my lord and master."

Jamie whirled on Jack. "I'll need you as a witness at the ceremony; then you're to come back up and deal with her. You begged me to let her remain at Gladstone. You claimed you could control her."

"*Control* me!" Sarah stewed, scowling at Jack.

He seemed chagrined but had no comment.

"She must be made to understand," Jamie continued, "that I will not be thwarted in my decisions. Can you get her to comprehend this fact? If you're not up to the task, admit it to me, and I'll handle her myself."

"She'll do as I say," Jack insisted, "and she'll do it gladly. Won't you, Sarah?"

"Go to Hell, Mr. Merrick," she sweetly replied, batting her lashes at him, showing him that she wasn't frightened in the slightest.

"Come, Anne," Jamie commanded.

He took her arm, and she dug in her feet, making a feeble attempt not to acquiesce. He sighed as if he were the most put-upon husband in the world and she the most shrewish wife.

"You've tried my patience beyond its limit," he pointed out. "You may walk down of your own accord, or you shall be hauled down like a sack of flour. The choice is yours. Which is it to be?"

"I'll walk," she grumbled like a petulant child, and she jerked away and started out.

The two brothers followed her, flanking her on either side in case she made a run for it. In a daze, she trudged down the stairs, stumbling along as if in a dream.

How had she arrived at such a bizarre fork in the road? The parents she'd never known, who'd died when she was a babe, came to mind, and she wondered what their opinion would be if they could see her predicament. Would they be horrified? Would they be enraged? Or would they merely think—as everyone but Sarah agreed—that Jamie Merrick was a spectacular catch and Anne was lucky to have him?

She stepped into the front parlor, where Ophelia, Percy, and Edith had assembled. The cowardly vicar was present, too, but no one else had been invited. They spun as a group, gaping at her with varying levels of incredulity.

Jamie entered and said, "Vicar, you may stay. The rest of you will leave immediately."

Percy had the fortitude to inquire, "Anne, are you injured?"

"No, but if you could just—"

"Be silent!" Jamie snarled, cutting her off.

Percy frowned at Jamie. "Are you sure this is the best way?"

"Out!" Jamie hissed.

Ophelia felt obliged to chuckle and butt in. "She seems a tad reluctant, Jamie. Are you positive you should go through with it? She might murder you later in your sleep."

"Out!" he said again, more loudly, and he swept them all with such a contemptuous glare that they scurried away. Jack slammed and locked the door behind them.

The vicar was standing by the hearth, and Jamie led Anne over.

"Get on with it," Jamie ordered, "and don't dilly-dally over the words. I want this concluded as rapidly as possible."

The vicar stared at Jamie, at Anne, at Jamie again. He studied her bound hands and gulped with dismay.

"Lord Gladstone," he tentatively ventured, "it doesn't appear that she's willing."

"So?"

"This isn't the Middle Ages. If she doesn't consent, I can't perform the ceremony."

"Get going, man," Jack Merrick barked, "or I'll take you outside and you can explain to me why it's so difficult for you to do as the earl has requested."

Anne glanced at the Merrick brothers. They were resolved and ferocious, and though mayhem might result against the poor minister, she was certain this was her last chance to enlist an ally.

"I don't want to marry the earl," she interjected. "Any union would be a sham. He told me, just a few minutes ago, that the vows are frivolous and—"

"I never said that!" Jamie protested, seeming aggrieved.

"—and he has no intention of keeping to them. If you marry us, you'll be making a mockery of the entire notion of matrimony."

She deemed it an excellent, persuasive speech, and for a fleeting moment it looked as if the vicar might heed her entreaty and refuse to participate, but Jamie grabbed him by the arm and escorted him across the room. Jamie delivered a whispered, blistering diatribe that she couldn't hear, but whatever coercion he used, he definitely had the vicar's attention.

Obviously, the man was being terrorized with a severe fate. He shivered, assessed her with no sympathy, then hurried back to her, muttering, " 'Dearly beloved, we are gathered here in the sight of God'—"

"Vicar, please!" she begged.

"Trust me, Miss Carstairs," he responded. "The earl

is a fine man. A fine man! You're having reservations now, but in the long term, you won't regret it."

"Are you mad? He's insane! He kicked down my door, and he tied me up, and he threatened my sister, and he—"

"Anne?" Jamie interrupted.

"What?"

"I asked you to be silent."

"Well, I don't choose to obey."

"I haven't asked you to *obey*. I've merely asked you to be quiet. I'm exhausted by your constant harangue."

She opened her mouth to reply, when he shoved a wad of cloth between her lips, effectively gagging her as if she were a prisoner. In the brief amount of time since she'd met him, she'd suffered numerous indignities, but this was—by far—the most aggravating, humiliating thing that had ever happened to her.

"There! That's better," Jamie mused. He patted her on the head, like a pet dog, as he grinned at the vicar. "Now then, let's proceed. I'm hungry, and I want to enjoy my wedding breakfast before it gets cold."

The vicar began again, and Anne stood there, muffled, shackled, mortified, as he sped through what had to be the shortest recitation of vows ever uttered. Jamie answered his questions in the appropriate spots. Jack chimed in where—in a rational world—Anne would have spoken.

Quickly they were at the end. The vicar closed his prayer book, had Jamie and Jack sign some papers, then raced from the room.

Anne was married to Jamieson Merrick—without ever saying a word.

Chapter
FOURTEEN

Let me explain how you've failed me yet again."
Percy glared at his sister, then checked his bag to be sure the maids hadn't forgotten to pack any important items.

"I'm not in the mood, Ophelia."

"You're not? And why is that? Would my list of grievances be too long? I guess you're so busy running away that you wouldn't have time to listen."

"Jamieson Merrick is like a force of nature. He can't be deterred. You saw how he was with Anne. He's had his way at every turn. There's no stopping him."

"He just banished *me* to the Dower House—with Mother!"

"A fate worse than death." He gave a mock shudder, not really concerned over what happened to Ophelia. He had his own problems to solve, and they were much more pressing than hers.

"What am I to do?" she nagged.

"Go live with your mum, I suppose. At this late date, what else can you hope for?"

"You know what Edith is like. I will not care for her! I will not play nanny to the demented shrew."

"What would you have me say, Ophelia? Would you rather he tossed the two of you out on the road?"

"You said it would never come to this!"

"You said the same, but it appears we were both wrong. You'd best pack your bags—as I have done."

She grabbed the lapels of his coat and shook him. "You have to help me! I've been your countess-in-fact for over a decade. I won't sleep in some decrepit bedroom in a hovel down the lane, with only a smattering of the most slothful servants to attend me. I won't abandon my spot to Anne!"

"The wedding is over, which would seem to indicate that you already have."

"This is all your fault."

"How is it *my* fault? I followed every bit of your advice, and look where we are."

"No, you didn't! I advised you to placate him so that we could keep a hand in the family coffers. But you let your pride get in the way."

"What do you mean?"

"Jack tattled on you."

"About what?"

"You told Jamie that you wouldn't accept any compensation, so because of your arrogance, we're left with nothing."

He hadn't wanted her to hear of that stupid meeting, and his first instinct was to deny her accusation. He'd merely heeded his idiotic lawyers and proceeded according to their instructions. How could he be to blame?

He clasped her by the neck, tightening his grip, loving the fear that came into her eye. With his recent rough treatment of her, he'd learned a fascinating detail about himself: He had a nasty side that reveled in violence.

He hadn't realized how exciting it could be to force himself on a woman, although with Ophelia there wasn't ever much resistance. She was as dissolute as he—often more so—but the discovery had shifted their relationship into an entirely new realm.

He couldn't wait to try out his aggression on other females, perhaps a few of the housemaids, or maybe an innocent debutante in London. It would be the ultimate decadence to viciously ruin some snotty, irritating virgin.

"I'm sick of your denigrating me," he said. "Shut your mouth!"

"What if I don't?" She was clawing at his fingers, gasping for air. "You haven't the nerve to do anything to me."

"Haven't I?"

He shoved her onto the bed, as she sputtered and fought, but he was stronger and more determined. He climbed over her as he fumbled with his trousers and released his cock.

"Suck me off," he commanded, stroking the tip across her ruby lips.

"I won't. Not when you're being a beast."

"Do it!"

He reached inside her dress to painfully squeeze her nipple, and she moaned in agony and opened wide.

He flexed into her, as she gagged and fumed, and he was thrilled by his mastery over her. For much of his life, she'd ordered him about, had disparaged and maligned and insulted, and he was delighted to finally show her who was in charge.

Like a crazed animal, he thrust, and as his seed

poured down her throat, he could barely keep from braying in triumph.

How could he not have known how satisfying carnal supremacy would be? Why hadn't he ravished anyone before? His days of enduring her criticisms and complaints were over. *He* would make the decisions. *He* would formulate the plans.

With a deep growl, he pulled away, and he heaved her off the mattress and onto the floor. She was crouched on her hands and knees, muttering and struggling for breath.

"Bastard!" she mumbled.

"I certainly can be, and you shouldn't forget it."

She stumbled to her feet. Her hair was falling, her clothes askew, and he laughed at her disheveled condition. In the past few weeks, the balance of power between them had changed, but she hadn't figured out exactly how. He was tired of letting her walk all over him, and from now on, they would do things his way. Starting with Jamie and Anne and moving on from there.

He stood, straightened himself, then calmly closed the straps on his portmanteau, which had her aghast and scowling.

"You can't leave," she insisted.

"I have to. For *now*."

"You can't be serious."

"Oh, but I am. Jamie has demanded my departure, and I don't want him wary, so I'll comply."

"But how will you ever return? As long as you're here, you have a continuing claim. If you trot off to London, Jamie will have won."

"Jamie will never be victorious over me."

"He already is!" she hissed.

"Little sister, you're beginning to annoy me. Now, I must be off. Would you like to come with me?"

"Are you mad? One of us must maintain a presence on the estate."

"So you'd rather remain here and play nursemaid to Edith?" As if his burdens were the greatest in the world, he sighed. "I have everything worked out, Ophelia."

"Really?" she snidely goaded.

"Yes, *really*. At the moment, I've lost the legal battles, but there are other ways to fight Jamie. Can you honestly tell me that you think he'll make Gladstone his permanent residence?"

"No, I don't believe he will."

"Neither do I. So he'll go shortly, and Anne will be all alone. After all I've done for her, can you actually suppose she'd dare deny me anything?"

"No."

"So once he leaves, I'll come home, and I'll bait the perfect trap, then lure him back."

"What trap? What have you arranged?"

"I haven't decided on the particulars yet, but I'm debating them. In the meantime, I'm off to London to revel before total poverty sets in. When I return, it will be to assume my rightful place."

Jamie would be dealt with like the nuisance he was, and as to Anne . . . well . . . she needed to remember how much she owed Percy for his support over the years. And he knew precisely the sort of payment he'd extract.

❦

E dith peeked through the keyhole, catching glimpses of her son and daughter as they flitted past the small opening.

She couldn't see all of what they were doing, but a

clear view wasn't necessary to understand the depth of their depravity. At an early age, they had succumbed to unnatural urges, and Edith had never had a clue how to make them desist. She considered bursting into the room, shaming them for their obscene acts, but she was tired and hadn't the energy to endure one of Ophelia's bitter tirades.

Percy was speaking again, and Edith pressed her ear to the hole to listen. She managed a few sentences, enough to discern that she was being evicted from Gladstone—when no one had said a word to her about it. With the new earl arrived, her future was being bandied as if she were invisible, as if she were a person of no consequence in the ostentatious mansion.

It had always been so. She had always been ignored.

Where was she to go? What was to become of her? Why would no one say?

She was treated like a child, like a half-wit, and to learn that Jamieson Merrick would cast her out, that he would abandon her to Ophelia and Percy, was the most frightening notion imaginable.

She'd been positive Jamieson would help her, that he would change things for the better. How could she have been so wrong about him? After all her scheming, if he was no different from his worthless father, what would she do?

Suddenly, Ophelia marched out in a huff, and Edith reared away and stood. She would have run so as to avoid detection, but before she could, the door was flung open and she was confronting her odious daughter.

"You old witch!" Ophelia seethed. "What are you doing lurking out here? From how much you spy on us, I'm beginning to think you're a voyeur at heart."

"I'm watching you," Edith said, "and God is watching you."

"Then your *God* certainly got an eyeful. Tell Him for me that I hope He enjoyed the show."

She stormed off, the disgusting smell of fornication hovering in her wake. Edith stared after her, knowing she would eventually even the score. But which revenge would be the sweetest?

ꝫ

Y ou tug the cord like this and let fly."

"Can I try it?"

"That's why I brought it."

Jack offered the slingshot to Tim, and the boy eagerly took aim at a stick of wood they'd rested on the fence. He frowned and fussed, but after several attempts, he got the hang of it. When he finally knocked the stick to the ground, he whooped with glee.

He was a smart child, a respectful child. The deceased widow who'd raised him had been very poor, and they'd lived in squalor, but she'd done a good job with him. Tim was courteous and friendly, and Jack liked him very much.

"Did you see that?" Tim asked. "I hit it square on."

"You sure did."

Tim tried to give the weapon back, but Jack just smiled.

"You keep it," Jack said.

"But . . . why?"

"I made it for you."

"For me?"

Tim was confused, as if no one had ever given him a gift before, as if he didn't know how to accept it. His expression was so identical to Sarah's that it was almost painful to observe him.

Jack patted him on the shoulder. "Yes, for you. I want you to practice every day. I want you skilled enough to keep the rats out of the barn and the rabbits out of the garden."

"I will!" Tim vowed. "I'll be the best guard ever!"

"I know you will."

There were squirrels in the trees, and Jack taught Tim how to track the fleet animals. He had no chance of harming any of them, but it was humorous to observe as he concentrated and struggled to improve.

Jack was in no hurry for the lesson to end, and he planned to loiter in the forest as long as he could. The manor was in chaos, so he'd stay away till matters calmed. Percy had left for London. Ophelia and Edith were heading for the Dower House, but complaining every step of the way.

Jamie had wed Anne, against her will, and Jack had assisted in orchestrating the event, and he wasn't sorry. While others might curse Jamie for forcing Anne, Jack never would. No one at Gladstone could be allowed to countermand or disobey Jamie. He was fully in charge and would be from now on. Anne—and everyone else—had to get used to the idea, but it definitely made for a rough afternoon.

The servants were sullen and unruly, Anne was in a state of shock, Sarah was spitting mad, and Jack couldn't stand any of it. Shooting at squirrels with a polite and enthused young boy was preferable to any of the alternatives.

At least one person on the blasted property was glad for Jack's company!

Jack played with Tim till his arm grew tired, till they

could find no more stones on the path. They started toward the house, when they rounded a curve on the trail and they came face-to-face with Sarah.

She looked as if she'd been crying, and Jack steeled himself against feeling any sympathy for her. They'd had sex on a few raucous occasions, but he refused to read anything into the episodes.

She had too many problems, more than he could solve, more than he could assume, and he didn't like judging her, but he couldn't help it. Her silence regarding Tim's parentage had Jack wondering about her true character. If she was really as callous as her behavior indicated, he wanted no part of a relationship with her—despite the physical attraction they shared.

On seeing him, she stopped, and she was still visibly angry over his role in Anne's wedding, but it was best for Anne to be Jamie's wife. What other choice did she have?

Jamie had merely kept her from making a dreadful mistake, and one day she'd thank them. That's what Jack was telling himself anyway. If Anne never came round to their way of thinking, Jack cared not. Jamie's goals were paramount, and Sarah's and Anne's protests were naught but insignificant chatter out on the edge of the world.

For a moment, it appeared as if Sarah would stomp off in a snit, but she couldn't resist the opportunity to speak with Tim.

"Hello, Tim."

"Hello, Miss Carstairs."

As she noticed what was dangling from Tim's fingers, she frowned. "What have you got there?"

"It's a slingshot, Miss. Mr. Merrick gave it to me."

"He did?"

The information had her extremely upset, but Tim didn't recognize her pique, and he answered eagerly, "We've been practicing shooting at squirrels, so I can keep the rabbits out of the garden."

Her temper flared, and she focused her livid gaze on Jack. "I won't have him killing small animals. I can't believe you'd instigate such an activity without asking me."

"It's not up to you, is it, *Miss* Carstairs?" Jack taunted.

"I don't give my permission for him to own a sling-shot! I don't want him to have one."

Tim was unnerved by her fury, and he peered up at Jack. "It's all right, Mr. Merrick. If she'd rather I not, I don't need it."

"I gave it to you, Tim, and it's yours." Jack glared at Sarah and goaded, "Unless you'd like to enlighten him as to why your decisions should supersede mine?"

She blanched, turning so white that, for a second, he worried she might faint. Tears swarmed to her eyes, and she hurled, "I hate you, Jack Merrick. I hate you and your awful brother, and I wish both of you would slither back to whatever hole you crawled out of."

She began to cry full on, and she whirled away and ran. Jack's heart lurched in his chest, her terrible words hurting him in ways he didn't like or understand, but he wouldn't race after her like a besotted idiot. She was crazy as a bedbug, and he needed to involve himself in her troubles like he needed a trip to the barber to have a bad tooth pulled.

"She's very annoyed with us," Tim said, stating the obvious.

"Yes, she is."

"Should I go to the manor and apologize? I'm not sure what I'd be apologizing *for,* though. I'm not sure what I did."

"Let this be a lesson to you, Tim," Jack sagely advised. "With women, you never know what it is that you did wrong. As you grow older, that fact will never change."

He walked Tim to the barn, then went to the house, himself, slinking in a rear door, hoping to avoid any of the disgruntled occupants. He'd planned to head to his room, to wash and relax before supper, but his feet had a mind of their own.

At the landing on the stairs, where he should have proceeded to his own bedchamber, he turned to tiptoe to Sarah's, instead. The hall was empty, so he spun the knob and slipped inside.

She was on her bed, her face buried in the pillow, and weeping as if there were no tomorrow. He was as irate as she was, but he'd never been the type to make a woman cry, and he couldn't bear to see her so sad and to know that he'd been the cause.

"Sarah," he murmured.

She raised up and stared over at him. "Oh, go away! Just go away." Then she clutched at the pillow again, her sobs muffled, her shoulders shaking.

He stumbled over and stretched out next to her, and he drew her into his arms.

"Hush now," he soothed. "Hush. It will be all right."

"Where is my sister?"

"She's in the earl's suite—with Jamie."

"Will he beat her?"

"No! Gad! Is that what you think? He'd never harm her."

"I tried to talk to her, but he wouldn't let me."

"She'll be fine," he insisted. No matter Jamie's many faults, he'd never resort to physical violence against a woman. Well, unless the woman did something violent first. Then, the gloves would come off.

"He was so angry with her."

"Yes, he was."

"I swore to her that she wouldn't have to marry him. I swore that I'd protect her."

"She didn't need your protection. Their marriage was for the best."

"I couldn't stop him!" she wailed. "I couldn't help her, and I couldn't help my son, and they're the only two people who've ever needed me. What good am I? I've never done anything worthwhile in my whole life."

"They're *both* fine. You needn't fret so much."

"But I've failed at every turn. Who can count on me? Why would anyone?"

She was at the end of her rope, and he hated to witness the depth of her despair. He'd spent many hours grumbling over her lack of integrity, and he'd convinced himself that she was a cruel shrew, when he knew she wasn't.

It was simply easier to paint her with a brutal brush, for if he viewed her realistically, he'd have to admit that she was merely a lonely woman who'd made some difficult choices. Then he'd have to admit his strong feelings for her, which would give her too much power over him.

He didn't want to care for her, didn't want to put himself in a position where she could reject him or kill him with her disregard. He'd been snubbed or deserted too many times over the years, and he never attached himself to others.

Relationships were fleeting. People died. People were left behind. People moved on. It was better to remain separate, but Sarah had him yearning for something more, something different from the empty existence of traveling the globe with his rootless, itinerant brother.

He held her for an eternity, calming her as if she were a young child who'd awakened from a nightmare, and the experience was wonderful.

Her anguish had his masculine instincts surging to the fore. He wanted to cherish and shelter, wanted to love and bond. The sensations were new and intriguing, and during this odd period of his life, when his entire world was being transformed, he wouldn't discount them out of hand. He would embrace them and see where they led.

Finally, her tears dwindled to a halt. She shuddered and sighed.

"I'm so pathetic."

"Yes, you are. You're an absolute wretch."

His sarcasm earned him a soft punch in the belly.

"I don't need you agreeing with me."

He chuckled as she drew away to peer up at him. She was utterly despondent, and he was crushed that she was so unhappy.

"Don't be sad, Sarah."

"What's to become of me? What possible reason is there for me to continue on? I'm twenty-six years old, and I have nothing to show for it. No money. No home. No family of my own. I'm such a failure."

"You're very pretty, though."

"Talk about something that matters or be silent."

He grabbed the quilt, using a corner to dry her eyes.

"You don't have to figure it all out today."

"I suppose I don't."

She studied him, looking confused and morose, when suddenly she shifted nearer and kissed him. She'd surprised him, but he wasn't about to complain.

They couldn't seem to interact without a sexual incident occurring, especially when they were snuggled on a bed. Sparks always sizzled when they were together, and while he eagerly joined in, she was definitely the one in charge. She needed the contact, and he was enough of a cad that he would indulge her in any fashion she desired.

She groaned with pleasure and dismay, and she rolled them so that she was on top. Her mouth ravaged his, while her hands explored; then she climbed over him, her skirt floating over his thighs, her privates pressed to his loins. Her hot gaze locked on his, she tugged at the bodice of her dress, baring her bosom. Her breasts were full and round, the tips rosy and luring him to his doom.

All modesty gone, she arched forward, urging him to feast, and he clasped her nipples, playing with them, squeezing them so that she moaned in delicious agony. She opened his trousers and took hold of him, stroking him to a painful erection; then she centered herself and eased down.

He'd understood that she had a very sensual nature, but he hadn't seen this side of it. She was demanding control, and he was thrilled to let her have it.

"What do you want from me, Sarah?"

"Just this, Jack. Nothing more."

"But I want to—"

She rested a finger against his lips.

"Don't wreck the moment by speaking of what I can't bear to hear."

"There's something happening between us, and we have to discuss it."

"There's nothing happening. Nothing!" He was about to argue the point, and she said, "Just give me this."

She was on her knees, her toes digging into the mattress, and she was rocking across him, taking him deep, retreating, taking him deep again. As if she were performing for him, she pulled the pins from her glorious brunette hair, and it swirled down to her hips.

He'd never viewed such an erotic sight. Her eyes were closed, her head thrown back, her breasts thrust out, and she kept on and on. Her lust increased, and she fell forward, a nipple at his mouth, and he sucked at it.

"Harder," was all she could say. "Do it harder."

He bit down, making her beg, making her squirm.

So far, he'd restrained himself, but his lust was raging, too, and he needed more than to lie under her like a stump of wood. He began flexing into her, being rough and unrelenting, and as he reached between their bodies, her sheath tightened around him, spiraling her into a potent orgasm. He continued pumping into her, desperate for his own release. He rolled them again, so that she was beneath him, so that she was his, and he delayed the end for as long as he was able.

With a feral growl, he heedlessly spilled himself inside her, his seed flooding her womb. It was the most wild, most reckless thing he'd ever done, and he reveled in the decadence, not caring that she could wind up pregnant. He simply proceeded to the conclusion that seemed unavoidable, like a bad carriage accident.

He jerked away, both of them on their backs and assessing the ceiling like a pair of strangers. Their breathing steadied, and their pulses slowed. The quiet settled. Ultimately, she curled onto her side, away from him.

"Why don't you go?" she requested, dismissing him as if she were the bloody Queen of England.

"No," he replied. "I don't believe I will. Not this time."

He dragged her to him. Though he'd just fornicated like a randy adolescent, his cock was ready, and he slid over her and wedged himself between her thighs.

"What do you think you're doing?" she snapped. "I asked you to go."

"And *I* have decided to stay."

He pushed into her and started in again.

Chapter
FIFTEEN

J amie stopped at the door that separated the earl's
bedchamber from the countess's. As he'd expected, it was locked, and he figured Anne had
pulled furniture in front of it, too, as an added barrier
to keep him out.

When he'd wrestled her upstairs after the ceremony, and had unceremoniously deposited her inside,
she'd been more infuriated than he'd realized a female
could be.

His own temper had been in no better shape, and it
had taken many hours to calm himself sufficiently to
where he figured he could converse with her without
tossing her over his knee and giving her a good paddling. He'd never met anyone who was so contrary.

He didn't bother asking her to open up, for he knew
she wouldn't. He simply raised a foot and let loose. As
the wood shattered, it occurred to him that he ought to
have a carpenter reside permanently in the manor. She
had a knack for goading him to such violent rages that
he'd regularly need repairs.

As he'd predicted, she had items blocking his way,

so a few more heaves and pushes were necessary before he walked across the threshold. She was on the other side of the room, appearing as livid as he'd anticipated and clutching a fireplace poker that she wielded like a sword. At her bravado, he nearly snickered.

How could she assume that a flimsy piece of iron would prevent him from doing whatever he wanted?

"Hello, Anne." He grinned and stalked toward her.

"What do you want now, you beast, you dog, you swine?"

"I'm ready to consummate, but you haven't undressed."

At his crude pronouncement, she was so horrified that he laughed and laughed. She humored him in too many ways to count.

"After your antics this morning, you think I'd lie down with you?"

"Yes, and I can guarantee you'll like it."

"You are mad!"

"Not mad. Just lusty as the dickens and looking forward to some romping with my *wife*."

"I am not—and never will be—your wife."

"It says you are—right in the parish register. Your friendly neighborhood vicar even signed as a witness."

"The man is a weasel!"

"He certainly is, but his name is still there, bold as brass."

Jamie drew closer, closer, and she stepped back, back.

"Don't you come near me," she warned, brandishing the poker.

"It's too bad you were having such a tantrum that you couldn't attend our wedding breakfast."

"I'll show you a tantrum, you despicable wretch!"

He approached until he was an arm's length away

and she'd trapped herself into a corner and could go no farther.

"I'll kill you," she insisted. "I swear it!"

"If you did, my brother would miss me."

"He'd be the only one!"

"I'm sure you're correct."

"I hate you!" she seethed. "I will hate you till the day I die."

He lunged and grabbed the poker, and he fought her for it. He was bigger and stronger, and he could have yanked it away, but he understood pride and courage, and he allowed her to continue, letting her believe she had a chance, that she'd given it her all.

Ultimately, he snatched it from her and pitched it over his shoulder. They glared, breathing hard, as if they'd run a long race.

"I hate you," she said again, but with much less rancor.

"I don't hate you," he replied, and he dipped under her chin to nibble her neck.

There was something about her that drove him wild. It provoked all sorts of naughty thoughts, and he could have dawdled there for an eternity, sniffing and nuzzling her skin, yet she was stiff as a board, refusing to relax the tiniest bit.

He picked her up and tumbled them onto the bed, and he hovered over her, an arm braced on the pillow, a leg on her thighs and pinning her down. She was sweet and lovely and so much more than he deserved or ever imagined he'd have, and the strangest wave of tenderness swept through him.

His wife. His! Forever. He was so lucky!

"I'm sorry," he murmured, and he brushed a kiss across her lips. "Don't be angry."

The apology sucked the wind from her sails. She'd planned to argue and harangue, but what could she say to an earnest expression of regret? And it was *earnest*. For the most part.

He wasn't sorry that he'd bullied her, or threatened the vicar, or tied her up, or locked her in. He simply felt bad that she was so unhappy.

"Liar," she petulantly charged. "You've never been sorry for anything you've done in your whole life."

"I'm glad you're mine."

"I'm not."

He kissed her more slowly, easing her into the notion of a wedding night, even though it was early evening.

He intended to go at it till dark, till the next morning, and he'd keep on and on until she was reconciled to the idea of being his bride. He wasn't proficient at words or flirtation, but he knew more about satisfying a woman in the bedchamber than any man alive. As he'd previously discovered, she had a potent sexual nature, so he would soon have her melting with ecstasy.

She'd forget why she was furious, and her reservations would scatter like leaves on the wind.

She broke away and clasped his shoulders, giving him a slight shake.

"Why did you really marry me? Why go to so much trouble?"

"You know why: The Prince asked it of me."

"But he didn't *demand* it."

"No."

"Yet you pressed ahead."

He chuckled. "I certainly did."

"I don't suppose there's any way for me to get out of it, is there?"

"I don't see how you could. The vicar read the vows.

We repeated them." She scowled. "All right, *one* of us repeated them, there was a witness, and it's all recorded neat and proper."

"So it's final, then."

"It definitely is."

"And you forced me into it even though I was adamantly opposed."

"I prefer to say I *chose* you."

"You would," she dryly noted. "Are you always so adept at rationalizing your offensive behavior?"

"Yes." He grinned. "I'm never wrong. Just ask me; I'll tell you."

He'd thoroughly exasperated her, and she sighed, sounding like the most miserable person in the world, and her despondency was beginning to aggravate him.

He couldn't describe why he'd hounded her so relentlessly. Some of his resolve was spurred by her rejecting him. He was too vain to let Anne—or anyone at Gladstone—snub him, but there was more to it than that.

Though he couldn't fathom why, he'd been desperate to bind her to him so she could never leave. Whatever had caused the peculiar impulse, it had worked to her benefit, so why was she complaining?

She was now rich and powerful. Her sister, who'd done nothing but irk and chastise him, was safe under Jamie's protection.

What more could she want?

Well, maybe to have it all without his annoying self as her spouse, but that pesky detail couldn't be helped. He was part and parcel of the entire package, but he didn't plan to be in residence at Gladstone that much, so it would all be hers with hardly any bother.

"Apparently, it's my wedding day," she grumbled.

"Can't you at least lie and make a kind remark about why you proceeded? Can you stop being a brute for two seconds and tell me something nice?"

He pretended to ponder, then shook his head. "I can't think of a single thing."

"You are the most vile, unpleasant man I ever met."

"I'll grow on you."

"Like an irritating fungus."

He laughed and kissed her again, encouraged when she didn't shove him away. She didn't join in, but she didn't wrench away, either.

"Dearest Anne"—he rolled onto his back so she was draped across him—"how could we not have wed? What if we've already made a little Jamie Merrick?"

"A baby?" She frowned at her stomach. "Could I be in the family way?"

"That's the usual result from how we've been carrying on."

"But I thought we were . . . ah . . ." She blushed, not able to discuss fornication. "I hadn't considered the consequences. Not that it could happen so soon anyway."

"It can *happen* the very first time."

The prospect of her increasing, her belly swelled with his son, was oddly comforting, and Jamie suffered another possessive thrill that he couldn't comprehend. With her, the strangest sensations kept popping up.

He'd never wanted to be a husband, had never wished to be a father and was convinced he'd be a terrible one, but suddenly he was nearly giddy with what could only be joy.

"I'm a cad, I admit it, but after I ruined you, there was no alternative but marriage."

"So, you wed me because it was *honorable*?"

"No, I wed you because you make me happy."

"Because I . . ." She paused and glared at him. "You said something kind."

"Of course I did. I know how. I just don't do it very often. It wreaks havoc with my contemptible image."

"What do I do that makes you happy?"

"You're just *you*. Can we get on with our wedding night?"

"I know you don't care about our vows, but—"

"I care about them," he indignantly claimed. He'd merely be selective in which ones he heeded.

"Don't lie to me!" She shook him again. "I can tell when you are."

He shrugged. "I'll try my best to live up to them."

"I realize that's the most I can expect from you, but I need you to understand that whenever you take another lover, it will break my heart."

He scowled. She made it sound as if he'd have hundreds of lovers, as if he'd have thousands, as if he might rush out that very instant to see which females were lurking in the hall so he could lift a few skirts and have at it.

He didn't like her to have such a low view of his character. While he'd never given her a reason to have a higher opinion, and his moral fiber was nothing to brag about, he wanted her to regard him as a better man than he actually was.

"I'd cut off my right arm before I'd hurt you," he vehemently insisted. "How could you suppose otherwise?"

"I think you really believe what you're saying."

"You're my wife. I'll always respect and cherish you."

"I hope so, Jamie. I truly, truly do."

She studied him, her gaze astute and probing, and he

squirmed under the intense scrutiny. It seemed as if she could peer through bone and pore, clear down to the center of his black soul. She could see every falsehood he'd ever uttered, every swindle he'd ever instigated, every violent act he'd ever committed, and he detested her shrewd perception.

He wanted to be a mystery to her, and it was unsettling to know that he'd never be able to keep any secrets.

He rolled them again, so she was on her back.

"I'm tired of talking."

"I'm surprised you let me chatter on as long as I have."

"So am I, and we're done hashing things out. For the rest of the evening, I'm not listening to anything you say, unless it's, 'Oh, Jamie, do that to me again.'"

He'd finally managed to make her smile.

"You're impossible."

"I know, but as I told you: I'll grow on you."

"You already are, but remember this. . . ." She grabbed him, flipped him over, and pinned him down. "If you tie or gag me ever again, I'll wait till you let me loose, then I'll murder you in your sleep."

"It's a deal," he fibbed. He'd behave however he pleased—even if it drove her to distraction. "Now can we get on with it?"

"Yes, now we can."

With the haggling over, he was awkward as a lad with his first girl. She wasn't a virgin anymore, so he didn't need to delay or worry about maidenly anxiety, yet he was suffering from the most insane urge to make the interlude special for her.

All women dreamed of their wedding day, but he'd given her none of the fancy fripperies for which they yearned. She'd have no pleasant memories of the actual day, itself, but if he could proceed in a tender and passionate manner, he could give her the night to recollect fondly over the years.

He slowed, reining in his rampaging desire.

He didn't want to rip off her clothes, to ram his phallus into her and call the marriage an accomplished fact. He wanted to woo and seduce and, in the end, he wanted her to be glad he was the one.

He pulled away and took her hand.

"Come with me."

"To where?"

"We're going to do this like an ordinary married couple."

"In light of our dubious beginning, is that possible?"

"Yes."

He led her to the dressing room that separated their bedchambers, and with it containing only her meager wardrobe, the space seemed very empty. He made a mental note to remedy the situation immediately. He'd accouter her in a way that would accentuate her new status, that would have fussy, fashionable Ophelia looking like an old frump.

"Turn around so I can unbutton you." He hesitated. "Unless you'd like me to ring for a maid?"

"At this late date, I don't see why we should be too conventional."

"Neither do I."

He spun her, taking a quick nibble at her nape, then he unfastened her garments, but he didn't remove anything. Instead, he retrieved her robe and offered it to her.

"Put this on," he explained. "Then come to my

bedchamber. Whenever you're ready. I'll be waiting for you."

He'd decided they should finish it in the earl's bed, not the countess's, and she needed to join him of her own accord. He was positive he'd calmed her sufficiently so that she'd accede to his polite request.

She peered over her shoulder, her bodice loose, a fist clutching it to her chest, and the gesture reminded him that though he had stolen her virginity, she wasn't much past it. The realization made him feel like a heel. He was too used to dabbling with whores, and he had limited notions of how to carry on with a genuine lady.

He was always pushing her further than she knew how to go, but then, it was her own fault. She was so wonderful, and he lusted after her as he'd lusted after no woman before her.

He leaned in and kissed her on the cheek; then he left for his own room, and he stripped to his breeches and reclined on the bed. He was so impatient that it seemed an eternity before she arrived, and his relief was so immense that it was a good thing he was lying down or she might have perceived his peculiar fit of nerves.

She came in, and he was tickled to see that she'd taken down her hair, but her robe was cinched so tightly that barely an inch of skin was exposed.

She appeared so young, so shy and lovely, and he smiled and held out a hand to her. With a few faltering steps, she was at the bed, and he seized her fingers and kissed her knuckles.

"Welcome, Mrs. Merrick," he murmured, and he helped her climb up next to him.

"I feel so . . . scared." She chuckled self-consciously. "Like I'm a real bride and I don't know what's about to happen."

"You silly goose! You are a *real* bride."

He eased her down on the pillows, and as he studied her, his heart did the oddest flip-flop, his earlier possessiveness sweeping through him again, but there was another emotion, too, a deeper one he didn't recognize. He was just so very, very thrilled that she was his, and he would never let her go.

"I'm delighted that you're my wife," he blurted out when he hadn't planned to wax on, and she assessed him with a great deal of suspicion.

"You're not just saying that, are you?"

"No. I'm very glad."

He commenced, dawdling as he never had in his amorous pursuits. He had all night, he had the rest of his life, to make love to her, and there was no reason to hurry. He could take his time, and as he did, he was stunned to learn that the journey was as enjoyable as the conclusion—maybe more so.

Gradually, he opened her robe, slackening the belt and tugging at the lapels so he could slip his fingers inside. He toyed and played with her breasts, massaging and stroking, then meandering down to suck a nipple in his mouth.

He nursed till she was groaning in agony, till she was begging for mercy; then he continued on, blazing a trail down her belly, her abdomen. As he reached her woman's hair, she tensed and raised up to glare at him.

"What are you doing?" she asked.

"Let me show you something."

"Tell me what it is first."

"You trust me, don't you?"

"No farther than I could throw you."

He grinned. "Lie back."

"Jamie!"

"It'll make you feel better."

"I already feel pretty good."

"Lie back," he repeated, and she acquiesced, flopping down and staring up at the ceiling, looking miserable, as if he were about to perform an unspeakable surgery on her innards.

He eased her thighs apart and wedged himself between them; then he leaned in and licked her. She lurched away and sat up.

"What was that?"

"Everything's allowed, Anne? Remember?"

"I know, but when you said that, I never imagined you'd do anything quite so . . . so . . ."

To stifle further complaint, he simply dragged her to him and tossed her legs over his shoulders. He laved her again and again, while she moaned and writhed.

Her taste and scent inflamed him, luring him to his doom, and he could have kept on and on, but she was rapidly losing the fight against desire. He slid two fingers inside her, and the instant he did, she came and came, bucking and wrestling to escape his torment.

As she spiraled down, he was nuzzling his way up her torso.

"You are so wicked," she said, giggling.

"I can't deny it."

"Can we do that again sometime?"

"Whenever you wish, my little beauty."

"You are going to kill me with pleasure."

"That's my intent."

He gazed down at her, letting his affection shine through as he fussed with the buttons on his trousers.

He was so aroused, and she was so eager.

He clasped her hips and entered her in one smooth thrust. As they joined together, he decided that the wedding vows had to be more powerful than he'd understood, because the strangest sensation rushed over him. He felt as if he was finally home, as if he'd finally arrived right where he belonged.

For a fleeting moment, the world narrowed to just her, and it seemed as if it hadn't been Gladstone and the earldom at all that had brought him back to England, but his chance for the universe to ensure that he found her.

He wasn't a romantic, though, and he paid no heed to ridiculous, maudlin premonitions. He wanted only to copulate with her, and to do it over and over again till some of his mad attraction was sated. No woman could keep his interest, and there had to be a limit to his infatuation. He merely needed to reach it, which he was certain would happen soon.

"Mine, Anne," he murmured, his seed rising, the end coming.

"Yours, Jamie," she agreed.

"Mine forever."

He flexed and let go, flooding her womb with a relish that bordered on desperation. The novel coupling had bonded them in ways that went beyond vows or human comprehension, as if they truly could never be separated till death.

He pumped into her till every drop was spent, till his heart was hammering so hard that he worried it might quit beating. Then he fell onto her, crushing her with his weight, as he struggled to breathe, to think.

His erection hadn't waned in the slightest, and it occurred to him that he could have sex with her for a hundred years and never have his fill.

Alarmed, disturbed, he closed his eyes, wondering what he'd gotten himself into and frantic over how he'd ever get himself out of it.

Chapter
SIXTEEN

I had no idea it would be like this."

"I'm glad for you."

"He's a marvelous husband."

"I must say that I'm extremely amazed to hear it."

Anne smiled at Sarah, then stared out the window toward the stables. Jamie was leaned against a fence and talking to his brother, and she relished having the chance to spy on him without his being aware.

He wasn't a typical aristocrat. He couldn't abide sloth, and he worked from dawn till dusk, fixing and changing things so they were done his way instead of Percy's. The tenants and servants seemed to like Jamie, when they'd never liked Percy, so he was gradually winning them over.

It was a hot afternoon, and he pulled off his shirt and dipped his hands in the water trough, splashing his hair and face. As he stood, water trickled off him, the summer sun shining on his bronzed skin, and her breath hitched with delight.

At his instigation, she'd become a wanton, a slave to

him and the naughty deeds he'd taught her to perform. There was nothing she wouldn't do to please him, nothing she wouldn't try at his suggestion. He could be sweet and tender, or stern and demanding, and she was so consumed by desire that she felt he was a sorcerer who had cast a spell on her.

He seemed equally obsessed, and there was no sight in the world so fine as Jamie Merrick gazing at her with love and affection.

And she was positive he was starting to *love* her. A person couldn't fake such devotion, so her dream was coming true. She was cherished by her husband, and she couldn't believe how lucky she was that he'd forced her into their marriage.

Whenever she remembered how she'd fought to escape his clutches, she shuddered at her stupidity. What if he hadn't been so adamant? What if he'd given up on her?

"Look at him," she murmured, her fondness clear and difficult to mask. "He's posed like a Greek god."

"He certainly is. It annoys me that he's so handsome."

"He knows it, too. The man doesn't have a humble bone in his body."

Sarah chuckled. "You love him, don't you?"

Did she love Jamie? Was it possible? Her feelings were so conflicted, so new and raw. When he was near, she suffered such quivery, insane surges of joy, and if that was an indication of *love,* she'd never admit it. Sarah would deem her mad.

"No, I don't love him." She scoffed, struggling to appear blasé about the topic. "I just find him so . . . so . . . remarkable."

"You don't have to explain it to me," Sarah said gently. "I'm happy for you. I just hope . . ."

"*Hope* what?" Anne asked when Sarah couldn't finish.

"It's nothing. Don't pay any attention to me."

"No, tell me."

"I hope he stays, that's all."

"You think he won't?"

Anne was horrified that Sarah could have so little faith in him, but then, in the beginning, before she and Jamie had grown so close, Anne had worried over the same.

But no longer! He'd stay because *she* was at Gladstone. He would never leave her.

"Don't mind me," Sarah said. "He's totally besotted with you."

"He is? Really?" At the prospect, Anne was as excited as an adolescent girl with her first crush.

"He's too smitten to hide it."

Sarah came to the window, too, as Jamie turned to the trough again, and he soaked his shirt in the water and stroked it across his heated chest. He was sexy and decadent, too delicious for words.

They could see all of his back, and old whip marks were visible, providing silent evidence of his hard life as a boy. Anne had gotten used to all his prior wounds and had ceased to notice the numerous spots where he'd been marred by violence.

Sarah mentioned, "I hate those scars."

"So do I. They're awful."

"Jack has them, too. I can't bear that they were beaten so viciously—and at such a young age."

Sarah froze, realizing how peculiar her comment

had been, and there was an awkward pause as Anne tried to digest it.

Tentatively, Anne inquired, "How would you know that Mr. Merrick has flogging scars?"

"I don't," Sarah insisted, her panic palpable, "and I have no idea why I said such a thing."

The two sisters stared and stared. Finally, Anne broke the tense moment.

"Sarah, is there something you'd like to tell me?"

"No."

"Are you sure?"

"Very sure. I . . . ah . . ." She wrenched away and headed for the door. "It's been a tiring afternoon. I should take a nap."

She raced out, and as Anne listened to her go, she was unnerved.

Was Sarah having an affair with Mr. Merrick? How else would she have learned such an intimate detail about his anatomy? It wasn't as if Jack Merrick wandered the estate without his clothes.

If Sarah was cavorting with Mr. Merrick, why lie about it? Anne knew—better than any woman alive—how irresistible a Merrick could be. She was in no position to judge.

She scrutinized the two brothers again, curious as to their similarities and differences. Occasionally, she chatted with Jack, and he was always scrupulously polite, but she had trouble moving beyond his domineering behavior on her wedding day.

Had he seduced Sarah? If so, why hadn't he stepped forward to propose?

At the notion that he might be trifling with her sister, Anne decided she should speak with the earl. Jamie enjoyed reminding everyone that he was in charge, so she'd give him a chance to prove how much power and authority he actually had.

If Mr. Merrick and Sarah were involved, then another Merrick brother needed to tie the knot—and quickly.

Anne walked out to the verandah and down into the yard, watching Jamie as she neared. Where she was concerned, he'd developed a second sense, and as she approached, he spun toward her. His gaze was so hot and so potent that she was weak in the knees, and she pondered—as she often did—how she'd survived before he'd burst into her life.

She kept coming until she was directly in front of him. Her skirt swirled around his legs and she could smell the sweat on his skin. His brother had vanished like smoke, though she couldn't have said when, so they were alone. Not caring who might see, she brazenly wrapped an arm around his waist and pulled him to her, and she rose on tiptoe for a stirring kiss that he was happy to bestow.

He was surprised by the bold gesture, but humored, too, and he reveled in the embrace, being so thorough that he curled her toes.

They were the talk of the neighborhood. The scandalous news—that the earl and countess were wild for each other—had spread hither and yon, but she wasn't bothered by the gossip. The tongue-waggers could all go hang!

"Lord Gladstone?" she greeted, and he chuckled at her formal mode of address.

"Yes, *Lady* Gladstone?"

"Is your brother having an affair with my sister?"

He cocked his head, as if he hadn't heard her correctly; then he shrugged his shoulders. "I don't know."

"Would he?"

"Well, he *is* my brother."

"Which means he probably is."

"He hasn't confided in me, though. What makes you wonder about them?"

"It's nothing important. I'd just like you to speak to him for me. Would you?"

"For you, my dearest Anne, I would do anything. You know that."

"Anything? Hmm. . . ."

She grabbed his hand and started for the house.

"Where are we going?" Jamie inquired, following along like a trained pony.

"You did say *anything,* didn't you?"

"Yes."

"I want to see if you're serious."

"Now?"

"Yes, now."

He glanced back at the barn. "I'm a tad busy."

"I need you to attend me. Immediately."

She kept on, leading him to precisely where she wanted him to be, though not nearly fast enough. Between the spot where they were and the spot where they'd end up, there had to be a thousand stairs, each one a petty delay that seemed ridiculous.

Perhaps they should just bring their bed down to the front parlor and save all the climbing.

"I've created a monster," he muttered as she dragged him into the manor.

She glared over her shoulder. "Are you complaining?"

"Not complaining," he said. "Merely stating the facts."

She reached the stairs, and they ran up together.

※

M y wife asked me the strangest question."

"What is that?"

Jack turned to look at Jamie.

"She wants to know if you're having an affair with her sister."

"Nosy little wench, isn't she?"

"She is at that."

Jack kept his expression carefully blank and sipped at his whiskey.

It was early evening, the two of them out on the verandah and discussing the estate before supper, which had become a nightly ritual. Yet Jack vividly remembered when Anne had leaned out a window while they'd been discussing *her*. Jamie's comments had caused a peck of trouble, and Jack wouldn't make the same mistake.

While Jack usually told Jamie everything, and couldn't recall when he'd last had a secret from his brother, he hadn't confessed about Sarah. He and Jamie had an acute mental connection, and frequently they thought the same thoughts at the same moment, so it was pointless to conceal information from him. Still, for reasons Jack didn't understand, he hadn't mentioned his trysting with Sarah. Nor had he explained about her being Tim's mother, and he couldn't fathom why he hadn't. Women—and his and Jamie's peccadilloes with them—were a common topic of conversation, so Jack's reticence was baffling. Why couldn't he say anything?

"So . . . are you?" Jamie pressed.

"I might be."

"What does that mean?"

"It means I *might* be."

Jamie scowled. "You *might* be fucking her? You *might* not? You're thinking about it? What? Don't you know?"

Jack peeked around, searching for eavesdroppers but seeing none. "I've had sex with her a few times."

"Really?"

"Yes, and if you tell your wife, I'll cut out your tongue, then slice off your balls."

As if the bloodletting were about to begin, Jamie held up his palms in a sign of surrender.

"She won't hear it from me."

"She better not."

"What's she like?" Jamie crudely queried. "Is she any good under the covers?"

"Shut up, or I'll knock your teeth out, too."

"All right, all right." Jamie studied him, amazed by Jack's surly attitude. "Since she's my sister-in-law, I suppose I ought to learn if you have any intentions toward her."

"Intentions!"

"You know what those are, don't you?"

"Don't be a smart-ass."

"Is she going to wind up pregnant? Should I be demanding a wedding?"

Jack shrugged, refusing to discuss Sarah or his insane attraction to her.

She was everything he loathed in a female—fickle, flighty, unreliable, moody—and he couldn't comprehend why he'd been bewitched.

Like a puppet on a string, he kept crawling back to

her bed, each fornication dragging him deeper into the morass. Every time he trifled with her, he told himself it would be the last, but the second he saw her again, he instantly capitulated.

He was so weak!

"So there's nothing to worry about," Jamie said.

"No, nothing."

Except for vicious rumor, scandal, another illegitimate child, plus the chance of the countess's sister being exposed as a fallen woman.

"If I asked Miss Carstairs her opinion about your behavior, what do you imagine her version would be?"

"If you ask her anything—if you so much as glance in her direction—I'll kick your ass from here to Jamaica."

"My, my," Jamie mused, and he whistled softly. "You're hooked like a fish on a line."

"I am not," Jack insisted. "She's very nice, and we've passed some pleasant hours together. That's all there is to it."

If he believed in Hell, which he didn't, he was positive the huge lie would have guaranteed he spent an eternity there. He had jumbled but potent feelings for Sarah and would have proposed immediately if he'd thought she'd have him—but she never would.

He was a vagabond and uncouth sailor, who had naught to show for himself but the fact that he was Jamie's brother. Jack had nothing to offer a snooty, refined lady like Sarah Carstairs, and he wouldn't humiliate himself by giving her an opportunity to spurn him.

Jamie was about to start in with another ribald, offensive remark that would have had Jack out of his chair and eager for an all-out brawl, but an altercation was avoided because Sarah stepped onto the verandah.

Jamie peered over at her and grinned. He had the look

of the devil in his eye. Jack had seen that look before, and he knew it well. If Jamie could stir up trouble, he would, and there was no predicting what he might say.

Jack braced for a catastrophe.

"Hello, Miss Carstairs," Jamie welcomed, as he and Jack stood.

"Hello, Lord Gladstone." She was as formal as if they'd been loitering in a fussy London drawing room.

"Are you ever going to let me call you Sarah?" Jamie inquired.

"Probably not," she coolly replied.

Jamie laughed at the insult and gestured to the chair across from him. "Won't you join us?"

"I'm sure she'd rather not," Jack quickly interjected, and he flashed such a churlish glare at Sarah that he was certain she'd take the hint and scurry off, but Jamie added, "We were just talking about you."

With that bit of news provided, she couldn't resist sauntering over.

"What is there about me," she asked, "that could possibly interest you two?"

Without preamble, Jamie said, "Jack has advised me that you're having a sexual affair with him. Is it true?"

Sarah turned white with shock and muttered, "He told you that?"

"Yes," Jamie answered. "I questioned him about his intentions toward you, but he claims he has none, and I wanted to hear your opinion. Would you like him to marry you? If it's what you wish, I'll make him propose."

She spun to Jack and seethed, "You told him?"

Jack felt like a fly caught in a spider's web.

"He's my twin brother," Jack pathetically justified. "I tell him everything."

"Everything?" She was aghast.

"Well . . . not anything about . . . ah . . ."

"You, Mr. Merrick, are an unmitigated bastard."

For the second time in their convoluted relationship, she slapped him as hard as she could; then she whipped away and stomped to the house.

As she reached the door, Jamie called after her, "I take it that means *no*?"

"I'm not my foolish sister, Lord Gladstone. I wouldn't marry one of you Merricks if my life depended on it."

As the sound of her angry strides vanished, Jamie sighed and said, "She doesn't like me very much."

"Who does?" Jack responded.

"Yeah, well, she doesn't seem too keen on you, either."

"Bugger off."

"I'll send a note to the vicar," Jamie taunted. "I'll have him check his schedule, so we'll know when he's available to preside at the ceremony."

"Go screw yourself blind."

Jack stomped away, too, Jamie's laughter ringing in his ears.

❧

L et me in."

"No. Go away."

"Let me in, or I'll beat the door down."

Sarah stared at the knob as Jack rattled it, then began to pound on the wood.

"It's your choice, Sarah. You can open it, or I'll keep on till the entire household comes up to see why there's such a commotion."

He would, too; she had no doubt. If she was overly obstinate, he'd simply kick his way in as his brother liked to do.

Jamie and Jack Merrick were a pair of contemptible, uncivilized scoundrels. They would do anything to a woman, without regard to the consequences. Who could gainsay them?

She stormed over and hissed, "Be silent."

"I'll be *silent* once you open up."

She fumbled with the lock, yanked at the knob, then grabbed his wrist and pulled him inside. She didn't peer down the hall to see if any of the maids were lurking, for she was too terrified to know. After so many years spent guarding her reputation, if she lost it now because of such a blackguard, she'd be driven to commit murder and at the moment a messy, unrestrained act of homicide would suit her just fine.

"What do you want?" she demanded. "And might I suggest that you be quick about it?"

"I didn't confide any pertinent details to my brother."

"Oh, that definitely makes me feel better."

"I didn't! I swear it!"

"Then how did he know?"

"Your sister asked him about us, so he asked me. I couldn't deny it."

"What? You can't lie to the miserable oaf?"

"I never have before, and I'm not about to start."

"Perhaps you should consider turning over a new leaf. I won't have that horse's ass meddling in my private business."

Gad! What a disaster. Jamie knew, so Anne would know shortly. What would Anne say? What would she think? How would Sarah ever justify her conduct?

She couldn't believe how she'd dawdled in the parlor with Anne, the two of them mooning over Jamie and Jack Merrick as if they were handsome gods, instead of mortal men with plenty of flaws. Sarah hadn't meant to comment on Jack's flogging scars, and the words had slipped out before she could stop them.

Without her realizing it, Jack had become an obsession. She drooled over him. She fretted over him. She was so fixated that she could barely eat or sleep.

"Jamie may be an ass, but he was correct," Jack said.

"About what?"

"You have to marry me."

As far as proposals went, it had to be the most cold, unfeeling one ever uttered, and she was incensed.

She'd waited her whole life to wed, had dreamed of it as a girl and yearned for it as a woman. Once, she'd risked all—chastity, reputation, safety, security—in the hopes of having it happen, and finally there was a man who'd mustered the gumption to proceed, but he looked as if he'd bitten into a rotten egg.

"Marry . . . you?" she scoffed.

Her tone was much more snide than she'd intended, but she was irate and hurt, and she spoke without reflecting on how she'd sound. As she might have predicted, he didn't react well.

He blanched as if she'd slapped him all over again.

"What if you're pregnant?"

"What if I am?" she blithely retorted, as if she hadn't a care in the world, as if the frightening possibility weren't gnawing at her every second.

"Your history proves that you're awfully fertile."

"Yes, it does. I seem to breed like a rabbit."

"Aren't you worried?" He studied her, his temper as

hot as her own. "Or maybe you don't mind. Maybe you'll spit out another bastard and be done with it."

"It's what I'm best at," she sarcastically replied.

"At least this time, the father offered to stay around. When you disavow another of your children, what will your excuse be?"

It was the most despicable, hateful thing anyone had ever said to her. She understood that he was livid, that they were quarreling and ought to shut up till cooler heads prevailed, but common sense was nowhere in sight.

She wanted to slap him again, and she wanted to keep on slapping him till his cheek was raw and her palm bruised. She wanted to find a whip and beat him to a bloody pulp. She wanted to fire a pistol into the center of his cruel heart and smirk as he fell dead on the floor.

"Get out," she snarled.

"No."

"Get out of here—and don't ever return!"

"I'll be damned if you'll order me out."

No longer concerned about discovery, she stormed to the door and flung it open.

"Get out! Get out!" she bellowed like a deranged shrew.

He thought about arguing, but a maid was coming down the hall. She'd heard the shouting, and she tiptoed to the threshold and peeked in.

"Are you all right, miss?" the maid asked.

"I'm just dandy."

Jack glared at both women, then cursed and marched out without a backward glance. Sarah staggered to the bed and eased down on the mattress.

The silence settled, and the maid cautiously queried, "Would you like me to fetch your sister, Miss Carstairs?"

"No, I'm fine. Please close the door on your way out."

The girl wanted no part of whatever had transpired, and she did as Sarah had requested, then hurried away, no doubt to tattle to the other servants about the scandalous scene she'd witnessed.

Sarah sat in the quiet, all alone again.

Chapter
SEVENTEEN

Jamie dawdled in the doorway, staring at Anne and rubbing his wrist that was aching like the dickens. She was asleep on the bed, and he couldn't pull himself away.

It was still early, but the sun had been up for more than an hour. He'd planned to head out before dawn, needing to put as many miles between himself and Gladstone as he was able, but he continued to linger, and he couldn't understand why.

He'd accomplished everything he'd set out to do. He'd established his ownership, had chased off Percy, had relocated Ophelia and Edith, and had confirmed the loyalty of the tenants and servants. Anne and Sarah were protected as the Prince had requested. Jack would stay behind and manage Jamie's affairs as Jamie would trust no other to do, so there was no reason to delay.

He figured it was Anne who kept him from leaving, and the realization was so aggravating. In the beginning, he'd intended to wed her, then go, but it had all grown so complicated.

The estate was like a living being, his roots in the place deep and abiding—when he didn't want them to be. The fertile soil seemed to have talons that had wrapped around his ankles. They were holding him locked to the property until he could accept his connection to it, but he simply couldn't open himself to the possibility that he belonged at Gladstone.

He'd spent the summer with Anne, and it had been magnificent, but he had to move on. He had scores to settle, battles to wage, whiskey to drink, women to seduce, and he had to quit tarrying like a besotted idiot. His infatuation with Anne had gotten completely out of control, and if he remained another second, he was terrified of where he'd end up.

He wouldn't be bound! Wouldn't be tied down or fettered! Not to her or to anyone!

She stirred and touched the spot where he slumbered next to her, and on discovering that he wasn't there, she frowned. Her auburn hair was strewn across the pillows, and a ray of sunshine made the soft tresses blaze with color.

He didn't mean to ever return, and suddenly the thought of never seeing her again was the saddest prospect in the world. He rubbed his hand over his heart, feeling as if it was breaking, which was absurd.

He would be fine without her! Just fine!

Like an automaton, he stumbled over and eased a hip down on the mattress. She was like a weakness in his blood, and he had no idea why he couldn't shake his need for her, but time and distance would quell her allure, as would a few London strumpets.

If he felt a stab of disgust at the notion, if he felt a stab of guilt and shame, he pushed them away. His marriage vows were preposterous, and he wouldn't be constrained by them.

Her pretty eyes fluttered open, and she smiled and stretched.

"What time is it?" she mumbled.

"After six already."

"What are you doing up? And dressed, too! You know I hate it when you get dressed before I have my way with you."

She initiated a luscious, slow kiss, and as he drew away, she sighed with delight.

"Why don't you come back to bed?"

"I must be off."

Usually, he rose for morning chores, so she wasn't aware that this was farewell. Not eager for a maudlin scene, he'd given her no hint of his departure, had made no preparations, had packed no bags. The prior evening, he'd merely instructed one of the grooms to have his horse ready. The animal was down in the yard, sensing a journey, and excited to be away. Jamie need only walk down, mount up, and go.

Why was it so difficult to pry himself away?

"Did I ever tell you how beautiful you are?" he inquired.

"Yes, but tell me again. I'm a glutton for your compliments."

He stole a last kiss, a brief brush of his lips to hers; then he hugged her tight, his face buried at her nape to hide his tormented expression. Once he'd contained his careening emotions, he slid from her arms.

"Bye," he said.

He yearned to say more, to blather on about how much he'd enjoyed their time together, but he was too much of a coward to confess what he was actually doing.

Without another word, he left, marching down the hall, practically running when he reached the stairs. The worst wave of panic swept over him, and he felt that if he didn't escape the house, he'd be trapped inside it forever.

As he sprinted out the front door, Jack was in the drive, waiting by the horse, and Jamie wasn't surprised to see his brother. Jamie hadn't confided to Jack that he was going, but Jack had figured it out nonetheless. They had no secrets.

Jack had packed Jamie a bedroll and satchel, had a pistol loaded and strapped to the saddle. Seeming cool and unaffected, Jack watched as Jamie approached.

"Are you sure, Jamie?" was all he said.

"I'm sure. How about you? You claimed that you wanted to stay here, but have you changed your mind?"

"No."

"Are *you* sure?" Jamie pressed, wishing Jack would come along and not able to imagine how it would be without him.

"No, but I'm staying anyway. Have you talked it over with Anne?"

"No."

"She'll ask me why you went. What should I say?"

"Tell her . . . oh hell, I don't know. Tell her what a bastard I am. Tell her she's better off without me. She'll agree with you."

"Yes, she will."

Jamie nodded and peered up at the ostentatious mansion, the shiny windows glowing red with the rising sun. "You have my permission to do whatever you want to the property. I'll have the lawyers put something in writing, and I'll send it to you—in case there's any question."

"Good."

Jamie studied his brother, his fondness so severe that it was painful.

"We traveled a lot of miles together."

"We did at that."

"I'm glad I could bring you back," Jamie said. "I'm glad I could give you this place and this life."

"So am I."

"It's what you always wanted. Don't squander it."

"As if I would, you wretch." Jack chuckled. "Shut up and go before I start blubbering like a babe."

A rattling noise sounded overhead, and they both glanced up to where Anne was looming out an upstairs window. Jack and Jamie froze, looking like the guilty conspirators they were, and he was troubled and annoyed. He'd hoped to sneak off without any fuss, but there was about to be an enormous amount of it.

"Jamie?" she called down. "What are you doing?"

"It's too early to be up, Anne," he advised. "Go back to bed."

She scrutinized his horse. "Are you . . . leaving?"

There was a lie on the tip of his tongue, but he couldn't tell it. She appeared stunned and hurt, and any remark was crushed by the sense of loss he felt at seeing her one last time.

"Don't you dare move!" she scolded, slamming the window. He pictured her racing to the hall, flying down the stairs.

"You're in for it now," his brother muttered, and he strolled away, no more eager for the pending confrontation than Jamie was, himself.

"Dammit," Jamie cursed.

He patted his horse, desperate to leap on and ride away before she arrived, but it was a craven notion.

He'd suffered through many good-byes in his life, and he hated how wrenching they were, so he never willingly participated in them. Anne had never been anywhere but Gladstone, so she hadn't discovered how awful a parting could be, but she was about to learn, and he detested that he would be the one to teach her.

A quick and complete break was for the best, but now they'd quarrel, then Jamie would go anyway. No matter what she said, no matter how prettily she begged, she'd never convince him to do otherwise.

She rushed out the door, and she was a splendid sight in her robe and nightgown, barefoot, her hair tumbling over her shoulders. She kept coming till they were toe-to-toe, and Jamie steeled his expression, determined to conceal how he was raging on the inside. His hands were gripped behind his back, his fingers tightly linked, so he didn't reach for her.

On noting his indifferent gaze, she paused, not as certain as she had been. Nervously, she clutched at the lapels of her robe.

"Where are you going?" she asked.

"To London, Anne."

"For how long?"

He shrugged but didn't answer.

"Forever?"

"Not *forever*. I'll visit now and again."

"How often is that? Once a month? Once a year?"

"I'll stop by occasionally—to check on things." He pointed to the corner of the house, where Jack was loitering and trying to ignore them. "In my absence, Jack is in charge. If you need anything, let him know. He'll take care of it for you."

She frowned as if he'd spoken in a foreign language she didn't comprehend.

"I thought you were happy here."

"I was."

"Then how could you just . . . go?"

"I never planned to remain."

"Never?"

"No."

At the callous admission, she nearly collapsed to the ground in a swoon.

"Did I mean nothing to you then?"

"Of course you did."

"What? What did I mean to you?"

"I'm glad I married you. I'm glad you're my wife."

Tears flooded her eyes, and it was the worst moment for him. He couldn't bear it when she was sad, and her woe reinforced what an ass he was, but it didn't alter his decision.

"What will I do without you?" she inquired. "What will become of me?"

"Jack will watch over you."

"I don't want Jack." The tears were falling freely, and she swiped at them. "I want you. I want you here with me. Always."

"I can't be."

"Why?"

He couldn't explain his jumble of feelings. Gladstone was his, and he'd kill any man who tried to say it wasn't, but he loathed the property and couldn't imagine being tied to it.

He could never fully describe what his past had been

like, how he'd struggled to survive, how many times he almost hadn't. When he walked about the estate, every tree and stone seemed to cry out with reminders of how it might have been, how it should have been, and he couldn't stand it.

What if he stayed? What if they had children? His father's blood ran in his veins. Jamie could feel it flowing with wicked intent, and he had to acknowledge that he was the man's son, so he might be capable of any foul deed.

What woman would want such a despicable character around her children? He might do anything to them. He might do anything to Anne.

"It's simply not meant to be," he ultimately said.

"Don't do this, Jamie. Please."

"I have to, Anne."

"Will you . . . will you . . ." She had to swallow twice before she could continue. "Will you at least write once in a while, so I'll know where you are and that you're all right?"

"Jack will know where I am."

She sobbed with regret, and her response was too painful to abide. Jamie tried to hug her, but she stepped away, refusing his comfort, and he couldn't complain. He deserved the petty rebuff.

"We need you here," she claimed. "*I* need you here."

"No, you don't. You'll all get on fine without me. Better, in fact." He grinned, attempting to inject some levity into the horrid discussion. "Why . . . in a week or two, your life will have returned to normal, and you'll be relieved that I left."

"It will be so quiet without you. How will I bear it?"

He raised a hand to rest it on her shoulder, but she spun away and raced for the house. Though it was the hardest thing he'd ever done, he didn't go after her. He tarried—alone—staring at the spot where she'd been. His heart was pounding, her last comment ringing in his ears.

Eventually, Jack joined him, a look of censure in his eye, but he wouldn't give voice to it. They knew each other too well, and Jack was aware that it was futile to chastise Jamie about anything.

"That was badly done, Jamie," he gently chided.

"Yes, it was."

"She loves you something fierce."

"She'll get over it," Jamie insisted.

"You can always come back," Jack said. "This is your home now. If you don't find what you're searching for in London, come home."

Home . . .

The word rushed through the grass and trees like a breeze on the wind. It promised and cajoled, and he nearly succumbed, suddenly wanting it more than he'd ever wanted anything, but he shook away the tempting impulse.

"I don't belong here," he asserted. "I never have."

He moved to his horse and swung up in the saddle.

"Be careful," Jack advised, "and keep me posted about your doings."

"I will."

Jamie paused, examining the windows of the manor. He'd hoped that Anne might be there, that he'd catch a final glimpse of her, but she was nowhere in sight.

He bent down, his hand extended, and Jack clutched it with both of his own, the two of them bonded as no other pair could ever be.

"So . . . this is good-bye," Jack murmured. "I can't believe it."

"Neither can I." Was he really going? Would he and his brother actually part? If they weren't together, how could either of them manage? "If you get sick of country living, come to London."

"What would I do with myself in London? You know how I hated it there."

"Then we'll ready the ship and set out."

"To where?"

"To wherever you want. To hell with this place."

"We'd just walk off and leave it?"

"Sure. Why not?" Jamie gazed around again; then abruptly he said, "Marry that girl, would you? Make Sarah an honest woman. Be happy with her."

"As if she'd have me," Jack scoffed. "She thinks I'm too much like you."

Jamie laughed, jerked on the reins, and cantered away.

⚓

Anne huddled behind the drapes in the earl's bedchamber. She was blocked from view, but *she* could see the drive down below perfectly well.

She watched as Jamie chatted with his brother and, as nimbly as a circus performer, leapt onto his horse. He leaned down, their dark heads close, their hands clasped in friendship; then, with a quick flick of the reins, he galloped away.

He was smiling, excited to be away from Gladstone—to be away from her!—and as he wound down the lane to the road that would take him to London, he never looked back. Not once.

She touched her fingers to the glass, wishing, praying, letting her mind reach out to connect with his.

At least wave good-bye! she implored, but if her message was received, he gave no sign.

Would he stay in the city? Or would he travel even farther away? Would he simply board his ship and sail away from England, never to be heard from again?

When they'd first met, she hadn't thought he'd remain at the estate, but after their marriage, she'd assumed he'd changed. He'd seemed so content, but apparently it had all been a charade.

How could she not have seen it coming? He'd provided no hint, had uttered no prescient remarks, hadn't even been particularly sad as he'd wakened her for a farewell embrace. Only the odd tension in his shoulders as he'd exited the room had indicated something might be wrong.

If she hadn't run to the window and peeked out, she wouldn't have known his plan. She'd have lounged in bed for hours, presuming him to be riding the fields and unaware he'd gone.

She dawdled till he was a tiny speck on the horizon, till he'd disappeared, and she continued to tarry. Pathetically, she told herself that he'd get a distance down the road and realize he'd made a mistake and he'd return to her.

But he never did.

Like a blind woman, she stumbled to their bed, and she fell onto the mattress, his pillow crushed to her chest. The sheets were still warm from his body's heat, his scent lingering in the fabric.

She stared up at the ceiling, contemplating how quiet it was. The house seemed bereft, as if it sensed the loss of his energy. Everything was gray and fuzzy, indistinct, as if nothing were real.

How would she survive it? How would she keep her heart from breaking?

"Oh, Jamie . . . ," she whispered, wondering how anything would ever be right again.

ॐ

O phelia? What are you doing here?"

"Hello, Sarah. It's so dreary down at the Dower House. I sent Mother to visit friends in town, so I'm lonely. I've decided to move home."

"To stay?"

"Of course to stay. What would you suppose?"

As if she hadn't been gone a single moment, Ophelia pulled off her gloves and tossed them on the hall table, and Sarah suffered from the strongest urge to march over and push her out the door. Sarah didn't want Ophelia coming back. The manor was in chaos. The servants were moping as if someone had died, and Anne was in a state of shock.

Ophelia would add to the turmoil, would set everyone more on edge than they already were, yet Sarah had no authority to deny entrance. Anne and Jack were the only two people who could tell Ophelia *no* and mean it, but Anne was ill with grief, and Jack was away, shopping for a new plow.

"Where's Anne?" Ophelia queried. "I imagine I should ask her permission—though it galls me that I should have to."

"She's a bit indisposed."

"Is that how you're explaining it?"

"Explaining what?"

"The entire county knows he's left her. It's all anyone

can talk about. She's a laughingstock, but then, Jamie is a lunatic. What did she expect?"

Ophelia went to the stoop and gestured to someone in the drive, and Sarah walked over to see who'd accompanied her. There was a teamster's wagon parked out front, loaded down with Ophelia's belongings, and she gave brisk orders to have the items hauled upstairs.

Sarah observed, aghast, panicked about what she should say or do.

Ophelia turned, her expression grim. "I guess it would be too much to hope that I could have my old bedchamber."

"The countess's suite?"

"Yes."

"Anne is countess now."

"I heard that she's lodged in the earl's quarters since her husband abandoned her."

"Well . . . yes, she is."

"Then what does she need with *my* room?"

"We should probably check with her, to be certain. . . ."

Sarah trailed off as some men tromped in, grappling with a large trunk, and she stood in silence, gaping, as Ophelia directed them to the countess's boudoir.

"Ophelia!" she finally protested. "You can't just come in and . . . and . . ."

"And what, Sarah? This was my home long before you two charity cases ever arrived. Don't presume to command me about."

"But . . ."

"Look, if it will make you feel better, we'll seek Anne's opinion—once she's up and around. If she wants me in another bedchamber, I'll go. In the interim, I don't think it's any of your business. Do you?"

Sarah was so close to letting loose, to giving the obnoxious shrew the tongue-lashing she'd always deserved, but she couldn't bring herself to expound. It simply wasn't in Sarah's nature to cause a huge scene.

"I'm starving," Ophelia commented. "Go to the kitchen and fetch me a tray of my favorite dishes. You know what I like."

"I . . . I . . . ," Sarah stammered, stunned by how quickly they'd reverted to form.

"Do you have some problem with doing as I've bid you?"

Ophelia neared, appearing determined and menacing, and Sarah grumbled, "No. I'll see to it immediately."

She stepped aside, and the men passed to the stairs, Ophelia following them up.

At the landing, she leaned over the rail, a smile on her painted lips.

"I have good news," she cooed.

Sarah was terrified over what it might be. "What is it?"

"Percy wrote from London. He's homesick, too. He should be here any day now. Isn't it marvelous?"

"Yes, marvelous," Sarah concurred, but her mouth puckered as if she were sucking on a lemon.

"It will be just like old times."

Ophelia studied the foyer with a proprietary air; then she kept on to her reclaimed boudoir.

Chapter
EIGHTEEN

M y, my, would you look at that?"

Anne glanced across the breakfast table at Ophelia, who was skimming the London gossip news and grinning slyly. Some things never changed, one of them being Ophelia's penchant for sowing discord.

Anne should have ignored her, yet she caught herself asking, "What is it?"

"Perhaps I should go to London, too," Ophelia mused. "Obviously, he's having more fun *there* than I am having here."

"Who are you babbling about?"

"Read this paragraph." Ophelia pointed to the appropriate spot. "The author refers to 'the Rascal Roué, Lord G.S.'" Sarcastically, she added, "Whoever could he mean?"

Anne snatched up the paper, poring over the lurid account. The details—that the man was new to the aristocracy and had previously been a notorious privateer—definitely ruined any attempt at anonymity.

Apparently, Jamie had cut a wide swath through

High Society, having engaged in every decadent deed a person could devise. He was throwing wild parties, consorting with Jezebels, and gambling away his money as if he had no responsibilities, as if he didn't own vast estates that employed people who depended on his fiscal restraint.

Anne knew she shouldn't give the rumors any credence, but stories usually started with some basis in fact, so she imagined at least some of his antics were true.

What had happened to him? Why was he doing this to himself?

She didn't understand him and never had.

Eager to annoy Ophelia, she was all innocence. "This Lord G.S. is certainly a wicked character. Who do you think he is?"

"It's Jamie, you silly goose."

"How could it be? Last I heard, he'd gone to Scotland on business. He's not even in London."

"You're receiving regular correspondence, are you?"

Ophelia chuckled cruelly, her raised brow signifying that she was aware Anne had had no mail and couldn't possibly know where Jamie was.

"He posts a letter once a week," Anne insisted. "Like clockwork."

"Give over, Anne," Ophelia scoffed. "He's an illiterate barbarian. Any note from him would simply contain a large *X* in the middle of the page. He never learned to read and write."

"That's a lie!" Anne hissed, her undeserved loyalty to Jamie making her ripple with fury.

Jamie was smart as a whip and shrewd like a fox, so

the notion that he hadn't been schooled had never occurred to her, and she was embarrassed to realize that
she knew so little about her husband that she had no
idea if Ophelia was correct or not.

"Poor Anne," Ophelia clucked. "So devoted. So
misguided in the affairs of the heart."

She rose, giving Anne a condescending pat on the
shoulder, then sauntered out. Anne watched her go and
gnashed her teeth.

When Ophelia had initially arrived, Anne had been
too distraught to care. By the time she'd been feeling
stronger and might have put her foot down, Ophelia
was ensconced in the countess's rooms. It would have
taken a shovel to dig her out of them.

Jack had begged Anne to evict her, but Anne
couldn't muster the energy to wage battles that seemed
ridiculous. As she'd explained to Jack, it was a huge
mansion. There was space for all of them.

Once Percy arrived, too—an event that Ophelia kept
promising—Anne might change her mind and eject
both of them, but for the moment she merely wanted
peace and quiet.

She reread the torrid article, and she supposed it was
an indicator of her improved condition that the information made her fighting mad. While she'd been lan-
guishing at Gladstone, grief stricken and bereft over
being abandoned by Jamie, he'd been in London, wa-
gering and carousing with loose women.

She scanned the words over and over, and with each
repetition her rage sizzled a tad more. She envisioned
him adrift in a sea of corruption and vice, his very soul
in jeopardy from his dissolution. He needed to come
home, where he was safe, where he belonged, where he

was loved. And she *did* love him. She had no doubt. She'd had to lose him to figure it out.

She sat in the silence, mulling, fuming, when a resolution presented itself to her. It was diabolical, it was foolhardy, it was destined to fail, but she had to try.

She folded the paper under her arm and marched outside to where Jack was working with the horses.

She and Jack were necessary companions, charged by the absent Jamieson Merrick with keeping the immense property functioning. Even though they had no concept of how to go about it, they'd muddled forward together, and in the process they'd become friends.

He saw her storming across the yard, and one corner of his mouth quirked in a smile that was an exact duplicate of Jamie's.

"What is it now?" he inquired.

"Tell me why your brother is such an idiot."

"I only plan to live another forty or fifty years, so there wouldn't be enough time."

She snorted. "Was he always this way?"

"What *way*?"

"Heedless, arrogant, and exasperating?"

"Yes, always."

"How did you bear it?"

Jack shrugged. "He grows on you."

"Did you ever think that you'd like to simply reach over and throttle him?"

"On a daily basis."

"Come with me to the house."

"Why?"

"We're packing our bags for a trip to London."

"To London!"

"We're going to fetch him home."

"I don't imagine he'll come peaceably."

"It doesn't matter," Anne said. "I'm going to kill him first."

"So we'll just be bringing the body for burial?"

"If that's what it takes to get him back here."

Jack chuckled. "I can't wait to see his face when you show up."

"Neither can I."

"He never lets anyone tell him what to do."

"Well, someone needs to start. It might as well be me."

&

W hat are you doing here?"

"Can't I attend my own brother's soiree without undergoing an inquisition?"

"No, you can't," Jamie retorted, glaring at Percy.

The more Jamie got to know Percy, the less Jamie liked him. Jamie saw Percy at engagements all over London, had ignored and endured him, but he shouldn't have to tolerate him at his own party, in his own foyer.

"You weren't invited," Jamie continued, "so what do you want? If you're about to beg for another handout, you'd best do it quietly or your snooty acquaintances might overhear."

"I didn't *beg*—as you so crudely put it. I've never asked for anything that wasn't rightfully mine."

"No, of course not. Why don't you swallow your pride and agree to a stipend, after all?"

"I don't need an allowance from you," Percy boasted. "I'm about to wind up with everything I ever wanted."

"And what would that be?"

"Why, Gladstone; what would you suppose?"

"You've repeatedly proven that you're too stupid to wrest it from me. Now why don't you go away before you hurt yourself? Or before *I* hurt you."

The place was crammed with guests. People were watching them, whispering and curious as to what was being said. Most likely, they were commenting on how much Percy had begun to resemble Jamie. Over the previous few months, dissipation had wreaked havoc on Percy's anatomy, and he'd lost a significant amount of weight.

Jamie had always understood that they were the same height and had similar features, but looking at Percy now, he felt as if he were staring into a mirror and seeing a blond version of himself staring back. Jamie was no longer a twin but a triplet, with Percy the third identical brother.

They were a spectacle, which Jamie typically didn't mind, but he was in no mood to tangle with Percy. Each time Jamie ran into him, Percy's condition was worsened. With no funds, no line of credit, and no true friends, he was in dire straits, but too conceited to admit it.

On one dubious occasion, Jamie had deigned to be charitable and had given Percy some money, but after receiving it, Percy had hurled so many insults that Jamie's patience was exhausted. He wouldn't spit up any more cash.

He studied Percy, disgusted by his deteriorated state. The man was falling apart, his clothes disheveled, wine spilled down his jacket, but he was too intoxicated to notice. He was a lousy drunk, prone to swaggering and confrontation, so eventually he'd cause trouble.

Jamie motioned to a servant—one of his crew members dressed in livery—and he came over and took Percy by the arm to escort him out, but Percy was determined to be obstinate and shook him off.

"I'll have Gladstone in the end," Percy swore, his words slurred. "My lawyers promised me."

"Your lawyers are fools."

"Then again, you might suffer a terrible *accident.*"

"You already tried twice, Percy, remember? Your aim is bad. Besides, if I die, Jack is the heir. Not you. So he'll have to have an *accident,* too. You're not brave enough or smart enough to murder us both."

"Once you're out of the way," Percy taunted, "don't you wonder what will become of Anne?"

It was a shock to hear him speak Anne's name. From the day Jamie had left Gladstone, no one had mentioned her, and if he hadn't thought about her so often and so poignantly, he might have suspected she'd never really existed.

"I always desired her," Percy absurdly claimed. "Did you know that? With you dead, the first thing I'll do is fuck her blind."

At the vile slur, Jamie was stunned and couldn't believe his ears. "What did you say?"

"I'll fuck her till she can't walk, but I won't marry her! Oh no. Not after you've stuck your filthy rod in her. I'll use her till I'm weary of her; then I'll cast her out. She'll wind up penniless and forgotten."

"Shut up, Percy."

"Is she any good under the blankets?" he coarsely asked. "Would she be worth the bother of raping?"

Jamie hit him so hard that he was lifted off his feet and flung backward into the crowd. He collapsed in a bewildered heap as Jamie stormed over and leaned down so that his face was an inch from Percy's own. Except for the color of their hair, they looked so much alike, and it was odd that they could be so similar on the outside but be so different on the inside.

Percy was Jamie's brother, but he was so weak, so lacking in character. From birth, he'd been given everything a man could ever want, but the largesse had been wasted on him. In a way, Jamie was glad for how their paths had diverged. Jamie's tribulations had made him tough and strong, had filled him with a righteous fury he wasn't afraid to exhibit.

He grabbed Percy by the shirt and threatened, "If you ever speak Anne's name again, I'll kill you."

"She's a cheap whore," Percy replied, too foxed to recognize that he should remain silent.

Jamie hit him again, harder, and he slumped to the floor, his nose oozing blood.

"When next I lay eyes on you," Jamie vowed, "I intend to murder you. Because we're kin, I'll give you a chance to get away, but I suggest you leave London immediately."

Jamie stood, rubbing his knuckles, and he nodded to a group of burly servants who'd hurried over to assist. They seized Percy and dragged him away, the guests parting like the Red Sea, but Percy was too dazed to offer any resistance. He was tossed onto the stoop like a sack of rubbish, and as the door was closed behind him, spectators smirked and murmured over the altercation.

Jamie worked his way toward the stairs, thinking he might sneak up to his room for a drink and some solitude, but he couldn't be gone long. By morning, news of their fight would be all over the city, and he didn't want anyone assuming that he'd been upset by it.

He was tired of London, tired of the rich, lazy nobles who now populated his world. He hated the noise and the crowds and the foul air, and he couldn't recollect what had driven him to come. Though he was loathe to stay, he was as stupidly proud as Percy. Having made one bad decision after the next, Jamie couldn't admit that he was miserable.

He missed Jack and yearned to fetch him, to board the ship and sail away, just the two of them out on the water, as it had always been in the past.

He missed Anne even more, so much so that the pain of it amazed him. Why did she have such a hold on him? Why was he so besotted? By fleeing Gladstone, he'd presumed his obsession would wane, but it hadn't. He wanted her more than ever, and he felt as if he'd lost a piece of himself, as if he'd hacked off a limb and couldn't grow it back.

He knew he should go home, that he should get down on bended knee and beg her to take him in, but he couldn't do it. She deserved better than a philandering libertine who had no loyalty and no constancy, and if he humbled himself by returning, what guarantee was there that she'd have him? Why would she want him?

He reached the staircase, and from the bottom step he could survey the crush of people. There were so many present, but he couldn't stand any of them. He had no friends, not even any cordial acquaintances. They'd come to see and be seen at the earl's latest decadent fete, but if he suddenly dropped dead, nary a one would rush to his aid.

An actress with whom he was regularly linked espied him, and she grinned and pushed her way over.

She pressed her voluptuous body to his, whispering a salacious proposition that made his cock stir, and she pointed up to his private quarters, where he never let any of them go.

Her cloying perfume was suffocating, and she clutched at his arm as if she owned it. He slid away and continued on alone, wishing they'd all leave but not having the energy to instruct the servants to usher them out.

He went into his room, shrugged out of his jacket, and poured himself a whiskey. As he was about to relax in a chair by the fire, he realized that there was someone in his dressing room, and from the sound of it, the person was . . . having a bath!

He frowned. Who would dare?

Had some strumpet violated the sanctity of his bedchamber? Would any of them be that brave? That daft?

He gulped his liquor, then stomped over and marched in. The sight that greeted him was so shocking that if the Queen, herself, had been there, he couldn't have been more surprised.

"Anne?"

"Hello, Jamie."

She was lounged—naked—in his bathing tub, and before he could focus on the fact that she'd arrived, she stood, water sluicing down her thighs.

"Would you hand me that towel?"

"Anne?" he muttered again, too astonished to say more.

"The towel, Jamie, if you please. I'm in a hurry."

Certain he was hallucinating, he physically shook himself.

"Who the hell let you in?"

"Why . . . the butler, who else? I'm your countess; I don't need permission."

"But why are you here?"

He couldn't move, and as it became evident that he'd be of no assistance, she climbed to the floor and grabbed the towel on her own. Like the most seasoned courtesan, she stroked it slowly, sensually, across her creamy shoulders, her perfect breasts, down her alluring belly, between her long, shapely legs.

Instantly, he was hard as stone. Though he'd tried his damnedest to forget her, it was obvious he still desired her more than ever. Would this insane lust never fade?

"It was so boring in the country without you," she was explaining, her busy hands meticulously drying every inch of her delectable skin. "And then, when I heard how much fun you were having in the city, I decided I should see for myself what it's like. Did you know I've never been to London before? I can't wait to try *everything*."

"Everything?"

"Yes. I'm told there are all sorts of amusements for a woman—if she's game."

"Game?" His voice came out as a squawk, and he coughed to clear his throat. "I don't want you here."

"Don't worry; I won't be underfoot. You'll scarcely notice I'm around."

"Not bloody likely."

She wrapped the towel over her lush, curvaceous torso, tucking a corner between her breasts like an African savage; then she went into the opposite bedroom, the room where his wife would sleep—if he had a wife. Which he did, but in name only.

Two maids had accompanied her from Gladstone. One was clutching a curling iron, and the other had fancy undergarments and a red ball gown strewn across the bed.

Anne glanced over to where he was loitering in the threshold like an imbecile.

"Do you mind?" she said. "I need to dress." He didn't budge, and she added, "In light of our estrangement, it's really not appropriate for you to watch."

He scowled. "Where are you going?"

"Jack and I are invited to a dozen parties, and I want to take in as many as I can before dawn."

"Jack is here?"

"Yes, just down the hall. He's getting ready, too. I didn't suppose you'd care, so I picked the bedroom for him that was nearest to mine. It's so convenient that way, isn't it?" She chuckled and winked. She winked!

"What are you talking about?"

"Me? Why . . . nothing. He and I have just grown so *close* since you left. I do so enjoy his company. It's like having you there, but without all the arrogance and bluster."

She made it sound as if she and Jack were . . .

Gad! He couldn't finish the thought!

Would his brother have the nerve? Would Anne? She was Jamie's wife! She couldn't start an affair with his brother! It was unseemly.

Was she mad? Was Jack?

A peculiar gurgling noise emanated from Jamie's chest, a growl or a bubbling rage, but she disregarded it and gestured to the door.

"Jamie, I can't dawdle, and I can't dress with you in here."

"It's my fucking house. I'll stay if I want to."

"Oh, don't be a beast. And I don't appreciate that kind of language being used."

He strutted over and pulled up a chair, a boot braced on the end of the mattress, the chair balanced on its hind legs. He studied her, his fury wafting out, his insolent attention raking her exposed body.

"Very well." She sighed with displeasure, then turned to her servants. "Help me, ladies, would you? If we ignore him, maybe he'll get bored and go away."

The maids tittered, then proceeded with their task, and Jamie observed, fascinated, as they curled and combed, as they laced and tied.

With each flick of a brush, with each knotting of a ribbon, Anne was more stunning, and he was disturbed by the transformation. He'd always thought she was lovely, but he'd known her at Gladstone, where the highlight of the day was a casual family supper.

He'd never seen her like this: bejeweled, fluffed, painted. She was . . . was . . . the most gorgeous sight he'd ever laid eyes upon. At last, corset taut, garters straightened, her gown was carefully drawn over her shoulders, the skirt smoothed down her legs.

Anne scrutinized her face in the mirror, her shapely ass stuck out, all that red silk taunting him with what he'd relinquished. As she smiled at one of the maids, he was miserably uncomfortable, his pants too tight, the temperature too hot.

"What do you think?" Anne asked the girl. "How about a little beauty mark right about here?"

"Oh yes, milady. A marvelous idea."

The girl took a pencil and dabbed the tiniest black dot on Anne's upper lip, which made Jamie vividly recollect the many times he'd kissed that very spot. He couldn't bear to have it emphasized. Every lecher in the world would gaze at it and ponder kissing her, and it was all Jamie could do to keep from rushing over, grabbing her, and rubbing it off.

Anne peered in the mirror again. "Is it too much?"

"No, milady, it's perfect. *You* are perfect."

"I am, aren't I?" Anne concurred.

She was exhibiting a conceit and confidence he'd never previously noted in her. When had this happened? How had it happened? He hadn't been gone that long!

He felt as if—in his absence—she'd metamorphosed into someone entirely new. The Anne of whom he'd dreamed, the Anne he'd mourned, had vanished, to be replaced by this purring, shimmering goddess.

Anne twirled in a circle, earning oohs and aahs from her servants, and as she spun, Jamie caught a glimpse of her bosom. His brows raised to his hairline. The bodice of her gown was cut so low that he could see nearly all of her breasts.

He leapt to his feet and snarled, "No. I will not allow it."

The three women whirled in unison, gaping at him as if he'd sprouted a second head.

"You won't *allow* what?" Anne inquired.

"You will not go out in public in that dress."

There was a bewildered pause; then Anne laughed and waved him away as if he were an irksome fly.

"Men!"

She rolled her eyes, and the maids snickered as she sauntered out. Jamie stomped after her, mad as a hornet, but she appeared to have forgotten his existence.

"Anne!" he snapped when she didn't stop. "I don't give you permission to go out like that."

"Oh, Jamie, don't fret over it. I'm really none of

your business. Isn't that what you wanted? Now that I've learned how much freedom a married woman has, I have to agree with you. Our split was for the best."

A door opened down the hall, and Jack stepped out. He was so formally attired that he might have been off for a presentation at Court. He was wearing an expensive, exquisitely tailored coat and trousers, his cravat flawlessly tied, his hair slicked back.

"Hello, Jamie," was the only welcome he had for the brother he hadn't seen in months; then Jack noticed Anne, and he lit up and gave a wolfish whistle.

"Look at you!"

"And look at you!" she gushed in reply. "My goodness, you handsome dog!"

She raced to Jack's side. He extended his arm, and she took it, the two of them as cozy as an old pair of slippers. Together, they hurried off.

"We'll be very late," Anne called to Jamie. "No need to wait up."

"When we get home," Jack felt compelled to add, "we'll be busy anyway, so we won't be in the mood to chat."

"We most certainly won't." Anne giggled in a sultry, seductive way Jamie had never heard from her; then she asked Jack, "Where to first?"

"Did Jamie ever teach you to throw dice?"

"No."

"It's my favorite game of chance."

"You'd actually take me to a gambling club? Aren't females banned from them?"

"They're admitted—in *some* establishments. You have to know the appropriate ones, which I definitely do."

She chuckled again. "You are so wicked."

"I can't deny it." He leaned in and whispered, "While we're there, I intend to teach you more than a bit of gambling!"

They flew down the stairs, and Jamie collapsed against the wall, wondering what had just transpired—and what he ought to do about it.

Chapter
NINETEEN

Anne crept down the hall toward her room, she and Jack tiptoeing hand in hand, like two thieves.

Dawn was breaking, and she was exhausted. She wasn't cut out for city life and couldn't fathom the attraction that drove the existence of so many. Like Jamie. Like her cousin Percy.

She wanted to simply fall into bed and sleep for hours. Her back ached, her head ached, and her feet were throbbing with blisters from traipsing about in such uncomfortable shoes.

Jamie's house was quiet, which surprised her. She'd assumed people would still be present and reveling, or perhaps passed out in the numerous parlors, but as she and Jack had flitted down the dark corridors the place had seemed empty.

They arrived at Jack's door, and he whispered, "Good night."

"I can't believe Jamie wasn't waiting up." She was whispering, too, her frustration clear. She'd been positive their ploy would have goaded him into a jealous frenzy, that he'd have been determined to confront her so he could harangue about her behavior.

"We'll try again tomorrow."

She nodded with resignation and went on to her own room. As she slipped in, Jamie growled from the shadows, "Get your ass in here."

She jumped with fright, then did as he'd ordered, though she dawdled, closing the door and toying with the lock. She needed a few moments to compose her features, to wipe the smile from her face.

He was sprawled in a chair by the window, moonlight streaming in. His coat was off, his shirt open, the sleeves rolled back. His hair was loose around his shoulders, his cheeks stubbled with beard. He'd been drinking, and he looked angry and dangerous, on edge, like a cobra about to strike.

A sane woman would have been terrified, but Anne shielded any reaction and blithely walked past him to her dressing room. He caught her before she made it, grabbing her and pulling her to him.

"Where the hell have you been?" he demanded.

"Out dancing—with your brother."

"You are never to go out with him again."

"How will you stop me?"

"I am your husband. You will do as I say!"

She scoffed. "You've picked the strangest time to claim me."

He shoved her against the wall, and he leaned into her. Down below, his erection prodded her leg, and a little thrill of victory tickled her stomach.

"You will attend me, at once."

"In what fashion?" she asked, pretending not to understand.

"Take off your clothes and climb into bed."

"I most certainly will not."

He flexed, showing her how hard he was. She'd never doubted his physical desire for her, and she was pleased to note that it hadn't waned, but it was exasperating that she couldn't figure out how to spur him from corporeal lust to emotional affection.

"Do it!" he hissed.

"You're being a boor, and I've had a long night."

"Your night has not been half as long as mine."

He clasped the neckline of her dress and ripped it down the center. She clutched at the fabric, feigning outrage, acting as if she were desperate to cover herself, but in reality, she loved him like this, so obsessed, so wild for her.

He smirked, relishing her predicament, his authority over her. "Pretty, pretty Anne, have you been giving away what should only be mine?"

"What if I have? Why would you care?"

"Have you!" he bellowed.

"You have paramours lurking around every corner. If your marriage vows mean nothing to you, why should they mean anything to me?"

"I could kill you for that remark, and there's not a man in England who would gainsay me."

"I'm not afraid of you," she boldly insisted.

He gripped her waist and spun her, her palms braced on the plaster, as he reached for something in his boot. When she saw that he'd retrieved a knife, she grew alarmed. Had she finally pushed him too far?

He dangled it over her shoulder so she could assess the sharp blade.

"Ah . . . I see I have your attention," he said. "Are you worried that I might use it?"

"No."

"If I learn that you've been fucking my brother, have you any idea of what I might do?"

With a quick flick of his wrist, he sliced through the laces on her corset and yanked it away. She shivered, naked, except for her stockings and shoes.

He leaned in again, his front pressed to her back, his arms circling her so he could massage her breasts, so he could painfully squeeze her nipples.

"Should I take you like a whore?" he taunted.

"You couldn't do anything to me that I wouldn't enjoy."

"I'm sure that's true."

Slowly, he unbuttoned his trousers, freeing his phallus from its confines, and she was eager to feel him plunge into her, but he didn't. He held himself in check, rubbing against her buttocks, moving her where he wanted, teasing them both with what was coming.

"Turn around," he commanded. "Get on your knees."

She whirled and dropped down as he glared at her, silent, angry, almost daring her to proceed.

Foolish man! She'd be his slave if he but asked it of her.

She stroked his balls, his cock, licking the length, the tip, till his sexual juice seeped from the end; then she sucked him inside.

He groaned—in agony, in ecstasy—and started to flex. He was being a beast, but she didn't mind. She knew how much he treasured the dissolute deed, and she could have knelt there for an eternity, loving and pleasing him, but rapidly he was at the edge. He pulled away, his respirations ragged, his head hanging down.

"Go lie on the bed," he said, not glancing at her.

"No, I want to—"

"Go!" he fumed, and he urged her toward it.

She scowled, ready to argue, to fight, but ultimately, she complied. He was in a frantic, troubled state, and she couldn't wait to see where it would lead.

Scurrying away, she crawled onto the mattress and lazily reclined. She raised her knee and let it fall to the side so that he could view her most private parts.

"Do you want me, Jamie?" she needled. "Do you want me, or should I give myself to someone else?"

"Never!" He stalked to her, leaping onto the bed and covering her with his body. "You're mine! Do you hear me? Mine."

"Prove it."

He clasped her thighs, jerked them wide, and entered her with a hard thrust. She moaned and arched up, but he was in a heedless fury and oblivious to her needs. He slammed into her, his lust at a level she'd never encountered with him prior, his hips pounding like the pistons of a huge machine.

She couldn't delay or calm him. She could only hold on through the tumult. With her legs wrapped around him, her ankles locked, she gave him greater access, and he drove himself deeper and deeper. His passion spiraled, and so did her own.

Her orgasm commenced at the center of her womb, the waves of pleasure shooting out to her belly, her limbs, and as she cried out, he finished, too, roaring with the fervor of his release.

Time seemed to stop as they soared together, as they raced to the pinnacle, then plummeted to earth, crashing with an echoing finality that frightened her, that saddened her.

Surely, he'd have been swayed! Surely, he'd understand that she loved him, that she needed him! But what if he didn't? What if her scheme had all been for naught?

He collapsed onto her and rolled away. They were side-by-side, on their backs, not touching, like strangers, like enemies. His distance from her was so blatant that if he'd handed her a few coins for services rendered, she wouldn't have been surprised.

"Tell me there's been no one but me," he said.

"Oh, Jamie, how could you think it?"

"Tell me you haven't lain with my brother."

"I haven't. I swear."

She snuggled herself to him, but she might have been cuddling a log.

"I was trying to make you jealous," she admitted.

"Why?" He peered over at her, his expression unreadable.

"I love you," she staunchly announced, but he looked as if she'd hit him.

"Don't say that."

"But it's true, Jamie. I love you, and I miss you. I want you to come home."

"Home!" He scoffed as if the word were an epithet. "And where is that?"

"It's Gladstone, you silly oaf. It's with me at Gladstone."

He relaxed a bit and drew her closer, her cheek on his chest. She couldn't see his eyes, but she could sense that he was awhirl with anguished thoughts. She didn't comprehend his demons, and since she didn't know what they were, she didn't know how to vanquish them.

He stroked her hair and sighed. "You shouldn't have come to town."

"I had to. I couldn't let you continue on as you are."

"I'm fine, and I don't need you playing nursemaid."

"I'm not *playing*," she insisted. "This is for real. This is for keeps."

"It was never meant to be forever."

"It was, too! I love you."

At her repeating the strident declaration, he winced and pressed a finger to her lips, silencing her, preventing any further pronouncements he couldn't bear to hear.

"Hush now."

"Jamie!"

"Hush."

She ceased her protests, but she refused to be discouraged by his adamant assertion that they had no future. It was only her first night in London, and she would stay as long as necessary, would use every feminine wile she possessed to change his mind.

The sound of his breathing soothed her, as did the steady beating of his heart under her ear, and eventually she dozed.

When she awoke, the room was flooded with sunshine. She peeked over at the clock, seeing that it was afternoon and she'd slept the morning away.

Jamie wasn't with her, and she was very still, hoping he was nearby, but it was so desperately quiet. There was an emptiness in the air, the same one she'd felt the day he'd left Gladstone, and she knew—without having to search—that he had left her again.

She climbed out of bed, the floor cold on her bare feet. She tugged on her nightgown and robe, and she hurried downstairs, stumbling into the dining room, where Jack was eating breakfast, but Jamie was nowhere to be found.

As she entered, Jack glanced away, his pity obvious as she sat across from him.

"Where is he?"

"He left. I'm sorry."

"Where was he going?"

"He . . . ah . . . he and some friends went to the horse races."

"Which *friends*?"

"It doesn't matter."

"Tell me, Jack. I won't faint. I promise."

"Two loose women, Anne. Actresses, I presume."

"I see," she murmured, and she really, really did. "Do you think the stories are true, that he's . . . well . . . *involved* with them?"

"I couldn't begin to guess."

"But he might actually be betraying me?"

"He might."

She couldn't believe it. She just couldn't believe he would! She was such a naive little fool.

"Did he say anything?"

"The usual."

"What does that mean?"

He leaned over and patted her hand. "Let it go, Anne. He's my brother, and I've always loved him dearly, but he's not worth it."

"I know he's not, but I can't help myself."

Jamie was like an addiction in her blood. She couldn't shed her need for him, and she didn't understand how he could make love to her with such wild abandon, then trot off with a pair of strumpets a few hours later.

He had to be made of stone. Ice had to flow in his veins.

He wouldn't treat a dog as he'd treated her.

"Why does he despise me so much?" She hated the pathetic quaver in her voice.

"He doesn't."

"Of course he does. What other basis could there possibly be for his behavior?"

"You don't know how it was for us, Anne," Jack gently said.

"Then explain it to me."

"We figured out, at a very young age, that it was pointless to grow attached to anyone. He simply never learned how to care. It was easier that way."

"Easier for whom?"

Jack stared at his plate, nibbled at his food. "He . . . left you a note."

"He did?"

Jack had hidden it under his napkin, apparently debating whether to show it to her. He pushed it toward her, and it lay there between them, like the kiss of death.

Finally, she mustered the courage to unfold it. After scanning the words, her eyes glistened with tears. She chuckled miserably.

"What is it?" he inquired.

"And here Ophelia claimed he couldn't read or write. Well, he seems perfectly articulate to me."

She crumpled the letter into a ball, clutched it to her heart, then walked over to the fire and tossed the letter in, watching as it dwindled to ash in the flames. For a long while, she stood, pensive, her hopes fading to nothing.

"I know I told you," she ultimately stated, "that I wanted to stay in London until we convinced him to come home." She turned to him. "But I was wrong. There's no reason to remain. How soon can you be packed?"

꒰

Hello, Miss Carstairs," Jack politely said.

"Oh, for pity's sake, call me Sarah."

"As you wish," he agreed, but he didn't speak her name aloud. Silly as it sounded, it hurt him to say it.

Since the terrible evening when Jamie had questioned them about their affair, they'd tiptoed around one another.

Jack had once thought he might marry her, that he might build a life with her at Gladstone. But it all seemed to have occurred in the distant past, like a sweet dream he couldn't quite recollect.

He'd never again sneaked to her room, had never again fought or chatted with her. At all costs, he avoided her, even sleeping in the grooms' quarters over the stables with the other bachelors so he'd never see her. He was more comfortable there than in the fancy mansion filled with the feminine craziness generated by the Carstairs sisters and their wretched cousin Ophelia.

Over the months, he'd grown acquainted with Sarah's son, Tim, and their relationship made Jack realize how much he'd missed by never becoming a father. He was hungering for a different future, and he was determined to meet a woman who could overlook his faults and history and have him in spite of them.

He wanted to go somewhere where no one knew him, where he wasn't viewed simply as the useless, powerless brother of the wastrel earl. He was eager to start over, maybe in America or Australia. Men were equal in those places. He could have a plot of land for the asking, could create a humble but satisfying existence.

If he spent a few days in London, he was certain he could stumble on a female who shared the same vision. Not for an impressive house and an expensive wardrobe, not for a snooty husband and a lofty position in the neighborhood, but for stability and constancy, for serenity and permanence.

He wasn't choosy. Nor did he expect the type of passion he'd experienced with Sarah Carstairs. He needed a tough partner, a pragmatic and sturdy ally, and he imagined that, without too much trouble, he could find someone who would be happy to accompany him.

"Where are you off to?" Sarah queried, studying his heavy coat and scarf, his hat pulled low on his head.

"I'm leaving."

"You oughtn't to go anywhere. The temperature is so frigid; I swear it's about to snow."

"I've seen better," he churlishly replied. "I'll see worse."

It had been a beautiful summer, but the harvest was completed, and autumn full upon them, winter close behind. A smart fellow would be sailing south, with the wind at his back and the sun on his face, as he traveled to warmer climes, which was Jack's exact intent.

To hell with Jamie! To hell with Gladstone and the flighty, unappreciative females who roamed its halls!

Without another word, Jack stomped to the door. A packed satchel and a bedroll awaited him, but that was all. He hadn't advised anyone that he was going, so there was no one to see him off. No one rushed out to say good-bye or wish him Godspeed, but that's the way he wanted it.

Farewells were annoying and pointless.

He took a last glance at the fussy foyer, at the priceless carpets, the sparkling chandeliers, the paintings, and furniture, and all the rest. He could have gagged at the excess, and he was delighted to be departing with no more than he'd arrived with.

How many chattels did a man actually need anyway?

Sarah watched as he hefted his bag over his shoulder, and she inquired, "What are you doing?"

Irked at being delayed, he snapped, "I told you: I'm leaving."

"You mean *leaving* Gladstone?"

"Yes."

"Forever?"

"Yes. What did you think I meant?"

"But . . . where will you go?"

She acted as if he were begging for spare coins on a street corner, and her snobbery aggravated him.

"I'm sure it will come as a huge surprise to someone as grand and glorious as yourself, but before I returned to England I had a decent life. I wasn't a wealthy nabob, and I didn't have fashionable clothes to wear, or rich foods to eat, but I got on all right."

"But I . . . I . . . thought you loved it here. I thought you were happy."

"I guess that just shows how little you know of me."

His gaze was cold, and he was being cruel, but he owed her no courtesy.

He spun away again, but suddenly she was there, halting him with the slightest weight of her hand on his arm. Her touch was like a brand, and he shook her away, hating to be reminded of how he'd have once done anything for her.

"Does Anne know about this?"

"No."

"Let's speak with her, shall we?" Sarah cajoled as if he were a lunatic escaped from an asylum. "She wouldn't want you to go with this storm brewing."

"Anne is busy. She's upstairs in her sitting room with your cousin Percy."

"Percy is here?"

"I tried to tell her not to let him stay, but—"

"He's staying?"

Sarah was aghast, and Jack took some comfort from her reaction. At least one person in the blasted house realized that Percy's presence spelled disaster. Jack had warned Anne, but she viewed her cousin as a nuisance, not as a threat, so she refused to heed Jack's dire counsel.

Jack could have bodily tossed Percy out on the road, and he'd been seriously considering it, when it had dawned on him that he didn't care enough about the accursed place to fret.

It was Jamie's property and Jamie's authority that were being maligned, but Jamie couldn't be bothered. Why should Jack enforce the rules and douse the fires? Why should Jack bloody his knuckles over a pompous ass like Percy Merrick?

When Ophelia had first slithered home, Jack had pitched a fit, but it had been a waste of energy. The vexing shrew was quietly wresting control of the manor, though Anne hadn't yet noticed the small ways her orders were being contravened.

With Percy on the premises, it would only get worse, and Jack wouldn't tarry to observe the trouble

Ophelia and Percy would foment. It was obvious that they had schemes in the works, and when those schemes were implemented it would be bad for all concerned, but what could he do? It had been the story of his life that he had no genuine power or influence.

He'd cautioned Anne, he was alerting Sarah, and he'd stop in London to notify Jamie before he headed out. Whatever any of them did—or didn't do—after that was none of his affair.

"Yes," Jack said, "Percy's here, and he's already demanded possession of his old suite."

"Why . . . that's absurd. It belongs to your brother."

"I hate to break the news to you, but Jamie will never be back to claim it. He made his position very clear when your sister and I went to London."

At memories of that failed journey, Jack grimaced. Anne had been crushed all over again, and Jack had been left with no more illusions. He'd had to accept the fact that Jamie was an unredeemable lout and unworthy of any loyalty.

Most pathetic of all, during the short period Jack had been gone he'd missed Sarah, and if there was any greater evidence of how Gladstone had driven him completely insane, he didn't know what it was.

His mention of Jamie had set a spark to her temper, but he was too weary to bicker. During his last argument with Sarah, she'd spewed every harsh word he ever planned to listen to from her, and as he prepared to walk out the door forever, he wasn't about to go with her snide remarks ringing in his ears.

"So that's it?" she seethed. "The two of you swept in, wreaked havoc, and now, you're simply moving on?"

"That about covers it."

"But what will Anne and I do?"

"I don't know," he truthfully replied. "If you need anything, I suppose you could try writing to Jamie, but I wouldn't expect an answer. And were I you, I'd be extremely wary of Ophelia and Percy. I don't believe they have your best interests at heart."

Sarah studied him, her mind awhirl. She'd always had too much to say, more than he'd ever wanted to hear, and he wouldn't tolerate any nonsense.

"You're not going because of me, are you?" she pestered.

"Don't flatter yourself."

"Because . . . if that's why, we can talk this out. We don't need to quarrel."

"We're beyond *quarreling,* Sarah. You know that."

"Where will you be living? What if I need to contact you?"

"I can't imagine why you would."

"Humor me."

She appeared sincere, so he told her. "I'm off to London, where I intend to find a woman who'll marry me; then I'm taking our ship and sailing it to America. To start over."

"You'd rather wed a . . . a . . . stranger and trek off to the wilderness than remain here with me?"

"Yes."

"Don't do this, Jack. Don't go."

She stepped forward and laid her palm on his chest, and she gazed up at him with her pretty green eyes. It would be so easy to get sucked in by those eyes, to begin dreaming of things that could never be, but he'd learned the hard way that it was foolish to depend on her, foolish to hope she might turn out to be someone other than who she was.

"Good-bye, Sarah." He was proud at how he managed to quell any hint of lingering affection.

"If I did anything or said anything that—"

He snorted with disgust. "Just leave it be."

"Will I . . . will I . . . ever see you again?"

"If I'm very lucky—which I haven't been so far—no."

They stared for an eternity, and finally she ludicrously declared, "I think I could have loved you."

"I doubt it," he countered.

"I'm sorry it didn't work out between us."

"I'm not."

He pulled away, spun, and hurried outside.

Chapter
TWENTY

"Where is Tim?"

Ophelia glanced up from her breakfast plate. "Tim? Who is Tim?"

"You know who he is," Sarah growled.

"No, I don't. I guess you'll have to clarify who you mean."

"Where is he, you witch?" Sarah shouted.

At the outburst, Ophelia chuckled and kept buttering her toast.

"Honestly, Sarah, you're positively unhinged, and I have no desire to deal with you when you're in such a state. Perhaps I should advise Percy to find you a husband. Or perhaps I should simply have Percy get you under control, himself."

She laid down her knife, her warning clear. Percy could do anything to Sarah, and Sarah couldn't stop him. While he'd never made an inappropriate advance, there had been times when he'd unnerved her with a leer or a gesture. She didn't trust him and never had.

The Merrick brothers were gone, the scant protection

they'd afforded having vanished like smoke, and the family had resettled to its original condition. Percy and Ophelia were lording themselves over everyone, so the servants were in continual turmoil, wondering who to obey.

Anne quietly and discreetly rescinded their more outrageous demands, but it was impossible to assert any significant authority. What could Anne do? Was she to summon the law and have her own cousins evicted? Would she have them dragged out to the road kicking and screaming? Such a scenario didn't bear contemplating, yet Ophelia was more of a shrew than ever, and Percy was drinking too much and seemed downright dangerous.

Sarah had begged Anne to write to Jamie, but Anne wouldn't lower herself, and Sarah couldn't blame her, but with Tim missing, the gloves were off, and Sarah might contact him, herself. Ophelia had always claimed that she could make Tim disappear, and it would be just like her to seek revenge against Tim when she was actually angry at Jamie.

Feeling as deranged as Ophelia had accused her of being, Sarah went to the sideboard and grabbed a knife. She walked to Ophelia and thrust the blade under her chin.

"If you sent him away," Sarah threatened, "if you so much as harmed a hair on his head, I'll kill you. Now where is he?"

Ophelia shrieked and pushed Sarah away, as Anne hustled into the room.

"What is it?" Anne asked, frantic. "What's happening?"

"Your sister is mad," Ophelia fumed. "She attacked me for no reason."

Sarah felt capable of any violence. She lunged at Ophelia, and if Anne hadn't jumped between them, she would have been delighted to stab Ophelia through the center of her cold, black heart.

"Sarah!" Anne scolded. "What's wrong with you?"

"Shall we explain why you're upset?" Ophelia taunted. "Shall we destroy the pretty picture you've painted for her all these years?"

"What are you talking about?" Anne inquired.

"Sarah is a whore. She always has been."

Both sisters gasped at the harsh term, and Sarah hurled, "You bitch."

Ophelia was unfazed. "When she was sixteen, and she was away at *school,* where do you imagine she really went?"

"Sarah?" Anne frowned.

"She was pregnant," Ophelia crowed, divulging the secret that had tormented Sarah for over a decade, and to Sarah's amazement, the earth kept spinning. No one dropped dead in shock. No one leapt away as if she had the plague. The facts were just words spewing from Ophelia's mouth.

There was a lengthy pause, as the three of them digested the announcement; then Anne queried, "Is it true, Sarah?"

"Yes." Sarah turned to her sister, relieved that Anne didn't recoil in horror.

"Why didn't you confide in me?"

"Because I was young and afraid." Sarah reached out and squeezed Anne's hand. "Ophelia constantly berated me till I didn't know what to do. She said I'd disgraced the family and that if anyone ever learned of my shame, they'd cast me out."

"And the child?"

"A boy—named Tim."

"He's been right here," Ophelia raged, "all this time, rubbing his bastardry in our collective noses."

Anne was incensed and uncharacteristically ordered, "Shut up, Ophelia."

"I won't be silent. Your sister prances about as if she's the bloody Queen of England, and I for one—"

"Shut up!" Anne said more forcefully, then to Sarah, "Who was the father?"

"I'll tell you about it later," Sarah promised. "I won't discuss it in front of her."

"It could have been anyone," Ophelia sneered. "One of Percy's friends. One of the neighbors' summer guests. The vicar's brother. Did you know who it was, Sarah? Or did you refuse to identify him because there'd been so many you couldn't be sure?"

Sarah dived at Ophelia, yanking her hair and scratching her face. Ophelia was shrieking again and several servants ran in to check on the ruckus.

Ophelia would have charged at Sarah, but Anne's fury—and a footman's strong grip—kept her in place.

"Tim will be brought to live in the manor at once," Anne declared, her livid gaze locked on Ophelia.

"No," Ophelia hissed. "I won't allow it."

"*You* won't allow it?"

"I won't have that little urchin welcomed as if he . . . he . . . *belongs*."

Anne peered at the maids. "Lady Ophelia is leaving the property immediately. Go upstairs and pack her things."

"Don't you dare!" Ophelia countered. "If any of you try, my brother will have you whipped, then tossed out without a penny or a reference."

The poor maids were in a quandary, the standoff embarrassing and awkward, and it was precisely the sort of debacle Sarah had been expecting from the day Jack had left. When he'd still been present, Ophelia had been manageable, but without him to quell her influence, there was no stopping her.

"All of you! Out!" Anne commanded, and the servants were more than happy to comply. They raced away.

Once the door was closed behind them, Sarah said, "Tim is missing, Anne."

"What do you mean?"

"He's been working in the stables, but he's disappeared. I think Ophelia sent him away. In the past, she often bragged that she might. That's why she and I were quarreling. I'm worried that she's finally done something awful."

"Have you?" Anne demanded of Ophelia.

"What if I have?" Ophelia boasted. "Why would you suppose it to be any of your business?"

Anne stared her down, weighing their options, but there didn't seem to be many good ones. They could muster some burly tenants and have them wrestle Ophelia outside, but Percy would let her back in. So they'd have to bodily throw him out, too, the trick being to make him stay gone. He'd find a way to return, and when he did, there'd be hell to pay.

Sarah stepped in so that she and Ophelia were toe-to-toe, and Sarah's wrath was so evident that, for a brief second, Ophelia's smug expression flickered with alarm.

"I'm finished being terrified of you," Sarah stated. "My worst fear has always been that Anne would discover what I had done. You told her, and I survived. Your hold over me is severed."

Ophelia shrugged. "If you assume you can proudly introduce your bastard to the neighborhood, then carry on as you have previously, be my guest. I can't wait to see what happens to you."

Casually, she sat at the table to continue eating her breakfast, but Sarah snatched Ophelia's plate and flung it at the wall. It shattered, eggs and toast oozing down the plaster.

"You are insane!" Ophelia bristled.

"Your days of sponging off Anne are over."

"Says who?" Ophelia replied. "Since this is—and always has been—my home, your gall is astounding."

"We'll see, Ophelia. We'll see who is still standing at the end."

"Yes, we will. Why am I positive it will be Percy and me?"

Sarah looked at Anne. "I'm having the carriage prepared. Would you have the servants pack a bag for me?"

"Why?" Anne asked.

"Jamie Merrick needs to know what's occurring. *I* am going to London to fetch him to Gladstone."

"He'll never come with you," Ophelia insisted.

"We'll see," Sarah said again.

"Try his mistress's house," Ophelia snidely suggested. "I hear he spends every waking moment in bed with her."

The terrible remark was meant to wound Anne, but Anne would never let Ophelia know that it had had any effect.

"Sarah," Anne calmly said, "would you tell my husband that I wish he'd come personally, but if he's busy, have him send some of his sailors, would you? They're just as ruthless as he is. Advise him that they should be heavily armed and ready for trouble."

"That's a great idea," Sarah agreed. "I'll let him know. Will you be all right while I'm away? Would you like to go with me?"

"One of us should remain here," Anne asserted.

"If you stay by yourself," Ophelia simpered, "aren't you scared of me and what I might do to you?"

"No," Anne answered. "Jack taught me to shoot a pistol. I intend to load it, then follow you around so you don't have a chance to steal any of the silver."

"If I take anything," Ophelia retorted, "it belongs to me and Percy—not the paltry, common wife of an impostor."

"I'm certain Jamie will have an interesting opinion on the subject," Anne sweetly responded. "Be sure to mention it for me, will you, Sarah?"

"I'll make Ophelia's position very clear."

Sarah spun and hurried out.

❧

"A nne, there you are. I've been searching everywhere."

Anne whirled to see Percy lurking in the doorway of her bedchamber.

Without argument, she'd relinquished the earl's suite to him and she'd moved to the other wing of the large mansion. She'd wanted to be far away from him and Ophelia, and in light of the morning's events, she didn't care to have him dropping by.

In the months he'd been away, he'd begun falling apart. He'd lost so much weight, his pudgy torso turning lean and lithe, and his clothes—about which he'd always been so fussy—were stained and messy. She could smell alcohol on his breath and figured he was inebriated, which was his usual condition. She didn't like dealing with him sober, let alone half-foxed.

"What is it, Percy?"

"You've been quarreling with Ophelia."

"It's much more than a *quarrel,* Percy. She's pushed me to my limit, and we can't go on as we have been."

"I understand that you're upset, Anne, but it's not your place to order her to leave. I've notified her—and the servants—that she'll be staying."

Anne's temper flared, but she reined it in. At that moment, with little power on her side, it was pointless to fight with him. She would trust that Sarah could convince Jamie to come home as she—Anne—could not, but Anne wouldn't count on Jamie.

While Sarah was away, Anne would talk with the vicar, would perhaps discuss the situation with a lawyer and seek legal assistance.

Percy and Ophelia would ultimately be evicted, but Anne would inform them when she had a few brawny men to back her up.

"Sarah told me about her son," Anne said. "You and Ophelia constantly threatened her."

"We hardly *threatened* her. Everything we did, we did for her own good."

"How can you justify your conduct?"

"If she wants to make a fool of herself and publicly claim the lad, it's fine by me. The two of you simply need to consider the consequences before doing anything rash."

"I plan to have the boy found, then brought into the house to live."

"Then don't come crying to me if Sarah is shunned afterward."

He walked into the room, so he was between Anne and the door, and an odd prickle of fear slithered down her spine. She felt as if he was blocking her in, and he seemed bigger than she remembered.

He took a step toward her, then another, till he was very close, and she forced herself to keep from retreating. She'd never been afraid of him, and whatever peculiar whim had spurred him to visit, she wouldn't be intimidated.

"You know, Anne, I've always been particularly fond of you."

"I'm glad to hear it, Percy."

"And I've been very generous over the years. Haven't I been generous?"

"Yes, you have been."

"If you'd like Ophelia to go, I might be amenable. You'd have to persuade me, of course."

"What would you have me say?" she naively inquired.

"Well, you wouldn't have to actually *say* anything."

He reached out and trailed a finger down her neck, across her nape, and she was so shocked that she stood there and let him do it. When he kept on—as if he might continue down to her bosom—she slapped his hand away.

"What are you thinking?"

"It could be you and me at Gladstone, Anne. We could rule here. Would you like that? It would please me enormously."

"I'm married to Jamie."

"A minor technicality, I assure you."

He leaned in and trapped her against the bedpost,

his body pressed to hers, and down below, his cock was on her leg. He had an erection!

Was he insane?

What would make him suppose she'd welcome this type of behavior? He was her cousin, like an older brother. She had no passionate feelings for him, and she'd never given the slightest indication that she was interested in him in an amorous way.

"Percy! Stop it!" She shoved him, but he was heavy as a boulder and wouldn't budge.

"Jamie stole everything from me—even you. Do you have any idea how it galls me to admit that I could have had you, but he had you first?"

"You're mad to reflect on it. I would never have lain down with you."

"I shouldn't have given you a choice in the matter."

He cupped her breast, having the temerity to pinch her nipple. For a stunned instant, she wondered how one man—her husband—could have touched the sensitive spot and sent her into spasms of ecstasy, while another could do the very same but merely be an annoying and offensive nuisance.

Then her wits caught up with her brain, and she groped behind her on the mattress, where earlier she'd tossed a shoe. She snatched it up and whacked Percy alongside the head as she let out a bloodcurdling scream that had him staggering away.

Freed from his weight, she scurried to the hearth and grabbed a fireplace poker. She pointed it at him, menacing him, eager for an excuse to inflict more damage.

"Get out of here," she seethed. When he didn't move, she shouted, "Get out, or when Jamie returns, he'll kill you."

"He's never coming back, so you'll never be safe from me."

"He's on his way this very second," Anne retorted, feigning bravado, her knees knocking together under her skirt.

"So trusting," he crooned, "so gullible. You should have wed me, instead of him. You know it, and I know it."

"I know nothing of the sort."

He started toward her again, not deterred by the poker, and Anne swung it, just missing his ribs. He jumped out of range and reined in his aggressiveness.

"I'll go for now," he vowed, "but you can't keep me out forever."

"I have a lock on my door."

"I have many, many keys."

"If you try to use one of them, I have a pistol that's loaded at all times. I'll shoot you right between the eyes, and I won't even blink."

"Who says I'll give you opportunity to aim?"

He stomped out, and as his angry strides faded, she ran over, slammed the door, and spun the key in the lock. She studied it, deciding it seemed very flimsy.

If Percy truly wished to enter, how sturdy would it prove to be?

"Why aren't you at Gladstone?" Jamie snapped.

"I've left," Jack curtly explained.

"I thought you loved it there."

"I was wrong. I loathe it."

"But . . . who's watching over Anne?" Jamie sputtered. "You were supposed to; we agreed."

"I guess you'll have to find yourself another nanny."

"I don't want anyone else to do it."

"Well then, you're in a pickle, because you've ended up with Ophelia and Percy."

"They're at the estate?"

At least Jamie had sufficient concern to look aghast. On a half-dozen occasions, Jack had written him but received no response.

"Yes, with Percy fully ensconced in the earl's bed-chamber."

"He would dare?" For once, Jamie was completely at a loss, and he commanded, "Get your ass back there. Deal with him."

"No," Jack said. "I'm taking the ship and heading out."

"You're what?"

"I'm leaving England. I'm taking the ship."

"Like hell you are. I can't believe you have the nerve to ask if you can use it."

"I'm not asking, Jamie. This is merely a courtesy visit to say good-bye."

Jack walked toward the hall, prepared to depart that very moment, and Jamie huffed, "Just a damned minute. What are you doing?"

"I've told you, but you can't seem to get it through your thick skull."

"That ship is mine. If you presume you can simply take it and go, you've tipped off your rocker."

Jack was so furious that he wondered if he might explode. He stormed over till they were toe-to-toe, loving his brother, hating his brother.

" 'Mine, mine, mine,' " Jack mocked. "You sound like a fucking parrot."

"*I* won that ship. Not you."

As if Jack could ever forget the brash, reckless boy Jamie had been! How could it be fifteen years later and nothing had changed?

"I was with you, remember? I know how it was."

"I spent my life on that hunk of wood, and I won't let you have it without a fight."

"I was with you every step of the way," Jack fumed. "I did everything you ever wanted. I went everywhere you ever suggested. I participated in every foolish, dangerous raid you ever planned. I stayed at Gladstone for you, while you were here in London, screwing women and gambling your money away. In all that time, have I ever asked you for a fucking thing?"

"No, but that doesn't mean you can have my ship."

"Why is everything yours?" Jack bellowed, surprising them both with his rage. "Why can't something be mine for a change?"

"You don't want anything badly enough to make it yours. You always give in. You always give up. Now get your sorry ass back to Gladstone. You're trying my patience."

Jack hit him as hard as he could. Jamie hadn't been expecting a punch, so he stumbled to the side and knocked over a fussy decorative table, sending whiskey glasses and figurines crashing to the floor. In all their years together, they'd never come to blows, and Jack couldn't describe the careening emotions that had driven him to lash out.

He had such vivid memories of how it had been when they'd first arrived at Gladstone, and he was tormented by them. There'd been a remarkable sense that he was finally home, but it had all been a chimera, and he was frustrated by how little he'd accomplished, by how unwelcome he'd actually been.

He stood, rubbing his knuckles, as Jamie sat up, then stood, too. Jamie was massaging his jaw and eyeing Jack as if he were a rabid dog.

"What the devil is wrong with you?" Jamie seethed.

"I hate it here," Jack lied, in his heart, yearning for Gladstone as he'd never yearned for anything before, but it wasn't his and never would be. "I hate England, and I'm never coming back."

"Is this because of Sarah Carstairs?" Jamie probed, reading Jack's mind. "Why don't you propose to the blasted woman?"

"I did, and she won't have me."

"So you'd go off and leave me—just because she hurt your precious feelings?"

"No, I'm going because you're an obnoxious prick and I can't stand you anymore. Go help your wife. She needs you."

After that, there wasn't much else worth saying. Jack marched away, hoping Jamie would call for him to halt but also hoping he wouldn't. His pull had always been too strong to resist, and Jack was too weary to battle the subtle pressure Jamie could exert.

As Jack reached the threshold, Jamie said, "Just like that? You're really leaving?"

Jack spun around, studying Jamie, anxious to recollect every detail. "Yes, just like that."

Jamie scoffed. "I'm placing guards at the ship, to make sure it's securely tied to its moorings. Don't even try touching it."

"Fuck you. I don't need your paltry vessel. I have

my own funds; I'll book public passage." He started out again, then paused. "If Sarah Carstairs comes sniffing around, tell her I have what she's searching for. Let her know . . . that ah . . . that I'll keep it safe."

"Did you steal from her? Will she demand payment?"

"No. I have something invaluable that she never wanted. You couldn't put a price on it."

"What the hell does that mean?"

"She'll know."

Detesting how long their parting had turned out to be, he whipped away and left.

❦

W hat do you think?" Percy inquired. "Do I look like Jamie?"

"Oh yes," Ophelia responded, "you definitely look like him."

She assessed her brother, intrigued by the transformation. She'd known that he and Jamie had similar features, but with Percy's recent loss of weight and his having donned a black wig, a fake ponytail in the back, the resemblance was uncanny. Jamie and Jack Merrick could have been triplets instead of twins, with Percy the third wheel. If Percy was spotted, especially in the shadows, in the dark, any witness would absolutely swear that he'd seen Jamie.

She slackened the collar on Percy's shirt and tugged some of the hem from his trousers, so that the fabric billowed around his chest and waist.

"Jamie never wears clothes that are tightly tailored," she explained.

"He doesn't?"

"Haven't you noticed?"

"I wouldn't pay him that much attention."

"Relax your shoulders and hips," she advised. "You have to be more loose limbed." Jamie moved as if he anticipated trouble, as if he was a moment away from slipping a dagger out of his boot.

"Like this?" Percy mimicked as he scrutinized himself in the mirror.

"That's excellent. And your mouth . . ." She considered, then suggested, "Can you quirk your lips in a half smile, just there on the right-hand side?"

"How's that?"

"Perfect."

Too perfect. She scowled.

She still recalled the night early in the summer, when she'd gone to Jamie's bed and had been rebuffed. While he'd inflicted many indignities on her, she hated him for that humiliation most of all.

Percy was the only paramour she'd ever had, and she'd presumed herself content in their relationship—until she'd met Jamie. The fact that she desired Jamie and could never have him was infuriating, but she would have her revenge, and it would be so satisfying.

Suddenly, Percy spun from the mirror and lay down on the bed.

"Come here," he ordered.

"Why?"

"I want to fuck you while I look exactly like Jamie. I want to pretend I'm him and that I'm forcing myself on you."

"That's disgusting."

"Did I ask your opinion? Just come here."

She glared at him. He could be so tiresome, but she'd been bound to him her whole life and couldn't imagine another path. Yet she had to admit that it was titillating to picture herself trifling with Jamie rather than Percy. If she blew out the candle, it would be sufficiently dark that it would seem as if she were with Jamie.

Would it be more arousing? Or would it be no different, at all?

"If you want me to believe you're Jamie, you need to be a bit more demanding."

"How so?"

She shook her head in exasperation. The man was thick as a brick.

"You've watched him with Anne. He doesn't take no for an answer. So *no,* I won't climb into bed with you. You'll have to make me obey."

He frowned, ready to berate her for denying him, when he realized what an amusing game she'd devised. He was as excited to play it as she was.

Ever since Jamie had appeared on the scene, Percy had grown more violent in their couplings, but Ophelia wasn't complaining. She enjoyed his more spirited side. It was thrilling to know that—after so many years—Percy still wanted her so desperately, and that she would forever be his one true love.

He rose up, slowly, deliberately, precisely as Jamie might have done it, and he came to her and seized her wrist. She tried to pull away, tried to run, but Percy wrestled her onto the mattress and pinned her down.

"Don't ever tell me no, Anne." He was totally immersed in their fantasy. "Don't ever assume you can escape me. You can't."

His cock was harder than it had ever been, and Ophelia rippled with lust, certain it would be their best fornication ever, but he was so wrapped up in his vision of her being Anne that he merely rammed himself between her legs and thrust with a vigor he'd never exhibited prior.

He took her in a coarse, despicable way, and she was irritated to discover that he'd found the notion of copulating with Anne—instead of herself—to be incredibly stimulating. He quickly flexed to the end and finished with a loud grunt. Then he rolled away and went to preen in front of the mirror again.

"Jamie couldn't have done it any better," he boasted.

"*Jamie* would have taken his time."

"Shut up." He admired his reflection. "I wonder what he'd do if I raped her. He'd be so angry."

Ophelia simmered with jealousy. "Anne? You want to rape Anne?"

"Of course. I always have. You know that. Would you like to help me? You could hold her down while I proceed."

"You're going to murder Anne," she tersely reminded him. "You're not going to have sex with her."

"Perhaps," he aggravatingly mused.

"Percy!"

He glanced over and chuckled. "I was joking, darling. I've never desired anyone but you. So . . . when should we expect Jamie to arrive from London?"

Sarah had done them such a favor by totting off to London to fetch him. It would make everything so easy, would bring about a conclusion that was nice and tidy.

"Maybe tomorrow or the next day."

Percy strutted before her. "Will I pass for Jamie or won't I?"

The wig and the rough love play had altered him,

and he was starting to walk differently, to speak differently, as if he were gradually becoming Jamie.

"You'll pass," Ophelia said. "Anne will never suspect that you're not her husband."

"Until it's too late."

"Yes, until it's much too late."

Chapter
TWENTY-ONE

W hat do you mean, Edith? You're babbling again."

"Sin and damnation," Edith said. "That's what's coming to them."

Jamie laughed at the older woman. She wasn't nearly as crazed as she seemed, and she provided the most interesting messages, but they were always extremely subtle and convoluted.

"Cease with the biblical chatter. You know I can't stand it."

He went to the sideboard, filled a glass of whiskey, then handed it to her. She downed a hearty swig.

He wasn't sure why he'd let her stay with him at his town house, but he supposed he felt sorry for her. She'd been shipped to London by Ophelia, and was to have visited *friends,* but shortly after Edith had arrived, her hosts had fled to the country.

Edith had shown up on Jamie's stoop, a tad befuddled and thinking the residence was still Percy's. She—the former countess, his father's wife!—had wanted to return to Gladstone but hadn't had the funds to go. Jamie would have gladly sent her home, but she hadn't seemed in a hurry to leave, nor had he been in a rush to kick her out the door.

In the weeks she'd been living with him, she'd developed an affection for his favorite Scottish liquor, and he wasn't about to tell her to moderate her intake. She was so irritatingly religious and had so few vices. What harm could there be if she became an elderly sot? She couldn't possibly grow more annoying.

"You shouldn't trust Ophelia and Percy," she said.

"This is not news to me, Edith."

"Bad blood. Bad blood in all of them."

"I can't argue with you."

"Your father spawned devils." She frowned. "But Sarah was no angel, either, so perhaps there's something in the water at Gladstone that causes people to constantly transgress."

His curiosity was piqued. "What did Sarah do that was so wicked?"

"Well . . . the baby. The boy."

"What baby?"

"Her little bastard."

"Sarah had a child? Out of wedlock?"

Edith stared him down. "Did I say that? I must have misspoken. I'm not aware of any child being born."

Jamie chuckled. "You're sly like a fox, you old bat. Why don't you just come out and share all your secrets at once? Why reveal them one at a time, in riddles?"

"No one can ever know."

"Right."

So . . . Sarah had an illegitimate son. Was he still at the estate? Or had the Merricks sold him into slavery? There was probably another lost, disavowed boy traveling the globe on a sailing ship. Then again, they might have saved themselves the trouble and simply drowned him at birth.

Had Jack learned of the lad's existence? Was the situation at the root of Jack's problems with Sarah? After Jamie's last quarrel with Jack, it was likely Jamie would never know the answer.

Jack was leaving, and Jamie couldn't convince him not to go. Jamie had been able to deal with Jack being a long horseback ride away at Gladstone but couldn't bear to envision his brother across the ocean, in some unknown, godforsaken place.

A wave of grief swept over Jamie, but he pushed it away and had another drink. He poured one for Edith, too.

To hell with Jack! If he wanted to act like an idiot, he could. Jamie wouldn't beg him to stay. Jack could dig any damned hole he pleased, and Jamie would happily furnish the shovel.

"What is it about Ophelia and Percy that keeps you in such a dither?" Jamie asked. If Edith was in the mood to spill her guts, why not let her? "You're always haranguing about them. Why are they so awful?"

"Fornicators." She nodded as if that explained it all.

"I figured Percy was, but Ophelia? I thought she was a spinster." The remark was a bald-faced lie. Ever since the night Ophelia had slithered into his bed, he'd known she was as experienced as any courtesan. "Who is her lover? Or has she had many?"

"Fornicators," Edith repeated, and she made a crude gesture with her fingers that could only be interpreted one way.

"Fornicators . . . as in Percy and Ophelia . . . together?"

Jamie assumed he'd heard it all in his life, but this

was definitely something new. But then, he wasn't that surprised. From his own relationship with Jack he understood how close twins could be, but apparently, his half sister and half brother had taken the word *close* to a whole new level.

"Couldn't let such a reprobate be the earl," Edith muttered. "It would be a sin."

"What do you mean? You couldn't *let* him be earl?"

"Why . . . the papers. The hidden papers."

"Edith, are you telling me that you're the one who came forward? Are you the one who told what had happened to me and Jack?"

She grinned a cunning grin that could have indicated anything, but Jamie was beginning to unravel how her strange mind worked.

"Your father was an asshole, Jamie Merrick."

"Edith! Such language!" He laughed and laughed.

"I never liked the man."

"Neither did I, and I never met him. I can't imagine what it must have been like to be married to him."

"It was difficult."

Which had to be putting it mildly. He studied her, pondering her peculiar ways. Was her curious behavior simply a wall she'd erected to protect herself? Had she survived by keeping a mental barrier between herself and her cruel family?

"With me installed as earl, he's probably rolling in his grave."

"He probably is."

She appeared dreamy, as if she was merrily picturing her deceased husband's fury in the afterlife.

"Thank you," Jamie murmured.

"For what?" Her blank look returned.

"You know for *what*. I'm grateful. I'll always take

care of you, Edith. I'll make sure you're safe and that there's someone to watch over you."

"The Lord's will be done."

It sounded as if it had been the Lord's will, with a little help from a demented woman. Who would have thought?

The discovery certainly sucked the wind from Jamie's sails. He'd been strutting around London for months, insulting his father's peers, gambling, and cheating them out of their money and property. Though Jamie couldn't describe why, he'd been driven to determine who had revealed the secret that had brought him to England. Stupidly, he'd hoped that by inflicting himself on them, he'd learn what he was dying to know.

The lawyers claimed the papers had been delivered to their office anonymously, but Jamie had been positive that if he identified the informant he'd find the answers he sought. Absurdly, he'd yearned to ascertain that somebody had been worried about him, but evidently, it had been naught more than a senile woman's quest for revenge.

He sighed, dismayed at realizing how fruitless it had all been.

The longer he'd stayed in the city, the more lonely he was, and it was increasingly obvious that he'd made all the wrong choices. Anne and his brother—the only two people with whom he'd formed any attachment—had been at Gladstone, but having repudiated them, Jamie was too proud to admit his mistake and go back.

Even when Anne had come to London and tried to lure him home, he'd refused to grab for what he truly wanted. He'd convinced himself that he didn't need the ties she offered, but after spending the summer with her, he'd changed. He hated to be so alone, hated to acknowledge that there was no one in the world—save for Jack—who cared if he drew another breath.

And now, he'd even pushed Jack to his limit. Jamie had only rambling, bewildered Edith Merrick for company. No one else could stand him, which was a sorry state of affairs.

He was such a fool!

Why was he in London? Why continue to remain with nothing to show for himself but a shrinking bank account and a constant hangover? He was no better than Percy—who was now ensconced at Gladstone because Jamie was too lazy to keep him away.

Perhaps Edith wasn't the crazy one.

Needing solitude to fret and stew, Jamie spun to flee, when Edith suddenly, lucidly, nagged, "Don't you ever wonder how your wife is doing?"

"I think about her occasionally."

"I can't believe you left her with Percy and Ophelia."

Jamie glared over at her. "What are you trying to say, Edith?"

"They don't like you, so they don't like her."

"Would they harm her?"

"How would I know? I'm just their mother. What could I have overheard?"

He felt as if he'd tumbled off a high cliff. His half siblings loathed him, but the prospect that they might hurt Anne in his stead had never occurred to him.

Would they dare?

His wrist began to ache, his old childhood worry about his nearly severed hand suddenly plaguing him. He rubbed the throbbing spot, his mind awhirl with dread.

He'd sworn to Anne that she'd be safe at Gladstone,

and he'd persuaded himself that simply by establishing her at the estate, with a huge allowance, he was giving her all she needed.

What if something happened to her? What if Percy or Ophelia did something horrid? How would Jamie live with himself?

Confused, torn by what he wanted, by what he should do, he walked to the stairs and climbed to his room.

❧

"A nne!"

Anne forced herself awake and stared at the ceiling. It was so dark that she couldn't see the clock, but it had to be very late. She thought someone had called to her, but she'd been sleeping so hard. It might have been a dream.

"Anne!" the soft cry came again.

She crawled out of bed, went to the hall, and peeked out, but no one was there, so she hastened to the window and peered down at the moonlit park. There seemed to be a man hiding in the shadows, and she pulled open the window and leaned out into the cold night air.

"Who's there?" she whispered.

"Anne, it's me. I'm home."

Jamie stepped out from under a tree, the moon shining fully on him. A corner of his mouth quirked up in a smile.

After her failed seduction in London, she'd been positive she'd never see him again, and her heart pounded with equal parts excitement and perplexity.

"Jamie?"

"Will you let me in? The doors are locked, and I didn't want to bother any of the servants."

She hesitated, but only because she was afraid that she'd blink and he'd disappear.

"Yes, of course I will. I'll be right down."

She paused, watching him, and a spurt of gladness shot through her. She would always love him. Always. It was like a curse that couldn't be lifted. No matter what he did, no matter how he acted, or how he treated her, she would never move beyond that one true fact.

She grabbed a robe and tugged it over her heavy winter nightgown, but the garments provided scant protection against the frigid temperature. She drew on some woolen socks, too, then flew down the rear stairs and burst outside, but she couldn't locate him anywhere.

"Jamie?" she murmured. "Where are you?"

"I'm here. Down in the yard."

She proceeded toward the sound of his voice. There was a surreal quality to the moment, the shadows seeming very threatening. Her breath swirled about her head. Icy blades of grass crunched under her heels.

"Jamie?" she said again.

"Hush!" he cautioned. "I'm here."

"Where?"

He was down the path, lurking behind some hedges. She didn't understand why he hadn't approached the manor, or why he wanted her to be silent, but she was so surprised by his arrival that she wasn't about to question him.

She continued on till she was a few feet away, then she halted, and oddly, she didn't feel any compulsion to get nearer. In the past, she wouldn't have been able to maintain any distance, and she was saddened to admit that perhaps her attraction was finally waning.

He extended his hand.

"Come with me."

"To where?"

"To a cottage out in the woods."

"Why not just come inside?"

"I have to deal with Percy and Ophelia, and it won't be pleasant. You should be away from the house while I get things under control."

"But I'm in my nightclothes. I don't even have on any shoes."

"It doesn't matter. Let's go."

"Is Sarah with you?"

"Yes, and we found Tim. They're both waiting for you at the cottage. I brought a carriage and some men. The three of you will be escorted to London, and I'll join you there."

She yearned to do as he demanded, but she was unsure of whether she should. It was all too bizarre—the late hour, the chill, the intrigue—and he was different somehow, but she was anxious to please him. With it being his first visit in months, she couldn't have him thinking her obstinate or stubborn. If he grew annoyed, he might depart before she had a chance to spend any time with him.

"I have blankets in the carriage," he coaxed. "You'll be plenty warm."

She vacillated but ultimately replied, "All right."

She took the last few, faltering steps, and he clasped her wrist, spun, and hurried them away without another word being exchanged. Anne could hardly keep up with him and hoped she didn't fall into a hole or crash into a stump.

Shortly, they reached a clearing, and she could see the decrepit cottage he'd mentioned. The door was ajar, a candle burning in the interior and giving off an eerie glow. The threshold loomed, looking like a ferocious beast that was about to devour her.

"Jamie, stop." She was out of breath, uneasy, and she tried to dig in with her heels, but he was practically dragging her along.

"Come on. Almost there."

"Where's the carriage?"

"Out on the road. Where would you suppose?"

He sped inside the hovel, and with a quick yank he hauled her in, too, and hurled her into the center of the only room. The door slammed, and she whipped around, expecting to see Sarah, but being stunned to find Ophelia, instead.

Ophelia grinned. "I guess you were correct, Percy. She *was* foolish enough to follow you."

"Like taking candy from a baby," Percy agreed as he removed a black wig.

Anne's beloved Jamie wasn't Jamie, at all, and her spirits flagged.

"Where's Sarah?" Anne asked.

"I haven't the foggiest," Percy said. "Lie down on the bed."

Anne glanced to the corner where there was a rickety bed, with a lumpy mattress, a tattered quilt tossed over it.

"Why?"

"Just do it, Anne," Ophelia snapped. "We're not about to stand here debating with you."

Ophelia snatched Anne's arm, and Anne jerked it away.

"What are you doing? What do you want from me?"

"From you? Nothing." Ophelia chuckled. "Now what we want from your husband is another matter entirely."

Ophelia positioned herself in front of Anne as Percy closed in from behind, so that she was trapped between them. The feeling of menace was extreme, the interlude absurd and seeming too strange to be real. Her two cousins, with whom she'd lived all her life, were mad as hatters.

"You can't mean to keep me here," Anne blustered.

"Why can't we?" Percy inquired.

"I'll be missed."

"Not for hours," Ophelia responded, "and by then, it will be too late."

Percy gripped Anne by the waist, his loins disgustingly pressed to her bottom. He spoke to Ophelia over Anne's shoulder.

"Why don't you head back to the manor?"

"No. I'm staying. If you're intending to hurt her or scare her, I want to watch."

"Jamie could arrive at any second," Percy claimed. "You have to be there to intercept him."

Ophelia scowled. "Why would he show up in the middle of the night?"

"The man's a lunatic," Percy asserted. "Who can predict what he might do?"

"Before I go," Ophelia grumbled, "at least let me help you tie her to the bedposts."

"Fine," Percy consented.

"Are you insane?" Anne gasped.

"No," Percy replied. "I've never been more lucid."

He lugged Anne toward the bed, and she panicked and began struggling. She was kicking and scratching, swinging her fists.

"Grab her hands, Ophelia," Percy instructed. "She

might land a lucky blow, and I'd end up bruised, which would be difficult to explain."

Ophelia seized Anne's wrists, and in a trice the deranged pair had her wrestled onto the mattress. There were ropes affixed to the bed frame, despicable evidence of how meticulously they'd planned. As Percy pinned her down, Ophelia swiftly knotted the ropes at Anne's wrists and ankles so that Anne was trussed like a hog at slaughter.

Anne screamed, and Percy clamped a palm over her mouth and nose. Rapidly, she ran out of air and felt as if she was suffocating.

She stopped fighting; she stopped yelling.

"If you promise to be silent," Percy said, "I'll let go."

Anne nodded, and he pulled away. The instant he did, she resumed screaming, but the ruckus was cut off by his clamping down again.

"Stupid bitch!" he seethed.

"Percy, you are such a trusting idiot," Ophelia scoffed. "She's never listened to you her whole life. Why would she start now?"

"She'll listen to me," he vowed. The cold gleam in his eye was terrifying. "My words will be the last she ever hears. Now get out of here."

"Spoilsport," Ophelia complained.

She leaned over and snuggled herself to Anne, and she studied Anne as if memorizing the details. Then she laid her hand on Anne's chest so that it was resting on Anne's breast. Anne didn't think the casual touch was an accident, but she didn't react to it. She was frozen in place, wondering what Ophelia might do.

"You're too beautiful, Anne," she peculiarly said. "I always hated you."

"Why? What did I ever do to you?"

"Nothing. You did nothing, and I hated you anyway." She laughed, and it was the sort of cackle a witch stirring her cauldron might have emitted. "Good-bye, and don't worry about Jamie. After you're gone, I'll comfort him for you."

She narrowed the distance between them, her fingers taking a furtive squeeze of Anne's nipple. Anne was still as a statue, desperate to keep from screaming again, to keep from spitting in Ophelia's face.

To her surprise, Percy saved her by shoving Ophelia away.

"Get out of here!" he griped. "Go to the house."

"I'm having too much fun. I don't want to leave."

"If you screw this up—after all my hard work—I'll kill you."

"You haven't the nerve."

"I have the *nerve*. After tonight, I'll have the courage to do anything I please. I won't be foiled ever again."

"From your lips to God's car, Percy."

She slipped off the bed, and with an amused glance at Anne she left. The click of the door shutting was like a death knell.

"Be quiet," he ordered, "or I'll gag you."

He went and peeked out to ensure that his sister had truly departed. When he turned back toward Anne, he looked dangerous, demonic even, and she jerked on the ropes, but the more she yanked, the more taut the knots became.

He grinned down at her, enjoying her bondage, which was so at odds with the person she knew him to be. He was her oldest male relative, her guardian and benefactor, and she couldn't understand from where this unhinged villain had sprung. She had to reason with him.

"Percy, why are you doing this to me?"

"You know why."

"No, I don't."

"I'm very sorry that it has to end like this."

"Like what?" Anne demanded. "What are you planning?"

"You have to die, Anne."

"Die! You're mad."

"No, not mad. Your husband shouldn't have come to England. He shouldn't have poked his nose in where it didn't belong."

"But what has Jamie to do with your bringing me to this cottage?"

"He has to die, too."

Her heart lurched. She couldn't imagine vibrant, charismatic Jamie dying.

"You're going to kill him?"

"No, not him. I'm going to kill *you,* then make it appear as if he did it."

"No one would believe he'd kill me!"

"Wouldn't they? Everyone in London gossips about how enraged he was when he thought you were having an affair with his brother. And Ophelia and I will swear that you were having an affair with me, too." He feigned a sad expression. "You'll pass away with the whole world assuming you're a whore who'd have sex with anyone. Poor thing."

She frowned. "But how will any of this result in Jamie's death?"

"He's a jealous maniac. I'll claim that he found out we were lovers, that the news goaded him to a homicidal frenzy, and he murdered you. He'll be hanged for the crime." He smiled with glee. "I won't have to do anything. The precious legal system he used so successfully to steal my title will do it all for me."

"You'll never get away with it," she insisted, though she wasn't nearly as confident as she should have been.

Jamie was renowned for his violent temper, and he had no associates in High Society who would support him in a crisis. He would be deemed capable of murder, and he'd have no allies and no way of proving his innocence.

Percy crawled onto the bed.

"What now?" she asked, though she was afraid she knew.

"I'm going to rape you."

"Percy!"

"You shouldn't have spurned me, Anne. The other day, you shouldn't have told me *no*."

"Percy, you're my cousin! You're my friend! You're like a brother to me."

"A brother, yes, but haven't you heard? Incest is extremely satisfying."

"You can't do this!"

"I can. In fact, I have to. I've craved it for years, and I'm not about to strangle you before I find out what it's like."

"No!"

"Yes! Jamie took everything from me. So I intend to take everything from him."

"This is so unnecessary. He doesn't care about me! He won't be bothered by anything you choose to do."

"Oh, he'll be *bothered*, all right. He may not be fond of you, but he holds his possessions in a tight fist. I want him to go to his grave wretched because I had you in every way that counts."

He stretched out on top of her, and though she struggled mightily, she couldn't escape. He untied the belt on her robe, pushing at the lapels, so that the only barrier between them was the flannel of her nightgown.

He bent to kiss her, and she turned her head to the side, so that he grazed her cheek, instead. At her petty rejection, he chuckled.

"I don't have to kiss you to get what I want."

He gripped the front of her nightgown and ripped it down the center.

Chapter
TWENTY-TWO

J amie! You're finally home."

"Ophelia, what are you doing in here? Last I knew, that was my bed and this was my bedchamber."

Ophelia stretched and preened, the strap of her negligee sliding down to reveal a perfect breast.

"I've been waiting every night," she purred, "for you to come back."

She thrust out her chest, practically begging him to look, but the bastard's eyes didn't dip the smallest inch.

"I'd heard," he said, "that Percy had claimed this room. Were you sleeping in here with him? That seems a little perverted—even by your low standards."

"Of course I wasn't in here with him," she vehemently declared. "How could you presume something so ludicrous?"

Jamie shrugged, acting as if he had entirely too much knowledge. "Have you any idea where your mother is?"

"My mother! Well . . . she's in London."

"Were you aware that she's been staying with me?"

"With . . . you?"

"Yes, and she's told me the most intriguing stories."

"Were *you* aware that my mother is a demented witch?"

"Really? At times, I've found her to be quite lucid."

"And I've found her to be quite deranged."

He wasn't paying her nearly enough notice, so she climbed to the floor and snuggled herself to him, but it was like hugging a slab of marble.

"Aren't you curious," she asked, "to find out what it could be like between us?"

"No."

"We could be so good together. We could rule Gladstone."

"I already *rule* Gladstone."

"I could help you."

"I don't need your help."

"But I could prove to be invaluable."

She slithered down the bodice of her nightgown so that the fabric was bunched at her waist. Her bosom was bared, her breasts pressed to his chest.

He surprised her by grabbing her nipples and pinching hard. She'd had sex with Percy often enough to have figured out how to pretend arousal, and she moaned with feigned ecstasy.

"Is this what you want?" he murmured. "Is this what you need?"

"Yes, Jamie, yes!"

"Well, I don't. In my opinion, you're one step down from a harlot. At least they state their price up front. What's yours?"

He shoved her, and as she stumbled away, she struggled to straighten her negligee. Why did she allow him to continue humiliating her? If he didn't want her, if he couldn't see what he was missing, to hell with him!

"How dare you insult me!" she huffed.

"What's it been like," he replied, "humping Percy all these years?"

Damn Edith! Why couldn't she keep her bloody mouth shut?

Ophelia tried to appear hurt. "What are you implying?"

"Give over, Ophelia. Edith told me everything."

"I have no idea what you mean."

"I understand about being close to your twin, but for pity's sake! If *I*—with all my faults and vices—am shocked by the information, your behavior is really disgusting."

"You think that Percy and I . . . that we . . ." She managed a credible sob. "Is that why you're being so awful to me? If you've spent time with Mother, then you know what she's like. You can't believe her horrid lies."

"I've wondered why you were so hot to crawl between the sheets with me and you made a pass at Jack, too. Have you a fondness for fucking your brothers?"

"What a ghastly accusation! If you were any kind of gentleman—"

"But I'm not and never have been. Our dear, departed father saw to that. Now then, where's Percy?"

"Percy . . . oh my." She forced down a grin, faking distress. This was going to be so easy! "Don't ask me, Jamie."

"Why not? Where is he?"

"You don't want to know."

"Humor me."

She walked to the window and stared out at the night

sky, acting as if she were torn over her choices, when in reality she was simply hoping Percy was ready.

She might lure Jamie into the trap, but Percy had to spring it, and he'd only have one chance. He seemed more capable lately, but Jamie was no drawing room dandy. If Percy didn't kill him the instant he entered the cottage, Percy would be dead, instead of Jamie, and Ophelia couldn't guess what would happen to her then. If Percy failed, she couldn't claim that she'd been ignorant of his intentions. Anne would tattle, and Ophelia had no desire to incur Jamie's wrath.

He might not care about Anne, but he would fight to protect what was his. Ophelia felt as if she were about to leap off a high cliff. Anything was possible, any ending likely. A reckless wind blew through her, and she whirled to face him.

"Sit down, darling," she coaxed.

"No."

"It's such bad news. I'm not certain how you'll take it."

"Just tell me."

"It's Anne."

"What about her?" he casually inquired.

Ophelia had thought he was indifferent to his irksome wife, but there was a tension in his shoulders. His fists were clenched, the air surrounding him lethal with menace.

So . . . she'd been correct. If Anne was in danger, he would do any wild thing to save her.

"You've been gone so long, and she decided you were never coming back."

"And . . . ?"

"You taught her to enjoy having a man in her bed. In fact, you taught her a tad too well."

"Your point?"

"Percy was here, and you weren't, and he reminds her so much of you."

"What are you suggesting, Ophelia? And please get on with it. I've had enough of your drivel."

She sauntered over, oozing concern. She laid a hand on his stomach and stroked in slow circles.

"They're lovers, Jamie."

"For how long?"

"For several months."

"Where are they?"

"Oh, I can't bear to tell you." She groaned in agony and spun away so she could bite down another grin.

"I'm sure you'll find a way."

Was that sarcasm in his voice? Was he laughing at her? She peeked over, but he seemed stoic as ever.

"They've built a little love nest."

"A love nest."

"Yes. In an old cottage out in the woods. They were carrying on in the house, but I insisted they stop. You should have heard the servants gossiping!"

"Where is it?"

He went to the window and gazed out toward the dark forest, the night seeming unusually ominous. She stood next to him and indicated the path that would lead him to his doom.

"There."

"I know where it is. I've been by it before."

He whirled to depart, and suddenly she was panicked by all the things that could go wrong, by how Percy was destined to screw up.

"Would you like me to show you the way?" she offered.

"No."

"I could assist you. I could go in first. I could speak to Percy and advise him that you've arrived. I could try to talk some sense into Anne."

"Thank you, but you've done more than enough."

He started out, halting at the last second. He glared over at her in a manner that made her blood run cold.

"Be here when I return," he said. "If you're not, I'll find you—no matter where you hide."

Quiet as a mouse, Jamie tiptoed to the cottage, pleased to discover that there was no guard posted. Whatever Percy was doing, the fool was doing it alone. The door was closed, the sole window nailed shut with some old boards, a shaft of candlelight gleaming through.

At contemplating the ambush Jamie's half siblings had orchestrated, a bitter fury washed over him. They would both pay forever. He only hoped that Anne had survived unharmed.

At the notion that she might not have, that they might have hurt—or even killed!—her, he was so enraged that he could have murdered every person in the land.

Anne was his! He cherished her in ways he didn't comprehend and hated to acknowledge.

To quell his desperate need for her, he'd fled Gladstone, but it hadn't worked. He was more obsessed than ever. He'd toyed with the prospect of leaving England altogether, had almost sailed away a hundred times over, but he couldn't take the final step that would put an ocean between them.

Did he love her? Was that why he was so overwhelmed? He couldn't quit thinking about her, couldn't cease wondering how she was getting on without him. He was sick with wanting her each and every day.

When would it end? *How* would it end?

He walked to the window and peeked through the slats.

"Jamie took everything from me," Percy was saying. "So I intend to take everything from him."

"This is so unnecessary," Anne replied, and on Jamie's realizing she was alive and well, his knees nearly buckled with relief. "He doesn't care about me!" she declared. "He won't be bothered by anything you choose to do."

". . . I want him to go to his grave," Percy boasted, "wretched because I had you in every way that counts."

There were some muttered words, then the ripping of fabric, followed by Anne's soft cry of distress.

Like soup in a pot, Jamie's ire bubbled up and overflowed, his anger so potent that he felt he possessed the strength of ten men. He would tear Percy's head from his body, would slice off his cock and shove it down his throat.

Jamie marched to the door, planting a swift kick to the rotten wood. It flew to pieces, and like a wrathful demon, he loomed in the opening.

He hadn't known what he'd stumble upon, but the sight of Anne—shackled, her garment in tatters, Percy hovered over her and eager to rape—was the most despicable, most galling spectacle Jamie had ever witnessed.

"Get off the bed!" he bellowed.

Percy frowned and paused, so absorbed with his filthy deed that he couldn't focus on anything else. He

sat back on his haunches, pinning Anne to the mattress
as he peered over.

"Jamie!" Anne breathed.

Percy said the same, though Jamie's name was im-
bued with a bit of alarm. "Jamie? What are you doing
here?"

"Get off the bed," Jamie barked again, approaching.

"Sorry, old fellow, but we weren't expecting you.
Anne and I were about to . . . to . . ." Percy smirked. "I
guess you can see for yourself."

"You can stand on your own two feet," Jamie
seethed, "and die like a man, or you can perish on the
bed like a snake slithering through the grass. It's your
decision. What shall it be?"

"Why are you in such a dither?" Percy asked. "We
haven't been doing anything Anne didn't want to do."
He simpered at Anne. "Isn't that right, darling?"

"Jamie," she said, "I never would have! Never!"

"Hush!" he curtly ordered.

"You've married yourself a real whore," Percy
taunted, pointing to the ropes that were cutting into
Anne's wrists. "She'll fuck anyone. Even me. While
you were gone, she's had half the county."

"That's not true!" Anne jiggled her bindings,
squirming, trying to escape. "Don't listen to him!"

Jamie didn't glance at her but kept his eyes glued to
Percy.

"She likes it rough," Percy jeered, "but then, you've
had her enough times, so you probably already know—
shall we call them—her preferences?"

Quick as lightning, Percy's arm came around, and
he was holding a pistol, the barrel aimed at the center
of Jamie's heart. Jamie was surprised to find Percy so

prepared, but he wasn't afraid in the slightest. Percy was too cowardly to pull the trigger, and Jamie was too tough to die.

"You're an idiot, Percy," Jamie scolded. "You only have the one shot. Once you fire, I'll slay you with my bare hands."

"Perhaps," he agreed, "but by then, Anne will be dead. You see, Jamie, *she* was always the one we planned to kill. Not you."

To Jamie's horror, Percy yanked the gun away and pressed it to Anne's forehead.

Percy would murder Anne? He would do it as Jamie watched?

"No!" Jamie howled like a wounded animal.

A lethal tempest rushed through him, and in a single bound that defied the laws of gravity, he leapt toward Percy. At the same instant, Anne screamed and bucked with her hips, throwing Percy off balance as Jamie slammed into him.

Still, Percy was able to squeeze the trigger.

In such a cramped space, the roar of the blast was deafening. Dust and mattress feathers flew; smoke filled the air, obscuring everything in a murky haze.

Jamie's momentum carried him across the bed, his fists clutching Percy's coat. They tumbled to the floor, and Jamie punched Percy over and over and over again till the man was naught but an unconscious, battered hulk. Jamie lurched away and rose, kicking Percy in the ribs so forcefully that his torso raised off the ground.

The smoke was clearing, the ringing in Jamie's ears fading. Terrified as to Anne's fate, he scrambled onto the bed, not knowing if Percy had hit her, not knowing if his jump had been fast enough to deflect Percy's aim.

"Anne!" he murmured. "Anne! Say something."

"Is he . . . is he . . . dead?" she whispered.

Jamie hung his head, offering up the only prayer he'd ever uttered in his life.

"No, he's not dead."

"Cut me loose."

He drew a knife from his boot and sliced the cords. Once freed, she curled into a ball, showing him her back, clasping at the ripped bodice of her nightgown.

"I didn't lie down with him," she said. "I didn't!"

"I know that."

"I never would have."

She started to cry, and he reached out to comfort her, but she flinched, not wanting to be touched by him. He hesitated, then moved away.

Why should he be the one to console her? Why should he presume any attention would be welcome? He'd always been a brute to her.

"Take him away, please?" she implored.

"I will. I will right away."

He eased off the mattress, and as he gazed down at her, such a wave of affection swept over him that he could hardly function. She was weeping, shivering, and he grabbed the corner of the worn quilt and draped it over her shoulders.

On the floor, Percy was stirring, and Jamie leaned down, seized the front of his shirt, and hauled him to his feet. Percy winced in agony. His eyes were swelling shut, his nose dripping blood.

Percy gaped at Anne, who was obviously alive, and he complained, "Dammit! You were supposed to die. Why can't you ever do as I command?"

With one hand, Jamie lifted him into the air, his toes dangling, and Jamie wedged the tip of his knife under Percy's chin.

"If you speak to her again, I'll slit your throat."

In reply, an angry female voice ordered, "Drop the knife, and put him down."

Jamie spun to see Ophelia, who was over in the doorway and brandishing a pistol of her own, and he cursed his folly. He'd been so concerned about Anne that he'd forgotten all about Ophelia, and at the moment he hadn't the patience to deal with her. She'd be lucky if he didn't march over, snatch her gun away, and shoot her where she stood.

"Get out of here, Ophelia," he said. "I won't tell you twice."

"Drop the knife. Release him"—she gestured toward Percy with the gun—"then step away."

Jamie didn't budge, and she shouted, "Step away!"

Usually, Jamie wouldn't have listened to her, but Anne was still in the room, so he wasn't taking any chances. He wasn't worried that they might kill him, but he sure as hell wouldn't let them kill Anne.

He tossed his knife and shoved Percy to the side.

"Ophelia," Percy piped up, "thank God you arrived."

"Why wouldn't I come? I knew you'd mess it up! I knew it!"

"I didn't mess it up," Percy huffed. "I was . . . distracted."

"By what? All you had to do was strangle her. You had her alone and tied up, yet you couldn't manage to finish the job."

"Shut up!" Percy retorted.

Ophelia ignored him, her weapon remaining pointed at Jamie, which was right where he wanted it. The second it looked as if she might swing it toward Anne, Ophelia was dead. He had another knife tucked in the waistband of his trousers, and before she could blink, he'd throw it straight through her heart.

"I'm sorry, Jamie," Ophelia explained, "but your inopportune appearance has altered the conclusion we'd envisioned. We were just going to murder her, but now, I'm afraid we'll need to stage a murder-suicide."

"What?" he asked, frowning. The woman's mind was a mystery he didn't care to unravel.

"We were about to kill her, then claim *you* did it in a jealous rage—so you'd be hanged. Instead, we'll murder you both, then claim you caught her with Percy and were so grief stricken that you killed her and yourself, too."

"Very convenient."

He pretended to rest his fists on his waist, but his fingers were slowly sliding to retrieve his knife.

Suddenly, Anne sat up. "No, Ophelia. You will not do this! I forbid it!"

"You *forbid* it!" Ophelia scoffed. "Oh, that's hilarious. Do be silent, you stupid cow."

Ophelia adjusted her aim at Jamie.

"Ophelia!" Anne wrenched her legs over the edge of the mattress. In her haste, she was off balance, and the quilt flopped down, revealing her torn nightclothes. Desperate to conceal herself, she clasped at the fabric.

Scowling, Ophelia studied the ruined bodice, struggling to make sense of what it indicated.

"What happened to your nightgown?" Ophelia queried.

"Percy tried to rape her," Jamie said.

Ophelia gasped. "He what?"

"From how aroused he was when I first walked in," Jamie added, "he was extremely eager, too."

"That's a lie!" Ophelia insisted.

"Is it?" Jamie taunted. "Tell her, Anne. Tell her what he did."

He nodded at Anne, with that quick motion imparting what he wanted from her. She understood immediately, their strong mental connection not having waned in the least.

"It's true, Ophelia," Anne concurred. "Percy said he's always desired me. He even said that he liked me more than you, and he wished we were married."

Ophelia whirled on Percy, her glare spiteful and livid. "You were planning to have sex with her? Her?"

"Well . . ." Percy sheepishly responded.

"You're mine! You can't give away what belongs to me."

"Don't flatter yourself," Percy had the temerity to mutter. "I'm your brother and your elder. I can do as I please, and I've never needed to answer to you."

Ophelia was so irate that steam was practically coming out of her ears. "When I think of how I stayed with you, how I sacrificed for you, how I suffered under your obnoxious authority!"

"Get a grip on yourself," Percy admonished. "You sound like a shrewish fishwife."

"How many others have there been?"

"Really, Ophelia," Percy chided. "You're trying my patience."

"How many?" she shrieked.

Making the worst mistake of his life, he grinned through bruised lips. "A gentleman never kisses and tells."

Ophelia yanked the gun away from Jamie and pointed it at Percy's chest. For a hesitant instant, it wavered there; then she growled like a rampaging bear and lowered it—to his crotch.

Percy froze, shocked realization rattling him, as she pulled the trigger and shot him right between the legs.

He didn't even cry out. He gaped in horror, grabbed at his missing, bloody privates, and crumpled to the floor in a stunned heap.

Chapter
TWENTY-THREE

I need to speak with Mr. Jack Merrick."

A sailor peered down at Sarah and shook his head. "Sorry, ma'am, only passengers allowed on board."

"Please?"

"Captain's orders."

"Could you at least advise Mr. Merrick that he has a guest on the dock?"

The man hemmed and hawed, and she supposed she looked sufficiently miserable that he took pity on her.

"Wait there."

"Thank you."

He vanished, and she tarried, trying to stay out of the way of the hectic hordes. As far as the eye could see, there were ships being loaded and unloaded. Passengers, sailors, and merchants were milling, yelling, and working.

It was intriguing to observe so many industrious people, and as she watched them, she was envious. She'd never traveled much of anywhere but for the neighborhood surrounding Gladstone. What would it be like to simply walk onto a ship and sail across the ocean? She couldn't fathom it.

She studied the vessel upon which Jack had purchased his fare and would journey to America. It seemed too small, and she didn't like to picture it rocked by huge waves or blown off course by stormy winds.

For a fleeting instant, she thought about the strong, sturdy woman he might have wed and would take with him to begin his new life, but she chased the vision away. She couldn't bear to ponder Jack's marrying.

What kind of man committed such a reckless, impetuous act? Not reticent, reliable Jack Merrick, certainly. What had come over him? During their brief, aborted affair, she assumed she'd gotten to know and understand him, but obviously, any sense of familiarity had been an illusion.

Voices sounded up on the deck, and shortly Jack peeked over the railing.

For some stupid reason, on seeing him again she was on the verge of tears. She was so happy that he hadn't left England, that she'd caught him before he could go. Since their last fight, everything had seemed wrong.

"Sarah, what are you doing here?"

"Could I talk to you?"

"I can't imagine what you have to say that I'd care to hear."

"Jack—"

She broke off, not sure of what to tell him. He was the only person in the world, besides Anne, who would be concerned over Tim's disappearance, and the realization had jumbled loose many inconvenient emotions.

She wanted Jack's assistance and advice, but she wanted other things, too, things she was afraid to name.

For a long while, he silently debated, and just as she decided he'd refuse her plea for conversation, he shrugged and said, "Give me a minute."

After another lengthy delay, the sailor emerged with instructions to escort her to the captain's cabin, where Jack had received permission to chat with her privately.

Sarah climbed up the gangplank, then down a ladder, into the dank hold, and she paused at the bottom, adjusting to the dim lighting, to the subtle rocking of the ship that made it difficult to balance.

The sailor led her to a door at the end of a narrow hallway, and Sarah stepped into a small room with a low ceiling. The space was graciously appointed with dark paneling, bookshelves, a nook for the captain's bed, and a large table in the center that was strewn with maps.

Jack stood behind the table, using it as a barrier between them, and she was hurt that he would keep his distance, but then, she couldn't blame him. She'd always been cold and spiteful to him, though in her defense, he'd stirred feelings she never thought to feel again. He'd frightened and delighted her, and she hadn't known how to deal with him other than to push him away.

"Why are you here?" he commenced without any opening niceties. "We're sailing with the tide tomorrow morning, and I'm very busy. State your business, then go away and don't come back."

Prior to arriving, she'd rehearsed a dozen speeches she'd intended to give, but with them face-to-face, none seemed appropriate.

"I had to see you," she pathetically said.

"Now you have. Will there be anything else?"

"I need your help."

"No, you don't," he scoffed. "You've never needed me for anything, except a few tumbles under the blankets, and other than that, I don't see what I could do for you."

"You're being deliberately cruel."

"So leave. I didn't ask you to visit."

"Tim is missing." She raised the only topic that might break through Jack's hard shell. "I'm terrified that Ophclia sent him away from Gladstone, and I'm very scared. I'm not sure what to do or where to search."

"Why are you worrying now? After all these years?"

"I've constantly fretted over him; you know that."

"I know nothing of the sort. Why is it you never fuss about him till he's in trouble?"

Jack's flip, curt answers made her angry, and her temper flared. "You've continually berated me because I don't understand how it was for you and your brother. Why can't you offer me the same courtesy? Why can't you at least try to understand what it was like for me?"

"I don't care what it was like for you. After all this time, it doesn't matter. Your son is the one who's important, but you never figured that out."

"He always came first. Why do you think I gave him away? Have you any idea of how awful it was for me?"

The tears that had threatened surged to the fore, and she started to cry. She hated to be maudlin, but the past weeks had been so arduous, and the pressures had ignited memories of her earlier traumas. Every pain she'd ever suffered seemed to have risen up until she felt as if she was choking with what might have been.

"I was so young," she said, "and I was alone and afraid. I didn't have any parents to guide me. There was only Ophelia. I couldn't win against her, and I've regretted it every day."

"I can't abide a weepy woman," he snapped. "Stop blubbering."

"I can't help it." She swiped at her cheeks. "I'm so sad, and I don't know where to turn. Your brother has left London, and you're about to leave, too."

"Jamie left? Where did he go?"

"I don't know. The servants at his house wouldn't say."

There was a chair next to her, and she sank down onto it. She stared at the planks on the polished floor. At that moment, if someone had painted their portrait, they'd have made an odd tableau: the irate, taciturn man and the defeated, melancholy woman.

She heard him sigh, and he walked to her and rested his hand on the top of her head.

"Don't cry," he grumbled, but gently. "I can't bear it when you do."

He lifted her off the seat; then he slid under her and pulled her onto his lap. She snuggled herself to his chest, relieved, feeling that she'd finally arrived where she was meant to be.

"Tell me what's wrong."

"Everything is so mixed-up, and I'm so unhappy."

"What do you want from me, Sarah?"

"I don't want you to go to America. I don't want you to leave me. And don't you dare wed some . . . some . . . strapping, tough stranger just so you have somebody to take with you."

She halted, a horrid notion occurring to her. What if,

that very second, his bride was in his cabin, unpacking her bags and tidying her belongings?

"You didn't marry already, did you?"

"No. I couldn't find anyone as irksome as you."

He chuckled, and she mustered the courage to gaze into his beautiful blue eyes. He was the most handsome, most virile man she'd ever met, and she was attracted to him as she'd never been to another. He was strong and steadfast and true, and if she leaned on him, she just might end up with the man she needed.

She eased forward to brazenly kiss him on the mouth, and she was thrilled to discover that he wasn't immune. He drew her closer and deepened the embrace, savoring it as much as she. They might fight and argue, might rage and bicker, but despite it all, they had a connection that couldn't be severed.

"What should we do?" he inquired.

"I haven't the foggiest."

"What would you like to have happen? If you could have whatever you wished, what would it be?"

"I don't know that, either."

"Well, *I* know," he stated. "I want to get married. I want to have a family. I'm tired of wandering, and I'm eager to settle down."

"In England?"

"That remains to be seen."

Her heart pounded. Was he on the verge of proposing?

"What are you saying?"

"That I'd marry you—if you'd have me. So . . . I guess I'm asking." She was about to reply when he interrupted. "But before you answer, I have to confess something, and there's a decision you'll have to make."

"What is it?"

A knock sounded on the door, and Jack called, "Come in."

Sarah peered over and was stunned to see Tim in the threshold. She frowned, trying to make sense of what his presence indicated.

"Tim?"

"Yes, it's me, Miss Carstairs."

"What are you doing here?"

"I'm going to America with Jack."

She glared at Jack. "You took him from Gladstone? Without telling me?"

"Yes."

"I've been absolutely frantic with worry."

He wasn't repentant in the slightest. "In the eyes of the world, Tim is an orphan with no kin. So am I— except for my worthless brother. Tim has no one, and neither do I. I'm prepared to claim him as my son." He paused. "What about you?"

She probably appeared distraught, and she was, but not in the way they assumed.

Tim stepped farther into the room and said, "Jack told me who you are, Miss Carstairs. If you'd like to continue keeping my birth a secret, I'll understand. It's all right. Don't be upset."

"Oh, Tim . . ."

For such a young person, it was such a sweet, magnanimous comment. When his natural father had been a philandering libertine and his mother a gullible, impetuous fool, how had he grown to be such a mature, dear child?

She looked at Jack, who was pensive and on edge about what her response would be, and there were so many words bubbling up that she couldn't figure out where to begin. She felt as if a dam was about to burst, that she might start speaking and never stop.

"I don't want to keep it a secret," she declared. "I *never* wanted to keep it a secret."

Nervous and shy, Tim gave a curt, gangly bow. "I'm glad."

She extended her hand to him, and he walked over and took it. After that, she wasn't certain what to say next. The moment was exhilarating, but awkward, too, and Jack rescued her from it—as she imagined he would many times in the future.

"Tim, why don't you wait outside while your mother and I talk?"

At having herself referred to as Tim's *mother,* she grinned from ear to ear.

Tim hesitated, as if afraid to let her out of his sight, and she explained, "We just need a few minutes. I won't go anywhere. I promise."

At the minor assurance, he left, and once she and Jack were alone, she clasped him by the lapels of his coat and shook him.

"You rat!" She kissed him hard. "I'd nearly convinced myself that he was dead in a ditch somewhere. Don't ever scare me like that again."

He shrugged, not apologetic, not contrite.

"What's it to be, Sarah? You insist that you'll acknowledge the boy, but what does it mean to you?"

"I want to be his mother. It would be my greatest dream come true."

"But it has to be out in the open, where everyone can see. I won't have you acting ashamed or making excuses."

"Jack! I want this. You're giving me such a gift!"

He was silent, weighing her resolve, and finally, he nodded. "All right, then. Will you marry me?"

"Yes, yes, yes."

She wrapped her arms around his neck, holding on like a drowning woman grabbing a rope. He stroked his palms up and down her back, soothing her, claiming her.

"I suppose we don't have to leave England," he mused, "but I won't return to Gladstone. I won't live under my brother's thumb, and I won't have gossip following either of you."

"Whatever you choose is fine with me."

"We could move to a small town someplace else. We could say we've been wed for years. No one would know about his past—or yours."

She was so happy that she felt her heart might simply burst with joy.

"Thank you."

"You're welcome."

"I'll be a good wife to you. I swear it."

"I know you will."

He eased her to her feet, and he stood, too.

"What shall we do first?" she asked.

"Well, since I'm not heading out in the morning, I should pack my bags and relinquish my cabin." He leaned down for a quick kiss. "And I think the captain could marry us before we debark. Unless you'd rather find a church and a preacher?"

"No, no. I want to do it now."

"So do I."

He linked their fingers and ushered her to the door, where Tim was waiting impatiently on the other side. Jack laid a hand on Tim's shoulder.

"I guess we're not going to America, after all."

"Are you sure, sir?" Tim was courteous but unable to hide his disappointment at having their grand adventure canceled.

"We'll be too busy here in England. Now, I need you to run topside and locate the captain."

"Why? What should I tell him?"

"Tell him"—Jack smiled at Sarah—"that your mother and I would like to marry immediately, so we'll need him to perform the ceremony."

Tim let out a whoop of delight and raced for the ladder.

※

"D on't leave me here!"

Ophella clutched at Jamie's coat, her fists kneading the fabric as if she might tear it to shreds, and he pried her away.

The decaying mansion where she'd been delivered was touted as a convalescent home for the aged, infirm, and deranged, and it had become a veritable House of Merrick. Percy was mortally wounded and being nursed, Edith was senile and kept secluded so she didn't wander, and Ophelia was detained because she'd been judged legally insane.

And it was all Jamie's doing.

The hospital or asylum or jail, or whatever the hell it was called, was allegedly the most modern facility in the country, when Ophelia couldn't fathom why.

There were bars on the windows, and the individual rooms were little more than cells. The patients and prisoners couldn't be trusted with more than a cot and a chamber pot. Lest they hang themselves in despair, there were no hooks on the walls. They'd taken her clothes; they'd taken her jewels; they'd taken her only pair of shoes!

The property was situated in the middle of nowhere, and it rained all the time, so the roads were a mire of mud. If she could have found a carriage to steal—there wasn't one; she'd checked—it would have bogged down in a trice.

She would die in such a despicable place! She would absolutely die!

Jamie chuckled. "It's so amusing to see you beg."

"You swine! You churl! How can you be so cruel?"

"Actually, it's comes quite naturally."

"I didn't harm your precious Anne. It's absurd to punish me. I'm completely innocent."

He arched a skeptical brow. "Fine, let's just say I'm an unconscionable boor and I'm torturing you for sport."

"Oh, you . . . you—"

She broke off. She had to calm herself, had to try a different tactic. He was such a brute that insults didn't faze him. Pleading didn't faze him. Nothing bloody fazed him!

She smoothed her features into an expression of extreme regret.

"I'm sorry," she said.

His chuckling metamorphosed into outright laughter. "You've never been sorry for anything in your entire life. You don't know the definition of the word."

"I *am* sorry," she lied. "I didn't realize Percy would behave so horridly. I swear it!"

"Do you think I haven't spoken to Anne? Do you think I'm unaware that you helped Percy tie her to the bed?"

"But he was merely going to scare her. How was I to predict what he'd do after I departed?"

"Have you any remorse for shooting off your brother's balls?"

"Of course I do," she falsely insisted. "I feel terrible. It's my temper. It often runs away with me."

"It certainly does."

"He might recover."

"Not his balls! They don't grow back."

"I mean he should live," she petulantly fumed. "The doctors all say there's a good chance."

"He may survive, but being a male myself, I can attest that there will be many days he'll wish he hadn't. He'll blame you, and you'll deserve his scorn. I'll return in six months to see how his wrath is settling on you."

He sauntered toward the door, as if he'd walk out that very second, and she hurried after him and grabbed his arm.

"Jamie!"

"What?"

"You can't abandon me."

"I believe I already have."

Using Edith and Percy as his witnesses, Jamie had had her declared insane. He'd had himself installed as her guardian, too, and he could do anything to her without penalty—as he'd proven repeatedly.

After she'd wounded Percy, Jamie had pummeled her to the floor, then locked her in a closet until some burly men took her to a prison in London that had been filled with whores and criminals. Ultimately, she'd been shipped—in chains—to the rural, isolated sanctuary where she now resided. She'd been callously tricked, assuming that she was being sent home, only to find herself incarcerated against her will, with Jamie claiming it would be forever.

"Take me to Gladstone with you," she implored.

"No."

"Then buy me another house. In London or anywhere. I'm not choosy."

"No."

"Please!" she wailed.

"I know you'll be surprised to hear it, but I've noticed that you're dangerous. You can't be out among normal people."

"My brother attacked Anne! Not me! Why can't you understand?"

"Percy may have attacked her, but with his cock blown off, I doubt he'll assault anybody ever again. Besides, he won't ever leave this hospital. With the stories of his castration being bandied in town, he's a laughingstock."

"He wasn't castrated," she seethed.

"I guess it's all in the eye of the beholder, but I'm not worried about him. *You,* on the other hand, are a different kettle of fish."

Furious, exasperated, she studied him, wondering how to make him relent. She laid a palm on his chest.

"How can I change your mind, Jamie? I'll do anything."

"Anything?"

"Yes. Just name it. You can't hide the fact that you desire me. Set me up as your mistress. You could love me; Percy always did. You'd be so happy."

She snuggled herself to him, letting him feel her lush torso, and for a moment, she thought she was getting through to him. He smiled at her; then the smile became a scoff.

"You're crazier than I suspected," he charged. "With

every word you utter, I'm more convinced that I made the appropriate decision by keeping you here."

He started out, and she screamed, "Jamie! What is wrong with you? I'm not mad."

"Anne might have an alternate opinion. Shall we ask her? Or how about Sarah? What would she say about you?"

Ophelia gnashed her teeth. Anne and Sarah. Anne and Sarah. Who gave a rat's ass about them? After she sneaked to Gladstone and murdered Jamie, they'd be next!

"I was simply trying to help Percy regain his heritage," she grumbled. "Why is that a crime?"

Weary of dealing with her, Jamie sighed. "I keep talking to you, Ophelia, but you don't listen. So I'll say this one last time. Pay attention. You will stay here until—"

Like a spoiled toddler, Ophelia clamped her hands over her ears, and he grabbed her wrists and pulled them away.

"You will stay here," he began again, "until I'm persuaded that you've reformed sufficiently to be released. Should that day ever arrive—and I admit I'm dubious that it will—you will be transported to Australia on the first available prison ship."

"And Edith and Percy will remain in England as if they played no part in events?"

"Yes."

"But I can't bear being trapped with them. I'll end up killing them."

"You'll do nothing to Edith," he warned. "She will be safe around you, and should she so much as trip on the garden path, I'll come after you."

"And what about Percy? I suppose if he croaks, that will be my fault, too."

"Yes, but I won't care so much. He tried to rape Anne, so he shouldn't expect any mercy from me. Then again, a man who loses his privates to a deranged, gun-toting female has suffered plenty."

"So you won't mind if I finish him off?"

"It's your neck, Ophelia"—he smirked, looking evil and resolute—"and the hangman's noose is very tight. You might wish to consider the consequences before you act."

"Bastard!" she hurled.

"I'm many things, but I'm not a bastard. Our father married my mother, remember? That's why you're in this fix." He knocked for the guard. "I'll check on you in six months."

"As if I need a nanny, you contemptible lout."

She was so angry that she picked a figurine off the table and threw it at him, but as with so much of what she'd done lately, she missed. The figurine thudded into the wall and tumbled to the floor, but it hadn't the decency to break, so she didn't even receive the satisfaction of a loud crash.

"By the way," he mentioned as the door swung open, "I've provided Edith with several boxes of stationery. She's to write me once a week to inform me how you're behaving."

"She can sod off. You can, too."

"Have you ever been to Australia? The climate is very hot—sort of like Hell is purported to be. I don't imagine you'd like it there."

He marched out, the guard quickly securing the lock. With so many barricades in place, she couldn't follow Jamie, but that didn't prevent her from pounding and pounding on the door. She screeched his name till she was hoarse, sounding every bit like the demented shrew he insisted she was.

Finally, worn and exhausted, she slumped to the rug. Footsteps echoed behind her, and she peered over to see Edith watching her. Her mother's expression was much more lucid and clear than Ophelia could ever recollect it being.

"Go away, you crazy loon," Ophelia hissed.

"No, you little sinner," Edith responded. "I've organized a Bible study group, and you'll be required to attend every meeting. Class is about to start. Come."

"I won't participate in any stupid Bible reading with you."

Edith grinned a nasty, malevolent grin. "It appears I'll be using Jamie's stationery much earlier than I thought."

She spun and walked away.

Chapter
TWENTY-FOUR

Anne tarried in the woods, listening to the quiet. Snow was falling, huge flakes drifting down. Off in the distance, the manor beckoned, the windows twinkling in the dim light, smoke curling from the chimneys. It was such a pretty picture, like a scene in a painting, a fantasy spot that no humans inhabited, and often that's precisely how it felt.

Everyone had left her.

Sarah had gone to London to find Jamie but had found Jack and Tim, instead. She'd stayed on to marry; then the three of them had moved to the other side of England to build a new life. Anne had no idea when she'd see her sister again.

Edith, Percy, and Ophelia had been whisked away to a private hospital, but with the local surgeon having originally tended Percy's wounds, there was no keeping the type of damage a secret. The injury—and the means by which he'd received it—was so shocking that the rumors never ceased.

What with the furtive, reproving looks of both servants and neighbors, Anne could barely leave her room, and she definitely wouldn't brave a trip to the village. She wished the entire episode would fade away, but the scandal was too delicious, and the gossipmongers couldn't be silenced. They were having too much fun.

Jamie's disappearance bothered her most of all.

She hadn't had a chance to ask him what had brought him home on that fateful night. By the time Sarah had traveled to London, he'd vanished, so it wasn't Sarah's plea that had spurred him to Gladstone.

So why had he come? Had he missed Anne? Had he hoped to make amends and start over? The likely answers had her abuzz with constant speculation.

After he'd rescued Anne from Percy's clutches, he'd spent several days at the estate, but he'd been distant and excruciatingly polite. Then he'd departed—abruptly and without a good-bye.

She understood that he'd been busy resolving matters with Ophelia and Percy, but would it have killed Jamie to keep in touch? Would it have been too much trouble to inform her of where he was or what he was doing?

As usual, she was left to wonder if he'd ever return, if they'd ever be together again.

In one brief interview, he'd pressed her for the particulars of Percy's attack, and she'd shared every squalid detail, but what if Jamie hadn't believed her? He probably assumed she'd been raped. If so, he'd be disgusted and would never come back, and she was incensed to suppose that she was being condemned for something that hadn't happened.

She sighed, pondering what to do, how it would all play out, and she told herself—as she had a thousand occasions prior—that she was glad he was gone.

Who needed an overbearing lunatic for a husband

anyway? Not her! From the moment he'd arrived, there'd been nothing but upheaval and disaster, when she simply wanted peace and quiet. She was better off alone.

She'd reached the stone bridge where she'd first stumbled on Jamieson Merrick all those months ago. It had been such a bright, warm summer afternoon. As she'd watched him survey his property, she'd had such an alarming sense of impending destiny that she'd tried to run from it. At the memory of how she'd tumbled into the stream, how he'd rescued her, she smiled, when she didn't know why she would.

Any fond reminiscence was complete proof that he'd finally driven her crazy. She wouldn't regret his decision to stay away. It was for the best!

Movement caught her attention, and she stood very still, thinking it might be a deer in the trees. She focused in, and to her utter surprise, it wasn't an animal, but her magnificent, horrible, delectable, impossible husband.

He was up on the ridge where he'd initially been, peering out across the fallow fields, and she suffered the worst déjà vu—as if Doom was about to chase her down all over again. Her heart pounded, with both joy and dread, and she'd just eased away, anxious to escape undetected, when he spun to face her.

Snow dusted his hair and shoulders, his cheeks rosy from the cold, and—evidence of his improved status— he wore a heavy wool coat and fur-lined boots. In the stark, gray surroundings, his eyes were bluer than ever, and they held her transfixed until he grinned his devil's grin and headed toward her. She knew that look well. It was desire, mixed with some of the false affection he was so adept at exhibiting, and a wave of banked fury washed over her.

How dare he come home after all this time! How dare he absent himself—week after week—without sending word! How dare he blithely show up and expect to be welcomed!

The man was a menace. He shouldn't be allowed to inflict himself on sane, rational people.

"Hello, Anne," he said casually as he approached.

"Hello, Lord Gladstone."

He laughed. The swine!

"Are you still angry with me?"

"I'd have to care about you to be angry."

"But you only call me *Gladstone* when you're spitting mad."

"What are you doing here?" she asked.

"I live here."

"No, you don't."

"We'll see."

She didn't like the enigmatic retort. It conjured all sorts of happy endings that were an illusion. Did he mean he planned to remain forever? Or merely until he grew bored?

She'd been down too many devastating roads with him, and she was in no mood to hold on for dear life through another tumultuous ride.

He neared, causing her to ripple with panic. If he got too close, she was lost. She had no defense against him. She loved him, she hated him, and she swirled with every emotion in between the two extremes.

"Stay right where you are," she commanded.

"No."

He stopped a few feet away, studying her intently, his torrid gaze roving over her, burning like a brand all the way down.

"I don't want you here," she insisted.

"You're as uppity as you were the first day I met you."

"And you're still a horse's ass."

He laughed again. "Ah, it's just like old times."

"Not quite."

She wasn't the foolish, sheltered spinster she'd been. He'd seen to that, and she wanted no part of whatever new twist he might insert into her staid, solitary existence.

She was fine without him. Fine!

Pushing past him, she ran for the manor, her cloak billowing out, her breath swirling around her like a cloud. She raced in the rear entrance and up the stairs to her room. With trembling fingers, she slammed the door and spun the key in the lock. She dawdled, steadying herself, listening to hear how rapidly he'd follow. Shortly, he sauntered down the hall and halted directly outside.

"Open up," he cajoled.

"No. I'm pretending you're a bad dream. If I hide in here long enough, maybe I'll wake up and you'll be gone."

"Is that any way for a loving wife to behave?"

"At the moment, I'm not feeling very *loving*, and I'm barely your wife—as you've worked hard to ensure. Go away."

"Don't you want to know where I've been and what I've been doing?"

Her curiosity soared. "No."

"If you let me in, I'll tell you."

His voice was low and seductive, as if he had a secret he could share with her and nobody else.

"Go away," she said again, which made him sigh.

"I guess I should buy more locks. The ones I own keep getting ruined."

He kicked at the wood, and as it bowed with the force of the blow, she jumped with fright.

She should have simply let him in and avoided all the drama, but she couldn't. There was too much at stake. He'd tarry at Gladstone for a week or two, then he'd depart, and her poor heart couldn't survive another rebuff.

She grabbed the dresser and shoved it over as an extra barrier, but it provided scant fortification and only protracted the wreckage through a few extra jolts. The door gave, the dresser tumbled out of the way, and he marched in.

He took a step toward her, and she stepped back. He took another, and so did she, the two of them gliding across the floor like a pair of dancers until she was at the wall and could go no farther.

He advanced till he was so near that his boots slipped under the hem of her skirt. He'd shed his winter coat, and she could smell the cold air on his skin, the laundered scent of his clothes, the essence of him as a man, and she yearned to reach out and hug him, or to rest her palm on his cheek. He looked so inviting, and she was lured to him like a magnet to metal, but he was lethal to her well-being and, rigid with resolve, she kept her arms pinned to her sides.

After all he'd done—and not done—why couldn't she resist him? What was the matter with her? Had she no shame? No sense?

She flattened herself to the plaster, wishing she could be subsumed by the wall and vanish.

"You get prettier every time I see you," he absurdly said, the comment like a warning shot across her bow.

Buck up! she scolded. She wouldn't be sucked in by a few obsequious words from a maniac.

"Really?" She glared at the wrecked door. "You haven't changed a whit."

"Oh, I have. A little." A corner of his mouth quirked up in that fiendish smile that made him so enticing. "Do you want me to tell you how?"

"No."

"I'm going to anyway."

"Why am I not surprised?"

Stunning her, he dropped to one knee and clasped her hand in his own.

"I'm sorry."

It was the very last remark she'd expected, and she frowned. "You're . . . sorry? What for?"

"When I married you, I swore that I'd always protect you, that you'd always be safe here at Gladstone, and you weren't. Can you forgive me?"

He appeared so young, so torn, and she couldn't bear to see him prostrate and begging for absolution. If he was repentant, it would be so difficult to keep him at bay.

"Yes, yes," she hurriedly declared, "you're forgiven, so if that's all you came to say, you can leave now."

"There's a tad more."

"What is it?"

He kissed her knuckles, and at the feel of his delicious lips on her skin, she lurched away and went to the window. She peered out across the park, watching the snow trickle down.

Behind her, she heard him rise, heard him approach, and she stiffened as if bracing for an attack. Didn't he understand that each touch was painful? His presence was a petty torment that was deadly in its intensity.

He placed his hands on her hips, and he snuggled himself to her backside.

"You didn't let me finish," he complained.

"That's because you've already said more than enough."

He chuckled and nibbled her nape, and she sucked in a sharp breath.

"Let's have sex," he suggested.

"Are you insane?"

"No. I want to make love to my wife. It's been ages."

Inundated by fury, she whipped around, eager to do battle, but on seeing the odd, tender expression on his face, she was flummoxed.

"I don't plan to lie down with you ever again," she asserted. "I can't believe you had the gall to ask."

"So who's asking?"

He picked her up and spun them so that they bounced onto the mattress. In an instant, she was trapped beneath him, which was precisely where she didn't wish to be.

"Let me up."

"No."

"Let me—"

He leaned in and kissed her, just a soft brush of his mouth to hers, and he was very tentative, as if he was afraid of being pushed away. Could it be? Could big, bad Jamie Merrick be worried that she no longer desired him? It was ludicrous to think so, but nevertheless, she experienced a vain thrill.

The arrogant prig! Although he had no heart, so he couldn't possibly feel any distress, she yearned to hope that he'd suffered as she'd been suffering.

"I missed you," he contended.

"I didn't miss you."

"Yes, you did. Quit lying. You're terrible at it. Now about what I've been doing . . ."

"I said I don't want to hear it!"

From how he was gazing at her, it was obvious that he was about to announce some perfectly charming gesture destined to placate and enchant, and she refused to be tempted with incentives to like him. She hadn't the wherewithal to deflect them.

"I sold my ship."

"You what?"

"I sold it, and I have to admit, it was deuced difficult to let it go."

"But . . . why?"

"I didn't need it anymore. I have the town house for sale, too." He frowned. "You didn't want to ever spend time in London, did you?"

"No, I hated it there."

"So did I. I didn't suppose we should keep a house we'd never use."

What was he saying? He seemed to imply that he'd come home for good, but she'd never trust that he was sincere. He'd tricked and hurt her too often to count, and they were far beyond the day when he could spew any story she'd deem credible.

"We've dispensed with the preliminaries," he continued, "so let's get down to business."

He started kissing her again, and she shoved at his shoulders till he drew away.

"Stop it!"

"Stop what?" he queried, appearing confused.

"You've been gone for months!"

"Yes, I have."

"You can't just waltz in here and expect that we'll take up where we left off."

"Why not?"

"How many reasons do you need? How about your

cavorting with strumpets?" She was amazed that she'd mention the humiliating fact aloud, and tears flooded her eyes. "It shamed me."

"Oh, Anne." He kissed one moist eyelid, then the other. "What would you say if I told you I haven't had a lover since I fled Gladstone?"

"I'd call you a bald-faced liar."

"There's been only you and no other. I won't claim I didn't have many chances to misbehave, but why do you assume I came home? I couldn't abide the frivolous coquettes I met in London, and I've been dying for female companionship!"

Could it be true? She had no idea, but she stupidly, desperately wanted it to be. She was struggling to remain firm, but the foundations of her anger slipped a little.

"I can't begin again," she moaned. "You've exhausted me. I can't keep on as we have been."

"But I relinquished my ship for you. It was like cutting off my arm. I need wifely sympathy to get over the loss. Aren't you going to give me any?"

He rolled onto his back, taking her with him so that she was draped across his torso. His hand was on her bottom, her loins pressed to his, and he rooted to her bosom and nestled at her breast through the fabric of her dress.

At feeling him so close to where she wanted him to be, she hissed with agony. He knew how to entice her, how to wear her down, and she was rapidly capitulating.

"What do you want from me?" she wailed.

"Let me show you."

In another quick flip, she was on the bottom, and he was hiking up her skirts and unbuttoning his trousers. To her ultimate disgust, she didn't put up the slightest resistance. Since he was extremely aroused, he didn't bother with any seduction. He simply gripped her thighs and impaled himself.

Immediately, he started to flex, and she groaned with delight and arched into him, meeting him thrust for thrust, and swiftly he was at the end. He came in a deep, satisfying rush of pleasure, and as he emptied himself against her womb, she joined in. They soared to the heavens, then floated down.

But as the commotion waned, he murmured, "I love you."

She froze. "What did you say?"

"I love you, Anne. That's what I hurried home to tell you."

The remark was the worst, most insulting thing he could have said. He had no notion of what *love* was, and she was crushed that he'd offer the pathetic sentiment.

"No, you don't. You don't love me."

Her dubious scowl humored him, and he chuckled. "It's shocking, I know. I can hardly believe it myself."

"No . . . no . . . no . . ." She shook her head, her dread rising, her heart aching. "You are not going to do this to me."

"Do what?"

"You are not going to lie—not when the subject matters so much to me."

She squirmed out from under him to perch on the edge of the bed.

He moved to the floor and knelt in front of her.

"How am I *lying* to you?" he gently asked.

"You've returned to Gladstone—when I have no clue why you would—and you've dragged me off and had sex with me, and now, you're whispering all these ridiculous comments."

"They're not ridiculous."

"They are when you don't mean any of them. This is all a big game to you."

"Is that what you think?"

"It's what I know! And I'm such a gullible fool that I'll sit here and listen to you and fall in love with you all over again. Then when you're bored, or your wanderlust takes over, you'll disappear." She grabbed his shirt and shook him. "I won't do this with you. I won't! You never get to break my heart again."

She slid by him, and she wanted to run off, to find a quiet place where he would leave her be, but where could she go that he wouldn't follow? Instead, she went to the window seat and climbed onto the cushion, and she gazed out at the gray day that perfectly matched her mood.

He came up behind her, but he didn't reach for her, and she was glad. When he touched her, she couldn't concentrate, and she made all the wrong decisions. They stood apart, silent and morose, like two strangers on the street.

"I always loved the snow," she finally said.

"I've rarely seen it."

"Really?"

"I hate the cold, so we mostly sailed in the south."

An awkward pause ensued, and she used it to muse over what a little gem of information he'd provided. He never discussed himself or his past. She didn't know his favorite color, his favorite food, or his mother's maiden name. What kind of a marriage was that?

"Turn around," he urged. "Look at me."

"No."

He sighed with resignation. "It's probably better if you don't. Keep staring outside."

"Why?"

"It will be easier for me to tell you things."

She'd rather have bitten off her tongue than inquire, but she caught herself asking, "What *things*?"

"While I was away, I had a lot of time to think. I couldn't eat or sleep, and I couldn't figure out why."

"And . . . ?"

"It dawned on me that I was in love with you," he claimed. "I'd persuaded myself that I didn't care about anybody, that I liked being alone."

"But not anymore?"

"No, not since I was with you over the summer." He swallowed twice and took a step nearer. "I've been so lonely without you, and I want to come home."

The request was so earnest, so filled with emotion, and she pressed her forehead to the cool glass and prayed for guidance.

"I thought you didn't have a *home*."

"Of course I do, silly. It's wherever you are."

It was the sweetest statement he could have uttered, and a spark of hope flared. She peered at him over her shoulder. He seemed weary and beaten down, his battles against the entire world having taken their toll.

"I left because I was afraid," he admitted.

"Afraid of what?"

"Of caring about you. Everyone I ever loved left me, so I learned to be the one who left first. I didn't know how to carry on any other way."

"You hurt me."

"For which I'm eternally sorry, and I will spend the rest of my life making it up to you. If you'll let me . . . ?"

He extended his hand, and it hovered there, a link, a

tether, to everything she'd ever wanted. Dare she believe him? Dare she trust him?

She spun toward him. With her on her knees in the window, and him standing on the floor, they were eye-to-eye for a change.

"Swear to me that it's forever."

"I swear it," he said without a flicker of hesitation.

"There can't be any other women."

"I don't want any other women. Only you."

"If I ever hear that you so much as glanced at a parlor maid, I'll do to you what Ophelia did to Percy. That kind of rage appeals to me."

He gave a mock shudder. "You drive a hard bargain, but I agree to your terms. If I hurt you again, I'll accept whatever punishment you choose to inflict."

"I want children."

"I'll give you a dozen."

"And I'll expect you to be around to help me raise them."

"I can't wait."

Tentatively, she reached out and twined her fingers with his.

"You'd better mean it," she warned.

"I do."

"If you leave again, I'll find you and kill you for going."

"I won't ever leave. I tried it before, only to discover that everything I need is here with you."

She studied his solemn expression. He seemed truthful, and his promises sounded genuine. She could believe him or not, and she decided to believe him.

Who could say what the morrow would bring? They might be together for the next hundred years, or tragedy could strike the following morning. Wasn't it best to grab for every chance at happiness?

She was an optimist. She would hope for the hundred years, and she would work to make it a reality.

"Stay here, Jamie," she implored, pulling him to her. "Stay right here with me."

"I will," he vowed. "I always will."

"I need you."

"I need you more."

He hugged her till she couldn't breathe, and when he finally drew away, he was shivering.

"This room is cold as the dickens," he said.

"Yes, it is, and you hate the cold."

"Would it be too much to ask that we go over and snuggle under the quilts?"

"To do what . . . ?" As if she didn't know!

"To make love till next week. What would you suppose? I have some catching up to do."

He swooped her into his arms and walked to the bed.

Look for these other sizzling reads
from *USA Today* bestselling author

CHERYL HOLT
*Named One of the Top 25 Erotic Writers
of All Time*★

FORBIDDEN FANTASY
ISBN: 0-312-94255-9

SECRET FANTASY
ISBN: 0-312-94254-0

AVAILABLE FROM ST. MARTIN'S PAPERBACKS

"Holt delivers a delicious erotic romance
with heart and soul."

—*Romantic Times BOOKreviews*★